White Wolf's Law

OTHER SAGEBRUSH LARGE PRINT WESTERNS BY
HAL DUNNING

White Wolf's Legion

White Wolf's Law

HAL DUNNING

Sagebrush
Large Print Westerns

Library of Congress Cataloging-in-Publication Data

Dunning, Hal, 1907-
White Wolf's law / Hal Dunning.
    p.   cm.
ISBN 1-57490-444-2 (alk. paper)
1. Large type books. I. Title.

PS3507.A848 W45 2002
813'.52—dc21   2002012114

Cataloging in Publication Data is available from
the British Library and the National Library of Australia.

26.95

Sagebrush Large Print Westerns are published in the United
States and Canada by Thomas T. Beeler, Publisher, PO Box 659,
Hampton Falls, New Hampshire 03844-0659. ISBN 1-57490-444-2

Published in the United Kingdom, Eire, and the Republic of
South Africa by Isis Publishing Ltd, 7 Centremead, Osney
Mead, Oxford OX2 0ES England. ISBN 0-7531-6699-2

Published in Australia and New Zealand by Bolinda Publishing
Pty Ltd, 17 Mohr Street, Tullamarine, Victoria, Australia, 3043
ISBN 1-74030-670-8

Manufactured by Sheridan Books in Chelsea, Michigan.

White Wolf's Law

APACHES OR LAVA GANG

DEATH HAD STRUCK TWICE ON THAT SEPTEMBER afternoon, and two riders returning to Cannondale had marked the glow from a fire against the early evening sky.

At first they had mistaken it for a brush fire and had swung their horses off the trail and headed toward it as rapidly as the going would permit. The brush was as dry as tinder, and a fire, unless checked, spelled ruin both to townfolk and plainsmen.

The two riders slid their horses down the shelving bank of a wide arroyo. After their horses had scrambled up the farther side, it was "Toothpick" Jarrick who first realized the truth.

"Hey, 'Dutchy,' it's a house on fire!" he cried.

"Sure is!" Dutchy grunted and checked his horse to a trot.

"Get goin'!" Toothpick cried impatiently.

"Not any," Dutchy said shortly. "Lava Gang."

"Yuh sure talk as if words hurt yuh," Toothpick grumbled.

His companion's taciturnity was always a source of irritation to the tall, lanky cow-puncher, and he lapsed into a sulky silence for a time, chewing the ever-present toothpick in his mouth, from which he derived his name.

"Yuh mean maybe the gents they calls the Lava Gang is makin' another raid, and they may be still hangin' about?" Toothpick asked.

"Yep."

"Why don't yuh open yuhr mouth and let the words

1

come out, instead of choking yuhrself on 'em, and makin' me explain to myself what yuh aim to say?" Toothpick asked scornfully.

Dutchy grunted, drew his rifle out of the boot beneath his saddle flap and balanced it across the pommel.

"If we're goin' to war, I'm sure plenty glad to have yuh along," Toothpick grumbled as he followed the example of his companion; "but yuh sure ain't no gent to relieve the tedium of existence with light chatter."

Accustomed as they were to the grim tragedies of the border, they were totally unprepared to find what they did close to the burning house. There was nothing left save smoldering rafters and bare adobe walls. Toothpick swung from his horse and quickly extinguished some brush that had been fired by a spark. Then he gave an exclamation and cried sharply:

"Hey, Dutchy, come here!"

Dutchy was a grizzled two-gun fighter who, rumor said, had once ridden "the long trail." He had lived close to the border all his life, yet he winced when he saw what the white-faced Toothpick pointed out to him.

A scant five yards from the doorway of the house, the body of a man lay half concealed in the brush. It was mutilated and scalped.

"Apache?" Toothpick queried as he slid a nervous hand to the hammer of his rifle and cast apprehensive glances into the darkness.

"Maybe so," Dutchy said shortly. "Let's see if we can find any others."

After a short search they discovered the body of a woman near a small shed. Powder marks on the back of her head told the story. She had been murdered deliberately—shot at close range.

"Skunks—downed a woman!" Toothpick swore.

"Cussin' never hurt no one," Dutchy growled. He wandered to the rear of the ruined house and a little later called: "Here's a gent what's got breath in him."

Toothpick hastened to the side of Dutchy and found him kneeling beside a middle-aged man who was unconscious. The two cow-punchers dressed his wound. After a time the man's eyelids fluttered open and he stared at them with frightened eyes.

"We're friends, old-timer," Toothpick told him. The man sighed with relief.

"Set fire to house to bring help," the man whispered.

"Well, it come," Toothpick soothed as he forced a little water between the man's parched lips. "Who done this?"

The man's eyes flashed and he raised himself on his elbow.

"*Le fils du Diable à Cheval—oui*—I knew him—"

The man sank back and grew silent. Toothpick gave him more water. "Who's the gent yuh knew?" he asked.

"*Le Diable à Cheval.*" The man's voice was nothing but a faint whisper. He sighed and closed his eyes.

"Dable Chaval—huh, that's a hell of a name," Toothpick grumbled. "Reckon we'll have to wait until he comes to again. Will he live?"

"Certain—then he'll talk." Dutchy was positive.

"When he does I'm aimin' to start gunnin' for the gent what murdered that woman," Toothpick cried savagely.

"Me, too," Dutchy said quietly.

They covered the wounded man with a blanket and once more continued their search of the surrounding bushes. Fifteen minutes later, just as they had decided there was nothing more to be found, a voice hailed them from the darkness.

3

"Hey, Dutchy, what's goin' on here?" the voice asked.

At the sound of the summons, both Toothpick and Dutchy instinctively leaped for cover. Recognition of the voice brought them to an abrupt halt.

"Huh, it's the sheriff," Toothpick said with a shamefaced grin.

Dutchy nodded and lowered the hammer of his rifle.

Three riders materialized from the darkness and entered the circle of light cast by the smoldering ruins. Tom Powers, the sheriff, came first. He was followed by his deputy, "Silent" Moore, and Sam Hogg, a wiry little man of fifty.

Tom Powers was a slender man of thirty. His face was gaunt, bony, and burned a brick red by the sun. At first his face looked hard, but his deep-set blue eyes told the character of the man. There was no hardness there, only force. He cast one quick glance at Dutchy's grim face and sensed the tragedy.

"Where's the Courfays?" he asked.

"Scattered about." Dutchy waved his hand.

Sam Hogg was good-natured and was forever cracking jokes. He now joined in.

"You two boys sure scattered yourselves when you heard us shout," he said, chuckling. "You acted skittish, like a pair of heifers just out of school."

A second later his mirth came to an abrupt end when he saw the sheriff, who had dismounted, kneel beside the body of the mutilated man. He swore excitedly and joined the sheriff.

Toothpick briefly told what he knew of the tragedy. He led them first to the body of the woman, then to where the unconscious man lay. The man was muttering in delirium. The sheriff kneeled beside him and listened, but after a

4

moment he arose to his feet and shook his head.

"Can't catch a word. I know him, though—he was a brother of the woman over there and came from across the border to visit last week," the sheriff explained.

"He was talkin' when we—" Toothpick began, but Dutchy brought his words to an abrupt halt by kicking him in the shins.

"Somebody comin'!" Dutchy warned in a low voice.

They listened and heard the noisy hoofs of a pair of horses and the crunching of wheels. A minute later two men in a buckboard drove up. The sheriff and Sam Hogg walked forward to greet them. Dutchy drew Toothpick aside.

"Some day yuh'll dig yuhr grave with yuhr tongue," he growled. "Don't tell no one that that gent talked to us private."

"But he didn't say nothin' I could understand," Toothpick protested.

"Maybe the Lava Gang wouldn't believe yuh," Dutchy said grimly.

Judge Ransom, one of the two men in the buckboard, climbed out and listened gravely to what the sheriff had to say. He was a man of fifty-five with the face of a scholar.

"Who's that jasper?" Dutchy demanded as he nodded toward the buckboard.

"With the judge?"

"Yeh."

"Gent named Bill Anderson. He's the new political boss around here," Toothpick explained.

The man was in his forties, of medium height and stockily built. He had a round, apple-cheeked face and a jovial manner—one of those men whom others like on sight and hail as a boon companion. Yet a close

5

observer might have detected something about the eyes that seemed to contradict the first impression.

"He rides around with the judge a hull lot," Toothpick explained further. "Why for did yuh ask?"

"Knew a gent what looks like him once," Dutchy muttered, with his eyes still watching Anderson, "twenty years ago."

"Then it can't be him."

"Might have been his father," Dutchy grunted.

They walked toward the others and arrived in time to hear the judge ask them:

"Who do you suppose did this?"

There was a moment of silence which was broken by Bill Anderson.

"I was over in Arizona last week, and the papers were talking about some renegade Apache who were raiding along the border. Maybe they have worked up this way," he suggested.

"Maybe so," the sheriff said doubtfully.

Silent Moore, the sheriff's deputy, carefully examined the mutilated man for a moment; then, for the first time since his arrival, he opened his lips.

"I've fit the Apache—'tain't their work," he said.

"Nonsense, man, it's impossible to tell," Bill Anderson exclaimed, and the others, with the exception of Toothpick and Dutchy, were inclined to agree with him.

"Greasers did that work—Apaches would have tracked down the man out there and killed him, and they would have used a club on the woman," the deputy insisted stubbornly.

"Sure yuh're right," Sam Hogg cried with an oath. "White men or devils started in to make it look like Injuns—got scared before they finished and run for it."

"The Lava Gang!" Toothpick cried excitedly. "Judge, where's 'Snippets' and Mary?"

The judge's face went white as he whispered: "You—you mean that letter from *them?*"

"Yeah, but where are the girls?" Toothpick asked again.

"They're safe. I took them over to visit Sam Hogg's wife at the Frying Pan Ranch this evening. Bill and I were coming back when we saw the fire."

Toothpick relaxed and uttered a sigh of relief. The Lava Gang sometimes stole girls for ransom and held them across the border.

"What's this—what letter?" the sheriff asked sharply.

"You all know that I am to preside at the trial of Pete Cable for murder, which takes place a week from today. Last week I received a warning signed by the Lava Gang, saying if I did not see that Cable was acquitted, some terrible thing would happen to me."

"What did yuh do with the letter?" the sheriff demanded.

The judge shrugged. "I tore it up."

"You are not going to pay any attention to the letter?" Bill Anderson asked curiously as his eyes searched the judge's face.

"I intend to see justice done," the judge replied firmly.

Bill Anderson pursed his lips and whistled soundlessly. The others turned and frowned at him. He smiled apologetically.

"No offense, judge. I was admiring your courage. If, as you seem to think, the Lava Gang did this, I would stay in after dark," the plump politician said.

"To blazes with the Lava Gang! We'll have the whole bunch in jail before the trial is finished," Sam Hogg

7

exploded.

Bill Anderson lit a cigarette, then smiled.

"You have to catch them first."

"We'll do it."

Sam Hogg spoke positively, but somehow his words brought cold comfort to the judge.

Some fifteen miles to the southwest there was a great barren waste of lava rock. The Lava Gang had received their name from the fact that after each raid their trail was lost on the smooth slopes of the lava fields. No one knew a single member of the gang. It was suspected that they had their real headquarters in Cannondale. They were as elusive as ghosts. The thought that a member of the gang might be present at that moment made the judge grow thoughtful.

Sam Hogg growled like an angry terrier.

"If we don't trail 'em tomorrow, I'll send for that little hellion, 'Jim-twin' Allen. I'm bettin' he'd trail 'em. I hears he's better than a bloodhound."

Bill Anderson laughed.

"He'd probably throw in with the Lava Gang himself."

"Him? Not any!" Toothpick snorted. "He wouldn't have no truck with hombres what steal girls. He'll come a-runnin' and a-shootin' if I tells him about it."

"Fairy tales," the judge snorted.

"You tell him to come, judge, and watch his smoke," Toothpick pleaded.

"A judge ask help from an outlaw who is wanted for murder in a dozen States?" Anderson laughed again.

"You gents stop gabbin' and help me get this hombre in the buckboard," the sheriff called.

A bed of blankets was made on the floor of the wagon, and the unconscious man was lifted in.

8

"Mr. Anderson, yuh drive him easy to town," directed the sheriff. "An' if he starts talkin', yuh listen hard, 'cause I got a hunch that hombre will sure tell us a heap more about the Lava Gang than we knows now."

"I'll certain listen if he starts talking," Anderson replied. He climbed into the buckboard and picked up the reins. Dutchy watched the team until it vanished in the night.

"I'd sure like to know where I seen that gent before, an', if I ain't seen him, who does he remind me of?" Dutchy muttered to himself.

Silent Moore was sent to town to gather a posse. The judge called Dutchy aside and whispered an order to him. Dutchy was known as a deadly fighter and a man who could be trusted.

"Dutchy, I want you to ride to the Frying Pan Ranch, and I don't want you to let my daughter or Snippets out of your sight until this is over."

The grizzled puncher mounted his horse and galloped off. The others remained.

Toward morning Silent Moore returned with the posse, and at the first streak of dawn they took up the trail of the murderers. For a time it led due south toward the Mexican border; then it headed sharply to the west, toward the lava fields. Here the trail was lost.

The lava fields were a maze of smooth slopes, abrupt ridges, and deep depressions. For seventy miles they roughly paralleled the border. And in all that expanse of rock there was no sign of verdure, save only an occasional cactus.

The posse scattered and searched for the trail. The sun blazed down and turned the desolate place into a furnace. The hunters were grim men, not easily turned aside. The sun baked them, they suffered from the lack of water, but they continued to search.

Toward noon, "Ace" Cutts, with five of the judge's riders from the Bar X Ranch, joined the search. The men dismounted and climbed the jagged slopes. They cut their hands and tore their boots on the knife-like edges of the lava rock.

The sun rose past meridian. The rocks and sand were too hot to touch. All that day the men of the posse continued their search, but found nothing. At last, toward evening, they realized their hunt was in vain. Beaten, baffled, they gathered for the return trip to town.

"Yuh figure Jim Allen could track those devils?" Tom Powers asked of Toothpick.

"Sure could," the lanky cow-puncher replied.

The sheriff reined in his horse. "Then if yuh know where he is, go get him."

Toothpick was about to answer when he saw Ace Cutts and three other riders were closely watching him. He remembered Dutchy's warning. He decided to remain silent. If he sought out Jim Allen, it would be well not to let people know it. He shook his head.

"The little devil is like a flea—no one knows where to find him," he declared. The remark seemed plausible enough.

They were close to Cannondale when another of the judge's riders joined them. The lathered flanks of his pony told of a hard ride. He swayed in his saddle as he sought out his boss.

"Judge, they jumped us an' downed Hank and Bill. They got me in the shoulder—"

"And those two hundred two-year-olds?"

The judge knew the answer even before he asked the question.

"They run 'em off."

10

Judge Ransom gripped his saddle. No one there realized what this meant to him—financial ruin. The Lava Gang had made good their threat.

The sheriff had hoped that the wounded man they had found the night before would be able to identify one of the murderers. But this hope was dashed when he met Bill Anderson as they entered the town.

"That poor fellow," Anderson told him, "got one of his bandages loose and bled to death. I never heard him move, but he was dead when I got to town."

The sheriff, followed by Toothpick, hurried to the doctor's house, where they were shown the dead man.

"Toothpick, yuh helped do him up; look them bandages over," the sheriff said.

After a brief examination Toothpick straightened, caught the sheriff's eye and nodded.

"I ain't no match for sneaks. If yuh know where to find him, go fetch Jim-twin Allen!" the sheriff cried passionately.

"Yuh might tell folks I've gone north to see my mother," Toothpick warned.

11

AN UNEXPECTED GUEST

IN SPITE OF THE FACT THAT CANNONDALE WAS THE county seat, and that it had also the advantage of being on the transcontinental railroad, it had always remained just a cow town.

Main Street, little over a block in length, was the business center. It was paralleled by Madison and North Streets. Madison was given over to one or two boarding houses, a few cottages, and many empty lots. North Street was closely lined with Mexican shacks. State and Depot Streets intersected Main.

The town had three hotels, two large, combination dance-and-gambling halls, and ten smaller saloons. Of the gambling halls the Red Queen was far the most pretentious. Located in the center of the block on Main Street, it was really the hub of the whole town.

On the day before the trial of Pete Cable for murder the Red Queen was doing a land-office business, for Dame Rumor had been busy, and it was freely predicted that there was bound to be trouble at the trial.

Just what form this trouble would take no one seemed to know, but a murder trial, with the added attraction of a possible jail breaking or lynching, was sufficient to send every able-bodied man within riding distance scurrying into town.

Thus, on this occasion, every hotel was full and the hitching racks along Main Street were lined with horses and buckboards; crowds milled about the courthouse, surged in and out of saloons, gathered in hotel lobbies and in the street, drank, sang, and excitedly discussed the coming trial. The general opinion was that Pete

12

Cable would hang. In spite of this, however, odds were offered freely in the Red Queen that the accused man would be acquitted.

In the late afternoon, "Tad" Hicks, "Windy Sam," and "Kansas" Jones, three Frying Pan punchers, rode into town. They tied their horses to the hitch rack of Aloe's Emporium and went across the street to the Comfort House. They pushed through the crowd at the bar and shouted for a drink. But, having thirstily downed that, they refused a second round virtuously. They had been ordered by their boss, Sam Hogg, to remain sober until after the transcontinental train arrived. Now they swaggered down Main Street; and as they passed the Hogg Hardware Store, run by Sam's brother, its owner greeted them.

"Howdy, boys. This town's so durned full of strangers, and I'm so glad to see a gent what I know, that I'll buy yuh a drink," Jim Hogg said heartily.

"Yuh're durn right. She's so full of strangers I don't know her," Windy agreed.

"An' they is all bad-lookin' hombres," Kansas said. Suddenly he was struck with an idea and he added hopefully: "Do yuh reckon there's anything in this talk about the Lava Gang bustin' up the trial tomorrow?"

"Hello, Toothpick, you ole hoss thief!" Kansas hailed a passing rider.

Toothpick Jarrick pulled in his pony and edged it toward the sidewalk. The pony's head drooped; its coat was rough with dried sweat and dust. Its rider's genial, grinning face was streaked with grime; dust covered his jeans. Both he and the pony bore evidence of having come far and fast that day.

" 'Lo," he greeted. "Mr. Hogg, ain't yuh afraid of being seen with three mutton eaters like them jaspers?"

"Howdy, Toothpick. Hit the ground and have a

13

drink," Jim Hogg invited.

Toothpick shook his head and turned his horse into the street again.

"Where yuh been all week?" Windy asked.

"Me? Fellow, I've been playin' the messenger of destiny." Toothpick grinned over his shoulder as he headed his horse toward the livery stable.

"Darn idiot!" Jim Hogg spluttered as the four lined up at the bar of the Lone Star. "I'm plumb sick of this here mystery. My brother Sam is packin' a gun under his vest and another on his hip. The sheriff is nutty with worry, an' if yuh ask him anything he looks sick and scared. Tough hombres drift into town, and the sheriff gets him more deputies. I hear gents betting the judge don't dare come back to town, and now I hears he's due to arrive. I'm bettin' Sam sent yuh boys to town to help guard him when he comes in."

"Safe bet," Windy admitted, "for he sure enough told us plain to stay sober and meet him at the depot."

"Why for, did he tell yuh? Not any!" Jim Hogg continued his complaint. "Yuh can't talk natural without some gent sayin', 'Hush!' Toothpick disappears and comes back an' says he's the 'messenger of destiny.' What in blazes did he mean by that, and where's he been for the last six days? Lava Gang! Why, this town is gettin' so scared it's going to drop dead of heart failure, an' if yuh ask someone what he thinks, he looks over his shoulder and says, 'Hush.' Maybe yuh boys knows what it's all about."

Windy put his finger to his lips, looked over his shoulder, then whispered: "This here town is goin' to have its sins wiped out, like Sodom an' Gomore."

"Yuh dang fool!" Hogg spluttered.

Here the bartender cut in. "I ain't boastin' that I knows anything, but I've kept bar all over this here

14

territory, an' I'm tellin' yuh I never see so many tough gangs gathered together as they is in this town. Hell is sure goin' to pop."

"Why? How? When?" The irate little storekeeper shot out his questions like a machine gun. "What makes yuh think so?"

"Feel it in my bones," the bartender hedged mysteriously.

They left the bar and headed toward the station.

The arrival of the Limited was a big event in Cannondale, and a large group of loafers always watched it hurl itself across the prairie and come to an impatient stop at the little station. On this night the three riders found nearly a hundred people lounging there. Sam Hogg was walking up and down impatiently and talking to Tim Lynch, owner of the Lone Star Saloon. The three punchers found perches on a baggage truck, rolled their cigarettes, and looked about for someone to annoy.

They saw Toothpick and the sheriff whispering together in the shadow of the freight house, but the lanky cow-puncher was too quick on the come-back for their taste, and Sheriff Tom Powers was touchy these days, so they continued to search for easier prey. Tad Hicks jerked his thumb toward Dutchy and Silent Moore, leaning against the wall.

"Wish I'd thought of tellin' Jim Hogg to go question them hombres," he grinned.

The others chuckled and then grew glum at this lost opportunity, for Dutchy and Silent had the reputation of being morose and taciturn.

Mrs. Ransom, the judge's wife, her daughter, Mary, and Snippets McPherson strolled by.

"Howdy, ladies," Kansas called.

Mrs. Ransom nodded, Mary giggled, and Snippets

15

smiled.

"Hello, boys," she cried. "Kansas, when are you going to bring me over that dun horse to break for you?"

Kansas flushed and the others guffawed. The week before, the said dun had set him afoot ignominiously, where he had been found by Snippets.

"Never mind, Kansas. I was only funnin'. I know your cinch broke, 'cause I found your saddle," she added contritely.

"Now, yuh darned tadpoles, will yuh believe what I tole yuh? Yuh know darn well *that* girl don't lie!" Kansas cried. He gazed after Snippets gratefully, for, if the truth be known, his cinch had not broken; that had been his alibi for the greatest disgrace that can happen to a puncher—to have a broken horse throw him and leave him afoot.

"She's sure a swell gal," Tad Hicks said admiringly.

"She's more like a fellow than a gal, an' she sure rides like one," Windy agreed.

The three women passed on down the platform. When they reached Toothpick and the sheriff, Snippets stopped and stared at the tall cowboy.

"Why, Snip," Mary giggled. "Are you in love with Toothpick? You're blushing."

Snippets did not heed her. When Toothpick failed to see her she plucked at his sleeve.

"Toothpick?" Her greeting was a question.

The lanky cow-puncher swung about and snatched off his hat. He had known Snippets ever since she was a child. Then he had worked for her father up North.

" 'Lo, kid," he greeted.

"Did yuh see him?" she asked in an eager whisper.

"See who?" Toothpick feigned ignorance.

"Don't tease. You know," she pleaded.

16

"Yuh can spill it to her," Tom Powers said as he went over to join Mrs. Ransom and Mary.

"Yeh, I seen him," Toothpick told the girl.

She waited for him to go on. Her dark eyes, wistfully eager, were fixed upon him.

"I goes to El Crucifixo, like yuh tells me to," drawled Toothpick. "An' I'm tellin' yuh I seen there a million dollars' worth of outlaws, 'cause a gent down there ain't known socially unless he carries a thousand, dead or alive. I ambles into the Palace Saloon, and the gents look hard at me, an' that bunch can sure look hard. A couple slid up to me and ask me bluntlike who I am. I tell 'em quick I'm huntin' Jim-twin Allen. At that they eye me different. Then I spots Jim sittin' at a table by his lonesome, and I calls him. He's darned glad to see me. He tells those hard hombres I'm his friend, and they get soft, pronto."

His deliberation irritated the girl.

"But is he coming?" she demanded impatiently.

"Sure is."

Snippets' eyes lighted with joy.

"I tell him about the Lava Gang, and he won't come. Then I tell him yuh want him to come, and still he refuses. He gets sorta bitter an' says he ain't no cow-thief catcher—that's his brother Jack's job. I plead with him and tell him how your uncle's in danger. He says he's not comin' up here to help your uncle hang a man. By accident I tell how the Lava Gang now and then runs off gals across the border fer ransom and how they murdered that Courfay woman. At that he says quicklike he'll come a-runnin'.'"

"When is he coming?" she asked quickly.

He shook his head. "I dunno."

"And when you told him I wanted him to come, he wouldn't?" she asked softly.

17

"Positively not," Toothpick said bluntly.

Another question trembled on her lips, but her eyes clouded and she turned away, leaving it unsaid. Toothpick called to her.

"Yuh know why he refused," he grumbled. "Yuh know darn well Jim Allen is an outlaw and hasn't a Chinaman's chance of being pardoned. He'd be a hell of a fellow if he came to see a girl like yuh. But I'll tell yuh this: He talked a heap about yuh and made me promise I'd tell yuh he was no good, an' that he thought yuh was only a fool romantic gal what thinks yuh like him 'cause he's the famous 'White Wolf.' "

"That's not true, Toothpick," she said quietly.

"Sure, I knows," he told her.

"It's not the Wolf I like, but—"

"Sure, you and me and Dutchy is the same. We likes the kid, Jim Allen, what blubbers about his hosses." Toothpick twirled his hat to hide his emotion.

"It's a damned shame!" he exploded. "Just the same, kid, yuh want to forget yuh ever see him and marry some nice tame gent."

"Like you, Toothpick?" she asked, smiling.

"Me?" Toothpick grunted. "Not any! I knows yuh too well. Yuhr tongue is too darned sharp. It keeps a man hoppin' all the time. Come on! Here's the train."

The Limited rose from a far murmur to a rasping, grinding rush of sound and roared to a stop, grumbling, sputtering, like some great steel animal suddenly foiled in its rush through the prairie night. Within the lighted cars, passengers turned in casual curiosity to look at the station throng. But, contrary to its usual custom, that throng did not return the stares. For once interest was not centered on the Limited itself; all eyes were turned toward one man as he descended alone, slowly, with dignity. He faced the

18

curious eyes calmly as he greeted his wife and daughter.

Erect, distinguished with his white goatee and the broad black hat that shaded sincere gray eyes, by no gesture did he betray excitement. And yet he knew that, of that crowd, almost every one knew his difficulties, knew why he had gone to the capitol, were avidly curious about the outcome of the visit, and were even more on edge concerning the trial tomorrow.

Cannondale knew that the judge had been in financial straits ever since the Lava Gang had stolen two hundred of his steers. He had tried unsuccessfully to get his notes renewed at the local bank; finally, he had made this trip to the capitol, where he had friends. But there, also, failure stalked him. His ranch was in debt, and it was hinted that his political position was none too secure.

Rumor said the judge had incurred the antagonism of the Mexican vote and would not be reelected. How this story had reached Washington he did not know. But of the two banks where he was best known, one refused outright to make a loan and the other postponed it until the judge was forced to leave for Cannondale to preside at the murder trial. Vaguely he suspected that the tentacles of the Lava Gang stretched even into the furthermost political and financial centers. As he boarded the train for home he resolved to fight the gang to the end, whatever that end might be.

No trace of emotion, beyond pleasure at seeing her, tinctured the greeting kiss he gave his wife; no hint of the sword above their heads. Yet one glance at his eyes told the kindly, white-haired little woman that their difficulties were still unsolved. She pressed his hand in the comforting reassurance of her own courage and understanding.

His daughter Mary gave him a resounding kiss and a

19

cheery "Hello, dad." The family troubles had as yet only vaguely affected Mary; they had not toned down her treble giggle nor her natural nineteen-year-old interest in the arrangement of her blond curls. Snippets, though a year younger, was far more seriously concerned than Mary, because she understood better the gravity of the judge's situation.

The conductor waved his lantern, the engine snorted response, and the Limited slid majestically past the spectators. At its rear there trailed a smoking car. As this drew abreast of the station platform, the door banged open and a husky brakeman appeared, dragging a small man by the scruff of the neck. The brakeman seized his victim by the collar and, catching him by the seat of the pants, he heaved him outward.

The small man rolled head over heels, to the spectators' howls of mirth. He fetched up at the feet of the judge and his friends.

"You darned drunken hobo, it takes money to ride on this train," the brakeman bawled as he shook his fist at the forlorn figure.

The little man stumbled to his feet and disclosed a dirty face largely obscured by blue glasses. His trousers were too large and bagged at the waist. His threadbare coat hung in tatters. A battered bit of felt draped his head in the semblance of a hat, and one toe protruded from an overlarge shoe. He clinched a grimy fist and shook it after the jeering brakeman.

"You mutton face! Just you dare come back here, and I'll give you a licking so your mother won't know you!" he cried shrilly.

His futile rage, his puny fists, brought another gale of mirth from the onlookers.

As if stirred by the laughter, his rage mounted, and he

lapsed into shrill abuse mixed with oaths. Toothpick seized him by the shoulder and shook him.

"Hey, you little runt, there's ladies present," he warned sharply. "Get out of here, pronto!"

He gave the hobo a rough shove that sent him staggering. The small man gave one glance at the tall Toothpick and limped forlornly up the platform.

"Poor fellow!" Mrs. Ransom fluttered after the tattered figure. Even in her own troubles she pitied this scarecrow of a man. "Why did they throw you off the train?"

He paused, then drew down his mouth and whined to gain her sympathy.

"I bought me a ticket to Chi—that's Chicago—where I live, ma'am. Me muvver is sick. That feller stole my ticket and guv it to a friend, then threw me off."

Mrs. Ransom struggled between the contrary emotions of pity and common sense. She knew the story was not true, yet he was so forlorn and hungry looking. Pity won.

"Here's a dollar. Go buy yourself some food," she said. Then, struck with an idea, she added sternly: "Promise you won't drink it up."

The tramp straightened up.

"Me, ma'am?" He was all injured innocence. "Why, ma'am, I never touch the stuff."

The crowd chuckled. Tom Powers snorted disgust. He seized the man's arm.

"What's yuhr name?" he snapped.

The hobo glanced at the star on the sheriff's coat and tried to slink away. Pinioned by the heavy hand, he cowered as if he expected a blow.

"Mister, I ain't done nothin'. I'll get out of town on the first train," he pleaded.

"You got until tomorrow afternoon to do it,"

21

warnedthe sheriff.

As the hobo slunk away the three Frying Pan riders looked after him longingly. He was an ideal mark for their humor. Sam Hogg sensed their longing.

"It's all right, boys," he said. "You can go along now. Looks like they ain't goin' to be no trouble here, after all. Not right now, leastways."

As one man the three humorists started after the scarecrow. Mrs. Ransom bristled to his protection.

"You bullies!" She shook a warning finger. "If I hear of you tormenting that poor little fellow, I'll —well, I'll be angry."

"Huh, ma'am," Tad Hicks stuttered. "We wa'n't thinkin' of doin' nothin', nohow."

"We figured we'd take him to dinner with us-all," Windy added with defensive genius.

Mrs. Ransom shook her head, smiling, as they joined the hobo. They towered above him—a tatterdemalion dwarf between three guardsmen.

She rejoined her husband. The sheriff nodded, and the judge and his family moved toward their home. Ransom was flanked by two deputies and further protected by Silent and Dutchy, who brought up a grim rear guard.

Snippets turned back and ran to Toothpick.

"Thank you for protecting me from that man," she smiled, teasing.

"Huh?" Toothpick queried dumbly.

"Oh, you men! How dumb you are!" She stamped her foot. Then, on tiptoe, she delivered a quick kiss on the nose of the astounded Toothpick and ran to rejoin her party.

Toothpick stared after her. He felt gingerly of his nose and scratched his lead.

"She meant somethin' by that. But what was it?" he asked himself, and gave up the answer.

KING OF LIARS

TAD HICKS, WINDY SAM, AND KANSAS JONES, OUT OF sight of the depot platform, seized the little hobo's arms and dragged him willy-nilly behind a saloon.

"Yuh promised yuh wouldn't drink up that cartwheel Mrs. Ransom guv yuh," Tad Hicks reminded him.

"Aw, get out and leave me be," the hobo said truculently, with an evident attempt at bravado.

"What's that?" Windy roared as he tightened his grip on the arm.

The hobo's truculence vanished, and he whined: "Nothin'—where we goin' to eat?"

They led him to a Mexican eating house on Depot Street, where they were joined by Toothpick. Having planked their charge in a chair and ordered food, they settled back to have a little fun with the victim.

"What's yuhr name?" Windy Sam commenced.

"Jim Anson. What's yours?" the hobo asked.

"Windy Sam, now—"

The man called Jim Anson interrupted him.

"Is you called that because you talk too much, or because what you say don't mean nothin'?" he asked innocently.

"Ha-ha!" the others exclaimed, and dug the red-faced Sam in the ribs.

One after the other they plied him with questions, but his answers always left them floundering. He had a way of turning a thrust into a boomerang. He did this with such a guileless, cringing air that they were never stare whether he was secretly laughing at them or if his answers were accidental. Before the meal was over he had them grinning at his absurd tales. In spite of themselves they listened, absorbed, and momentarily almost believed what he said.

"Rise up, liars, and salute yuhr king!" Toothpick shouted.

For a moment there was a change in the hobo's face. The fawning expression was replaced by a broad, lovable grin that made the punchers' hearts warm toward Jim Anson. Toothpick started. For a moment he studied the hobo's face, saw the fawning smile there again, and shook his head.

The five adjourned to Maria's Cantina, on the corner of Depot Street. Jim Anson insisted that the first drink was on him and ordered it in a loud voice. Another followed and another. Toothpick chuckled when he saw that, while Jim Anson always ordered the drinks, one of the three riders paid for them.

All the while Jim Anson asked them questions in such a way that they never realized they were being pumped. He turned on Toothpick and skillfully ferreted from him the story of the murder of the Courfay family two weeks before.

"When we got there they was all dead, except one gent what says: 'Fees do dible chable,' which I figures is French." Toothpick rambled on with his story, but Jim Anson was not listening.

"*Fils du Diable à Cheval,*" he muttered to himself. "Sons of the Devil on Horseback. Gosh!"

A little later "Mac" Kennedy, an Eastern dude, sauntered in. Jim Anson, after studying him a minute, turned to the others.

"Who's that gazebo all dressed up like a Christmas tree?" he asked.

"He's a white-livered dude," Windy snorted contemptuously.

24

"He comes out here about three months back and says it's for his health," Kansas elaborated. "Buys the Bar X, a little runt of a ranch what backs up against the lava fields."

"He don't look yellow," Anson said meditatively.

"He is, though. Plumb yellow, from the neck down and feet up," Tad Hicks hiccuped.

Ten minutes later Bill Anderson stepped into the *cantina*. He hesitated for a moment when he saw the group at the table; then he nodded to them.

"Boss in the back room?" he asked of Maria.

"Si, si, señor."

Anderson walked quickly to a door in the back, glancing over his shoulder at the five at the table. Apparently they were too interested in themselves to note his actions. Quietly he passed through and closed the door after him.

Jim Anson insisted on buying one last drink here, despite his comrades' urging to try the liquor elsewhere. Maria brought the drinks. Kennedy, the dude laughed as he watched them. He leaned over the bar and whispered something to Maria, then left the *cantina*.

The cow-punchers began to sing, and the woman came forward and ordered them to leave.

"All right, we'll go," Jim Anson said with drunken dignity. He staggered to his feet and swayed toward the rear door. He turned the handle and kicked it open. It led to a storeroom.

"That's not the way, stupid." The woman gave him a violent shove after the others. He grinned drunkenly at her and staggered out.

About ten that evening Bill Anderson swung in at judge Ransom's gate and knocked at the door. When he and the judge were comfortably installed in easy chairs before a fire, he looked squarely at Ransom.

"What are you going to do about the trial tomorrow?" he asked bluntly.

"My duty," the older man replied with equal bluntness.

"Judge, don't think I'm asking you to do anything else." Anderson added quickly. "You know I'm not in politics for my health. When I came here a couple of years ago, every one was at odds. The leaders of the party were fighting among themselves. I'm not flattering myself when I say that all stopped when I took hold. Judge, you understand that I'd soon lose my leadership if I nominated men who were not elected."

The judge had hoped against hope that Bill Anderson would back him because of his record, even if the Mexican vote was against him. He was sure, if he could get the nomination, he would be reelected. Now his heart sank.

"Let's be frank, judge. If you insist on bearing down too heavily in the trial tomorrow, you lose the Mexican vote, and, much as I want to, judge, I don't see how I can propose you for renomination."

The judge pulled thoughtfully at his goatee. For the first time since he had known Bill Anderson, he detected a certain sinister quality beneath his bland air of good fellowship.

"But, Anderson, this Pete Cable isn't a Mexican," he said.

"That's not the question," Anderson replied. "For some reason the Mexican vote is interested in him. Now, why not be sensible? Go easy at the trial. Cable was drunk, he made a mistake and killed this Easterner. Other men have killed in this town and gotten away with it. Why not be reasonable? Remember, you are not

26

being asked to do anything dishonorable. All these people ask you to do is to sit quiet—to do nothing."

"You ask me to do nothing—nothing but pervert justice," the judge said quietly.

The political boss' good nature and blandness dropped away. A stranger to the judge stood before him, with a face that was hard and cruel.

"This house is mortgaged, isn't it?" Anderson snapped.

This hit home, for the place was mortgaged to the hilt, and the notes were due the following month. Ransom paled, but his eyes were steady as he gazed into Anderson's granitelike brown ones.

"Is that a threat?" he asked.

"Only a reminder," Anderson said savagely. The next moment the judge heard the front door slam, and he was alone.

Slowly he paced the floor. He and his wife had struggled for his present position, for this home. What sacrifices she had made to allow him to finish law school, and through the years of poverty that had followed his graduation! Little by little, after that, came success, until recently they had dreamed of the time when he would go to Washington, a United States senator. All that rosy future had seemed assured—until last month.

Now, not only the future, but the present, might be wiped out. Their savings were wasted; his hope of reelection crumbled; their home would go next. All because of a murder trial with its mysterious ramifications. There would be no college for Mary, no ease in old age for his wife.

Rebellion and temptation seized him. What right had he to bring ruin on his family? All he had to do was to let events take their course, as Anderson had directed. His credit would be good once more; his dreams of Washington might come true. Back and forth he walked and struggled with the devils of temptation.

A door opened gently, and Snippets stood before him.

"Uncle." she said softly, "I heard. I couldn't help it."

"You heard?" he said, and his voice was harsh. "Then what shall I do? Ruin my wife and child?"

"No. Make them proud of you," she said firmly.

The judge's face cleared, and he smiled. "Thank Heaven for you, my child," he said. "You're right. That's the one thing I must do."

Anderson left the judge's house in a high rage, but the moment he was in the open his anger gradually left him, and he was once more his cool, calculating self.

"That's the first time I lost my temper in nine years," he told himself. "Now what's to be done? First thing tomorrow I've got to see the judge and apologize. I guess I better go and talk it over with my dear brother. How pleased he would be if he knew I'd lost my temper!"

He laughed and strode briskly down Main Street toward the Red Queen. Across from the Lone Star he saw Toothpick, Tad Hicks, Windy Sam, and Jim Anson, staggering along, arm in arm. They had left Kansas asleep at the Lone Star. Anderson waved at them; he was once more the politician.

"Come on, boys, I'll buy you a drink," he called.

They staggered after him into the Red Queen and lurched against the bar. The place was filled with shouting, singing men. The back of the long bar shone ornately, with polished glasses, mirrors, colored bottles, and other glittering paraphernalia.

Anderson ordered the drinks, and his four guests

28

drank thirstily, with profuse thanks. He nodded to them, told them he would see them later, and pushed his way through the milling crowd toward the gambling room. Unseen, Jim Anson slipped through the crowd in his wake.

The gambling room of the Red Queen was on the left of the dance hall. Here Francisco Garcia, the owner, could he found on any night. The Toad, as he was called by some, but always behind his back, acted as lookout for a big game. He sat on a raised platform between the two faro tables. He was so powerfully built that he looked squat despite his height. Heavy jowls, thick lips, and protruding eyes relieved the monotony of his full-moon face. His swarthiness hinted at Mexican blood. Garcia himself never carried a visible weapon; he relied on his two paid killers for protection—"Yuma Kid" and "Baldy" Flynn. And because his enemies had a strange habit of disappearing or ending violently, he was more feared than any other man along the border.

Bill Anderson, with Jim Anson, still unnoted, at his heels, sauntered to the table and watched the play for a moment. Then he smiled to Garcia.

"Having a big game?"

The Toad grunted.

"I wanted a word with you, but tomorrow will do." Anderson turned away.

Jim Anson, that ubiquitous hobo, flopped drunkenly at a nearby table. From beneath his tattered hat brim he studied the gross Mexican and the two killers who lounged against the wall behind him.

"Gosh! The Devil on Horseback," murmured Anson to himself. "And he had four sons! Horned lizards. Rattlers. Coyotes, mixed up with tiger and Spanish bull."

29

He wandered out to the dance hall, staggering; yet, strangely enough, when a bully struck at him, he seemed to float away to escape the blow.

His comrades at the bar were now noisy and riotous with drink.

"I'd sure like to see some of this money that's bein' bet that Pete Cable won't get his neck stretched," Windy announced to the world.

"Yuh wanta see it? Take a look at this." A wad of bills dropped on the bar. The three punchers swung about to stare at the money and at the man with the high, cackling voice who had produced it.

They met the toothless leer of old Baldy Flynn. Behind Baldy lounged the Yuma Kid, twenty-one-year-old, two-gun killer. The Kid's pale eyes met theirs, and his two buck teeth shone in a menacing sneer. Most men could easily whip the narrow-chested Yuma Kid in a hand-to-hand encounter, but he did not fight that way; and he was feared along the border.

Baldy and the Kid, Garcia's two hired slayers, were inseparable. They were bound together by the bond of skill with a Colt and by their unscrupulous cruelty, despite their varying characters. The Yuma Kid seldom talked, never laughed, and never drank. He avoided quarrels, save for profit. Baldy, on the contrary, loved his liquor, his own jokes, and above all loved to quarrel with those who failed to laugh with him.

Toothpick realized that he and Windy stood no chance against these two killers; he knew their reputation. Yet the bar was crowded; people were listening and were already commencing to shuffle to one side in the hope of a fight.

"Yuh gents is talkin' loud. I'm bettin' yuh my roll that Pete don't get his neck stretched," Baldy cackled.

30

Toothpick saw the menace in the killer's eyes, and it sobered him. He tried to gather his scattered wits. He glanced at his friends and saw that they were incapable of action. Tad Hicks, with drooping head, clung to the rail of the bar. Toothpick knew that Baldy would push the affair and try to force Windy to take water. This, no matter what the consequences, Toothpick would not permit; certainly not, with that crowd of spectators all watching and listening. Windy had been a fool; Toothpick would have to use his wits to get him out of it. He chose his words carefully.

"That roll of yallerbacks sure makes me hungry like a coyote, 'cause it's three days to pay day," he said, grinning. Both he and Windy moved to the left. If it came to gun play, their right hands would not be hampered in the draw.

Baldy cackled derisively again. He turned to the hushed bystanders and grinned. Out of the tail of his eye Toothpick saw Jim Anson squirm through the crowd toward them.

Baldy spoke slowly and raised his voice: "Gents, I'm askin' yuh to step up an'—"

Boom! A Colt roared behind Toothpick. Like flashes of light, guns leaped into the hands of Baldy and the Yuma Kid.

"What the hell?" snarled Baldy.

Toothpick swung about and saw Jim Anson looking foolishly at a smoking Colt on the floor.

"Darn it!" the hobo wailed. "The durn thing was loaded."

He looked so foolish as he stared at the gun that the crowd rocked with mirth, but Baldy spat like a wild cat.

"What did yuh expect, yuh bum?" he shrieked.

Tad Hicks had been aroused from his sleep by the

31

shot and stared stupidly at Jim Anson.

"When yuh guv it to me, yuh didn't say it was loaded." Anson stuttered reproachfully.

Tad held out a wavering hand and picked up the gun.

"Kick that hobo out o' here," cried Baldy. Hands seized Jim Anson and sent him spinning to the sidewalk.

Jim Anson disposed of, Baldy turned again to Toothpick and Windy; but before he could speak, Bill Anderson shoved his way to the bar between the killer and the two riders.

"It's right kind of you, Baldy," he remarked.

"Huh?" Baldy blinked with surprise. "What yuh mean?"

Bill Anderson looked at him blandly.

"Didn't you say, just as that fool hobo learned that guns are loaded: 'Gents, I'm askin' you to step up and name your poison'? There's your money on the bar."

The crowd chuckled and moved a step closer to the bar. Anderson, without waiting for a reply, called to the bartender:

"I'll take straight whisky for mine."

After one look into Anderson's eyes, Baldy grinned ingratiatingly.

Toothpick and Windy decided that discretion was the better part of valor. Dragging Tad Hicks with them, they slipped out of the bar.

"Huh!" Windy complained, as the cool air refreshed him. "I was lit up considerable, but now I'm plumb sober."

"Me, too. Baldy scared me sober," Toothpick agreed. "I'm goin' to buy that hobo drinks aplenty, 'cause he sure stopped Baldy from hurtin' my feelings."

"Sure did. But I'm tellin' yuh that Bill Anderson is some nervy hombre, runnin' in on a sidewinder rattler like that toothless old ape. Folks says he's a grafter, but I'll vote for a coyote, if he tells me to, just because he made that Baldy draw in his horns," Windy confided.

Toothpick did not reply. He was puzzling out an answer to a riddle. Why had Baldy backed down, when Anderson confronted him? He left Windy and Tad Hicks at the Lone Star and then went to look for Jim Anson.

"That little runt sure saved my reputation, an' he can have half of my bed, even if he is a dirty little tramp," he told himself.

He wandered about, searching bar after bar. At last he discovered the hobo asleep in Maria's. Before him on the table stood a half-empty bottle. Toothpick shook him awake. However, Anson refused to move until they had finished the bottle. Toothpick was agreeable because he was now stone sober. They had emptied the bottle when, to their surprise, Anderson stepped out of the back room. His face clouded when he saw them.

"Darned good of yuh, Mr. Anderson, to steer Baldy away tonight," Toothpick called.

Anderson smiled genially.

"That's nothing. Is that the little bum who just discovered guns are loaded?" he asked.

Toothpick nodded.

"Who is he?"

"A hobo what got hisself thrown off the train this evenin'."

Anderson called good night and left. The moment he was gone Jim Anson grasped Toothpick's arm and staggered out with him. To better support the drunken hobo, Toothpick slipped a hand beneath his armpit. He jerked the hand away suddenly.

"Say, who are you?" he demanded. "Yuh got a gun

33

there in a shoulder holster, and yuh made believe yuh didn't savvy guns."

The hobo dropped his stagger and stood erect.

"Where's my hosses, Toothpick?" he asked softly.

Toothpick jumped; the whine had left that voice, and he knew it now.

"Gosh! Jim-twin Allen!" he whispered.

Allen laughed.

"Huh! That's what Snippets meant by callin' me stupid," said Toothpick. "Yuh sure got everybody fooled except her."

"Maybe so," Allen said indifferently. "I give the brakeman five bucks to throw me off that train."

The two rode together out of town toward the lava fields.

"Why for did yuh watch Anderson at Maria's tonight?" asked Toothpick.

" 'Cause I was plumb curious to savvy why Anderson went in that back room and come out with straw on his boots. Is there a stable in that block?"

"Yeh. They's one behind the Red Queen."

"Thought so," Allen grunted sleepily.

SONS OF THE DEVIL

BY EIGHT O'CLOCK THE FOLLOWING MORNING, EVERY seat in the courtroom was taken; men crowded the aisles and perched on the window sills. At eight-thirty the sheriff closed the doors and refused to allow any more to crowd in. Exactly at nine judge Ransom stepped from his house and walked slowly down Main Street toward the courthouse. As he passed State Street, Dutchy and Silent Moore stepped up and followed him. The judge did not look back, but he knew they were there. He quickened his pace, for their presence reminded him forcibly of his danger.

The crowd before the Red Queen grew silent as the judge approached. He nodded to several friends on the porch of the Comfort Hotel, as he cut across Depot Street toward a small door which led to his chambers. At his knock it was opened by the sheriff. The judge and his two shadows passed in, and the door was locked behind them.

A few minutes later be entered the courtroom and took his seat on the bench; outwardly he was calm, inwardly he twitched with nervousness.

The prisoner was brought in, the charge was read, and the trial was on. Pete Cable, a big brute of a man, grinned insolently. The judge realized with something of a shock that, in spite of the prisoner's pale skin and American name, he was a Mexican; he understood now why the Mexican vote would be against him in the next election.

The Honorable J. T. Williams, the defense lawyer, had been imported from Washington at great expense.

He towered over Bill Herrick, the little prosecuting attorney, who was obviously nervous and frightened. The judge wondered if Herrick, too, had been threatened, and, if so, if he had weakened.

Tom Powers had seen to it that there was no chance to fix the jury. He had collected his panel only the night before, and no man knew he was to serve until given a summons, when he was straightway conducted to the jail and locked up in a large room.

From the first it was apparent that Williams sought delay. He did all in his power to make the trial drag and to encumber it with technicalities. He offered objection after objection, forced the judge to rule on a fine point of law at every opportunity.

One by one the jurymen were called, and Williams challenged them peremptorily. He had no idea of the size of the panel called by the sheriff and hoped to force him to call another. If he were successful, the defense would not be caught napping again and would see that among those called there were several who would bring in a verdict of acquittal, no matter what the evidence.

But by late afternoon Williams saw his challenges mostly used up, and still there was no sign of the end of the panel. The jury box was full before the court adjourned for the day.

The judge was thoughtful as, followed by his two shadows, he walked home that evening. The die was cast; he had clearly shown that he was in the camp of justice. He refused to think of the consequences.

Bill Anderson was waiting for him when he arrived at his house. The political boss apologized for losing his temper the evening before. His regret appeared so sincere that the judge almost forgot that momentary flash he had seen of the man's real character.

A little later Mac Kennedy and Ace Cutts arrived. Kennedy was a frequent visitor at the house and a great favorite of Mrs. Ransom's. Ace Cutts was a sleek-haired young fellow of twenty-three, who went in for flashy clothes and handmade boots. He had full charge of the Bar X, and the judge had brought him up as his own son, although he had never adopted the boy legally. At times Ace's wildness bothered him. Now Ace drew his foster father aside.

"Look here, dad. Why lean over so straight you fall over backward? Be sensible. Take things easy. They can't possibly acquit Pete Cable. Why not work things to have a hung verdict? Then you grant a new trial. You can be in Washington, and another judge will hang him."

"I'm sorry to hear you talk like that, my boy," the judge said severely.

Ace flared up.

"Rats! It's sense. They'll break you," he cried angrily.

"Ace, come on, if you're going to dinner with me!" Kennedy called sharply.

Kennedy said good night to the judge and departed, followed by the sulky Ace.

The judge watched them thoughtfully. He wished Ace would get control of that temper; he said foolish things when he was angry, and people might misunderstand him.

About ten that night Toothpick and Jim Allen arrived back in town. All day they had lain flat on their stomachs, under cover of brush, and watched the lava fields with a pair of powerful binoculars.

Now they had circled the town and entered it from the north.

Toothpick went to the jail, where he held a long,

37

whispered conference with the sheriff. Powers' expression changed from surprise to delight as he listened. Allen went to Maria's *cantina*. He staggered as he arrived, but he had money to pay for a bottle, so Maria allowed him to remain. He chose a table close to the rear door; here he drank the first bottle and called for another. He was halfway through this when Dutchy and another man entered. They argued drunkenly for a time, and ended in a fistfight.

A table and a chair crashed over. Maria screamed. She left her bar to stop the fight and assailed the two men with furious words. They mumbled and staggered out. When she returned to the bar she looked about for Allen; he had vanished. Puzzled, she stared about for a moment, then shrugged her shoulders with indifferent indolence.

Allen had slipped, under cover of the fight, out of the back door. He found, as he expected, another door beyond, that led from the storeroom into a path. This, in turn, led to an alley, which cut the block in two and was lined by shacks, little better than hovels. Directly opposite from the intersection of the path and the alley lay a corral.

"That's where Mr. Anderson got straw on his feet. He comes by that narrow alley so he won't have to go by them greaser shacks, 'cause, if he did, they might talk. Let's see what he comes for." Allen chuckled to himself.

He removed his blue glasses, took a Colt from his shoulder holster, and tucked it inside his belt. Then he flitted across the alley and ducked under the corral bars, silent as a ghost. He crossed the corral to a wall on the farther side. Music within told him that this was the rear of the Red Queen Saloon. There was no door here, so he slipped over to the barn and examined that. He passed the double doors that led to the stable. Beyond these he found a small door which was locked. He recrossed the corral, slipped under the bars, and tiptoed down the alley toward Depot Street. In one or two of the shacks there were lights, and once he passed two slovenly Mexicans seated in a doorway. They called to him, but he hurried by.

Back on Main Street he fell into his role once more, staggering and singing softly to himself. He peered through the doors of the Red Queen, not daring to enter, because of the danger of being thrown out. Yet if he found Anderson, he had a plan that he thought would reinstate him in the Red Queen. He waited until several men clattered in to the bar and slipped in after them. He ducked through into the dancing hall, unseen by the bartenders. By good luck he found Anderson watching a poker game. He plucked his sleeve.

Anderson scowled at him.

"Say, mister," he whined, "don't let that sheriff jug me. They tell me you're a good guy that don't kick a guy just 'cause he's down on his luck."

Several other men who heard the hobo's appeal looked curiously at the tattered figure and laughed.

"You just stick in here, an' Powers dasen't come in after yuh," one of them said.

"But them gents out front will give me the bum's rush," the hobo complained.

Anderson grinned good-naturedly. "I've been down on my luck myself. Tom Powers can't touch you, if you have a job."

The hobo drew back suspiciously.

"I ain't very strong, mister."

Again the others laughed, and the political boss

smiled.

"I wasn't thinking of anything that would hurt your health," he said. "How about doing odd jobs about the Red Queen?"

Anderson went over to the Toad and talked to him for a moment. The Toad grinned and assented. Allen had known there was no love lost between Anderson and Tom Powers, but, even so, things had worked out better than he had hoped. Now he was hired as handy man about the Red Queen.

He took up his new duties on the spot. And between errands he kept his ears open.

"Ace is sure shootin' 'em high tonight. I bet he's lost over a thousand," he heard a man say.

"It must come easy to him, because he lost more than that last night," another laughed.

Allen wandered over to the poker table. Ace Cutts' face was sullen. Ace was a poor gambler, for he became angry and forced his luck. He bluffed wildly and tried to outdraw the other players. Allen watched his chips melt away until the last one was gone. Ace leaped to his feet and went over to Bill Anderson.

"I'm busted, Bill; let me have five hundred," he demanded.

Anderson's face grew flinty, his eyes hard.

"And you'll pay me back out of the sixty a month the judge gives you," he said with a harsh laugh.

Ace Cutts' dark face flushed; his eyes grew stormy. He leaned forward as if to whisper something, but Anderson turned away. Ace glared at him, then jammed on his hat and went out to the bar.

"Where the hell does he get his money?" someone asked Anderson.

The political boss shrugged.

"Maybe he signs the judge's name to papers," he suggested.

The other nodded. But Allen was not satisfied with this explanation, for he knew that Anderson knew the judge was broke. A little later he walked out of the Red Queen and headed toward the Ransoms' house. As he passed it he whistled softly, then stopped in the shade of some bushes a little farther on. There he was joined by Dutchy.

"That was sure a realistic scrap yuh pulled in Maria's," Allen said by way of greeting.

"Yuh got what yuh was after?" Dutchy asked.

Allen nodded. They whispered together for a few minutes, until Toothpick rode up and dismounted. Without a word he handed his bridle to Allen, who mounted and trotted down the street.

"Damn the little cuss! Why doesn't he tell a fellow what he's doin'?" Toothpick said irritably.

"So yuh can tell the folks in the Red Queen about it?" Dutchy was scornful. "I'm bettin' he'll find a way through them lava fields."

The following morning, when court opened, the room was again packed. The judge took his seat, and the first witness took the stand. The prosecuting attorney, visibly upset, began the questioning. It was apparent at once that the attorney had been "fixed"; he might as well have been the defending lawyer, for he asked only questions that were favorable to the prisoner. The witness looked disappointed when he was excused. He had had something to tell and had not the chance to do it. He had been asked many questions, but none of importance.

Another witness took the stand, and the district attorney followed the same tactics. The judge saw

41

Williams frown. The local attorney was making the thing too obvious. The jury glanced at one another and whispered among themselves. But this witness was a pugnacious Irishman, and when he was excused he refused to leave the chair.

"Ain't yuh goin' to ask me if Oi seen Pete Cable down that dude?" he roared.

The district attorney paled. He glanced appealingly toward Williams. Before he could determine on a line of action, the foreman of the jury decided to question the witness himself.

"Did yuh see the prisoner down that dude?" he asked.

"Shure Oi did. The dude was skeered stiff whin Pete yanked out his gun. Pete said deliberate: 'Oi'll learn yuh to call me a card cheat.' Thin he plunked the dude twice in the stomach."

Williams shouted: "I object!"

The spectators began to move restlessly and mutter in low tones. The judge hammered on his desk. When silence was restored, he overruled Williams' objection.

The district attorney met the belligerent eye of the foreman; he sensed the angry restlessness of the spectators. He was between the devil and the deep sea. A coward at heart, he yielded to the present menace. He had started this trial crooked, but he would have to finish it straight. Instantly he did a right-about face and changed his tactics. He called witness after witness, and his questions were now keenly edged.

When the prosecution rested, not a man in the room would have taken the short end of a thousand to one that Pete Cable would not hang. The straight stories of those witnesses seemed already to have placed the rope around his bull-like neck. Confidence had left even the prisoner; pasty yellow mantled his usually red face.

Williams did what he could; he called witnesses who flatly contradicted the first evidence, but under cross-examination they floundered and contradicted themselves. By five o'clock the rival attorneys asked time to prepare their summing up, and court adjourned.

That night the district attorney made a wise decision; he slept in the jail. And two deputies reenforced the judge's usual escort of Dutchy and Silent.

Late that night Allen attacked the mysterious little door in the barn with a large variety of keys. It gave at last, and he slipped inside. A ladder led to a hayloft, and he went up. He had no light and fumbled for many minutes before he found another door in the farther end of the loft. More key manipulation and it, too, yielded. Cautiously he crept along the short hall beyond and listened at the door at the end.

"I've done all I will to save that fool," an unfamiliar voice rasped.

"He's your brother." Allen knew that heavy guttural. It belonged to Francisco Garcia, the Toad.

"You and he are alike. You lose your temper and kill," the other man replied.

Allen searched his memory. Where had he heard that voice? At the risk of missing something he hurried to the door at the other end and listened. If any one came in through the barn he would be caught like a rat in a trap. Five seconds later he was back again, straining his ears.

"We'll talk about that when he comes," the unknown man said. "We have got to start a clean-up pronto. It's our only chance. We got to get these gents out of the way." He read a list of names, which Allen carefully noted. When the man had finished, he added: "Jim Allen's in town!"

"The Wolf!" A chair crashed as the Toad leaped up.

"Skinny saw him and those grays of his over near the lava fields," the other added. "Skinny's downstairs waiting."

"*Dios!* The man who killed our father!" the heavy voice of the Toad cried.

"There's two people in town who may know where he holes out—Toothpick and that girl Snippets."

"Then we have to—"

Like a flash Allen slipped back along the hall. Already his exit was barred! A blurred figure stood at the top of the ladder. He waited, knowing that whoever it was had seen him in the shadows. The figure vanished behind a post.

"Francisco!" the man called. "There's someone out here."

The inner door to the room was flung open, and Allen heard a voice bawl for Baldy and the Yuma Kid. Noiselessly Allen circled the post which hid the man. He was within five feet of the square hole which led to the floor below when he heard steps pounding upstairs as the two killers answered the call of their boss. He picked up a board and hurled it across to the opposite wall; he knew that the man behind the post would look instinctively in that direction. He leaped for the trapdoor. He plunged through before the man had time to turn and fire. Allen landed on his feet, agile as a cat. The outer door was blocked now by another man. A Colt roared, and the door was empty. Allen slipped through the corral bars.

He ran down the alley and five minutes later entered the Red Queen. He was once more the hobo as he slouched into a chair where he could watch the door that led into the Toad's private quarters. He considered his

44

discoveries. He had learned that there was another brother mixed up in this affair. He would see to it that Toothpick was sent out of danger and that Snippets was guarded. He had a suspicion as to who this other brother was, but no proof. As a matter of fact, he had no proof of anything. He would have to get that, and there was very little time to be lost.

Fifteen minutes later the Toad, followed by his killers, entered. Allen waited for some time and then decided that the unknown man had left the barn by the back way. Shuffling, with his hands thrust deep in his pockets, he went to the bar. Here he had a couple of drinks, which, as usual, went, not down his throat, but into the cuspidor.

He staggered out to the sidewalk and commenced to sing. As he neared the jail Tom Powers came out and seized him by the arm.

"I told yuh I'd run yuh in if I caught yuh again," he cried, and, to the amusement of several spectators, he dragged the cursing little hobo to the jail door. When this was closed behind them the sheriff released Allen's arm and led the unresisting tramp into his own private office.

"I'm glad to meet yuh, Mr. Allen," the sheriff said as he studied the tattered figure opposite him.

Allen grinned.

"We sure worked that pretty. Yuh got to keep me in jail a couple of days. I found the way through them lava fields, and I want to see where it goes to, so I'm lightin' out for there tonight, and I don't reckon I'll be back until after tomorrow."

"And the people over in the Red Queen will think yuh're in jail," the sheriff chuckled. "A good alibi."

"I suppose yuh want to learn what I found out. Maybe

45

yuh recollect a hombre what used to hang out along the Texas border about seven years ago what called himself '*le Diable à Cheval?*' "

"Yuh betcha—and he was some devil, too," the sheriff said.

"He used to steal girls over the border and hold 'em fer ransom," Allen went on. "I followed the gent—the Devil on Horseback—for near a month, then I ketched him and downed him."

The sheriff stared.

"He had four sons by four wives, and all four sons is right here in town. One of 'em ain't far from us here."

"You mean Pete Cable?" the sheriff demanded.

"Sure. That's why the other three are raising such hell to keep Pete from stretching hemp. I betcha yuh could guess another if yuh thinks hard enough."

Without a moment's hesitation the sheriff answered. "The Toad! An' I'd say I knew the third if he weren't white."

"Didn't I tell yuh they had different mothers?" Allen grinned.

"Then Anderson did fix those bandages!" the sheriff cried with an oath. "Who's the fourth?" he asked.

"I ain't got no idea—don't even know what he looks like. But I did hear once that a gent in Texas who was called 'Cupid Dart' was a son of the Devil."

"The two-gun sheriff and bad man?"

"The same."

Briefly Allen told the sheriff about the death list he had heard the unknown man read out in the secret room.

"Two nights from now yuh have Tim Lynch, the Hogg brothers, Doc Robinson an' yourself meet me at the judge's, an' I'll have somethin' to tell yuh," he promised. "An' yuh can warn them gents that the bunch

46

they calls the Lava Gang is goin' to down 'em, 'cause if they can get the judge's crowd out of the way, they can run things as they choose. With Anderson controllin' the white vote, and the Toad the greaser vote, they'd sure break this country wide open and plenty. Yuh and yuhr friends be careful."

The sheriff shook his head. As yet they had no proof against their enemies. Yet there was something in the matter-of-fact way Allen spoke that made him hope their difficulties would be over soon.

"Yuh got a back door here?" Allen asked.

The sheriff led him to the small door that opened into a vacant lot behind the jail.

"Yuh tell Dutchy not to let Snippets out of his sight," Allen gave his final warning. He vanished into the night.

Scarcely had the door closed on him when someone pounded on the front door. The sheriff opened it to an excited news bearer.

"Someone knifed Doc Robinson," gasped the man.

The sheriff called two of his deputies and ran to the doctor's house. The doctor had been knifed in bed. No one had seen the murderer come or go.

With a sick feeling, the sheriff remembered Allen's story of the fatal list. He left the deputies in charge and went to warn the others of that death list. Each took it seriously and quietly, with the exception of Jim Hogg, who sputtered and insisted he had a right to know who was going to attack him and why.

"I don't know who, but the why of it is because yuh're an honest man," Tom Powers told him.

The sheriff found Dutchy in his usual place before the judge's house. When the sheriff gave him Allen's message his only reply was a grunt of reassurance.

THE WOLF SHOWS HIMSELF

ON THE FOLLOWING DAY, ABOUT ELEVEN O'CLOCK, A great shout went up from the crowd before the courthouse. The jury had brought in a verdict of first-degree murder against Pete Cable.

On Thursday night, after dinner, Tim Lynch, the Hogg brothers, and the sheriff met in the judge's house. They had been there but a short time when Ace Cutts, followed by Anderson, strolled into the room. The sheriff frowned when he saw them, but he realized that it would be better to keep them here now than to allow them to go away. They must suspect something about the gathering.

"Dad told me that little fake, Jim Allen, was coming here tonight, so I thought I'd drop in and look him over," Ace said sneeringly.

Sam Hogg bounced to his feet. "You promised to tell no one!"

"Ace is really my son, and it just slipped out," the judge apologized. He looked sternly at Ace. "You kept your word?"

"Sure thing. Bill, here, never heard a word about the Wolf until we came in here," Ace replied.

"That's true, gentlemen," Anderson corroborated him.

The sheriff doubted both of them. He considered swiftly. He could not reach Allen now and warn him not to come. Dutchy had gone downtown. If he himself left to find Allen he might miss him. Better to remain here and help the Wolf when he came.

Bill Anderson regarded the waiting circle sardonically. "I've always been curious to see Jim-twin

48

Allen," he said. "You'll forgive me if I mention that an alliance between a judge, a sheriff, and an outlaw has its humorous side."

"You're quite right," said the judge thoughtfully. "But if he can help us we are justified in allying ourselves with him."

"If he was the devil and could lead us into the lava fields I'd follow, hanging onto his tail," said the sheriff.

"If what I hears is true, that he can follow trail like an Apache or a bloodhound, I'm bettin' he can lead us through them lava fields," Sam Hogg cried warmly.

"You fellows are wastin' your time," Ace Cutts put in. "He ain't got nerve enough to come here."

"Yuh mean he ain't big enough fool to come into a town filled with gents what is longin' to plug him," Jim Hogg corrected.

"Call it that if yuh like."

"I am afraid I agree with Ace; whether it is fear or caution which keeps him away, he won't come tonight," the judge said heavily.

"He will come, because he said he would," affirmed a girl's voice. Snippets had entered the room in time to hear the last remarks.

Anderson laughed tolerantly. "That sounds like a schoolgirl's admiration for Robin Hood."

"Robin Hood—huh! Allen's rep is made by fools, girls, and old men," Ace snapped. "I'm tellin' yuh he ain't no good and he won't come. And we're wasting our time not havin' a rider beatin' it to Texas to get Cupid Dart, the gent I was tellin' you of."

His words held a word of hate. The other men looked at him curiously. Jim Hogg scratched his head. The judge looked questioningly at the others.

"I think Ace is right," Bill Anderson said judiciously.

"We have all heard of Cupid Dart. Why not send for him? Even if Allen does come, it is a question if we can trust him."

"Trust him? Of course you can't trust him! He's a bushwhackin' killer, who kills men by shootin' them in the back. I know men who have seen him do it." Ace's face was pale with rage.

"Why do you hate him?" the girl asked quietly.

"Because you are a sorta cousin of mine, and I hate to think of you having truck with a man like him," Ace replied bitterly.

"I have no truck with him; I have never heard one word from him since the day he rode away after saving my father. He told me then that friendship between a girl like myself and a man like him was impossible."

The girl's face was flushed. In spite of herself her voice trembled. But her eyes were steady as she looked into Ace's angry brown ones.

"Darn it, the girl's in love with the little runt," Sam Hogg whispered to his brother. He went over and placed an arm about the girl's shoulder.

"Ace, yuh got Allen wrong," he said defensively. "When I was in the Rangers and he hung out in Texas, I chased him plenty. And he had the rep then, among bad hombres, of bein' square. An' I don't believe he killed any gent what didn't need killin' bad."

"Only men who fear him hate him," the girl said softly.

Ace Cutts took a step toward her, but Anderson grasped his arm.

"You fool!" he exclaimed in a whisper.

His back was toward the others. His lips formed a sentence that could be read only by Ace. The young man nodded sullenly and made an effort to recover his composure.

"When he comes," Snippets said anxiously to Tom Powers, "remember you promised there will be no shooting."

"Are you scared I'll drop your hero?" Ace jeeringly asked.

"There's going to be no gun play," Tom Powers cut in sharply.

"Make him give you his word," she insisted.

The worry in her voice was apparent to all. Ace was triumphant.

"I promise you I won't—" he began.

Sam Hogg read the reason correctly for the girl's anxiety and he interrupted sharply.

"Yuh idiot! She ain't scared for the Wolf. But she's worried that yuh'll make a fool play so's the Wolf will have to drop yuh before the judge."

Ace Cutts jeered and slapped his holstered gun. The little cattleman looked meaningly toward Tom Powers, who nodded, crossed to Ace Cutts, and slipped the gun from its holster. Snippets smiled gratefully at the grizzled ex-Ranger. Ace Cutts lapsed into sulky silence.

Then a noise at the rear of the room made them turn. The door that led to the kitchen swung open. Just outside the doorway stood a shadowy figure. It moved forward into the lamplight.

"You bum, what you doing here?" Jim Hogg rasped.

The newcomer was the hobo they knew as Jim Anson.

"Howdy, gents," he said. "Yuh sent for me?"

He removed the blue glasses and tilted back his battered hat. As he advanced farther into the room they saw the two big Colts strapped at his thighs. His loose mouth split in a broad grin, and his big, uneven teeth

51

flashed white.

The clock on the wall ticked loudly in the silence. The assembled men stared wonderingly at the undersized boy. It was Snippets who broke the silence.

"Uncle, this is Jim-twin Allen."

The judge couched and said foolishly: "I thought you were Jim Anson."

Jim Allen grinned again. That contagious grin made the two Hogg brothers chuckle aloud, and even the judge and the sheriff smiled in return.

"No, I ain't Jim Anson. I knows there was gents in this town longin' for my scalp, so I sorta disguises myself. And as there was gents sneakin' around in the bushes out there, I had to pretend to still be Jim Anson. I reckon someone of yuh gents talked, 'cause the Toad's got all of his killers out there waitin' for me. I told the Yuma Kid I had a message for the judge, so he let me pass," Allen explained.

The men were amazed. It seemed unbelievable. Jim Anson, the cowardly, whining little bum! Jim-twin Allen! Their glances traveled from his shapeless moccasins to his boyish, freckled face. But from his strange, animal-like eyes, there could be no doubt he was the man for whom they were waiting. They also understood how he had come by the name of the Wolf.

Ace Cutts' face was ghastly white. With an effort he switched his eyes from Allen to Bill Anderson. The latter was licking his dry lips and staring at the famous outlaw, hypnotized. The realization that Jim Anson was Jim Allen had stunned the politician. Desperately he tried to figure what this would mean. At all costs Allen must not leave that room. He shot a glance to Ace Cutts. The latter began to slide unobtrusively toward the front door.

"I'm right glad to meet yuh, Jim Allen," Sam Hogg cried heartily.

His brother, Jim, chuckled. "An' you tole me yuh chased this feller ragged when yuh was in the Texas Rangers."

"I sure did," the cattleman said ruefully. "I bet the Rangers winded a hundred horses chasin' yuh when yuh was hangin' around lower Texas. An' we never got close enough to throw lead at yuh. Yuh still got them grays yuh had then?"

Allen's face clouded as he glanced quickly at Snippets.

"I got one of 'em—but Queen is dead. I got her son, though."

The ex-Ranger had heard that story. Snippets had told him how Allen had ridden his favorite horse to death in order to save her father. He understood what a sacrifice that had been—for to men who ride the long trail, horses become more than horses. They are friends, companions, and the only living things to be trusted. Sam Hogg cleared his throat.

"Heard about that," he murmured. "It was sure a fittin' end for a grand ol' hoss. When my time comes I hopes I go out like that. I hears the whole town turned out unanimous and planted Queen in style."

"Yeah," Allen murmured dully. The others watched the little rancher and the even smaller outlaw in wonder. Bill Anderson glanced at Ace Cutts, who was close to the door now. Then his eyes once more sought Allen, and he sneered. A man who could sentimentalize over the death of a horse could hardly be as redoubtable an antagonist as rumor painted him.

Allen stepped away from the girl, who had laid her hand on his arm. He looked at Anderson and grinned once more.

"Let's get down to business," Tom Powers spoke.

"Sure, we're wasting time," Anderson snapped. "Allen, we think, because you are an outlaw, you may know the whereabouts of the Lava Gang. If you will lead us to them we will pay you well."

There was something intolerably offensive in the way Bill Anderson spoke. Jim Hogg opened his lips to protest—but the expression on Allen's face did not change. There was nothing there to indicate he had noticed the veiled insult in Anderson's words; if anything, his grin grew broader.

"Yuh mean, I, bein' on the dodge, maybe knows some of the Lava Gang and will give up my friends if yuh pays me enough?" he asked gently.

"No, we don't mean that," the judge cried.

"Not at all," Tim Lynch added.

Allen ignored the judge, glanced meaningly at Tom Powers, then faced Bill Anderson, who was lounging against the fireplace. This maneuver placed Ace Cutts behind the little outlaw. Anderson had expected Allen to grow angry, to bluster, and this calmness disconcerted him. However, he had gained his objective, which was to concentrate Allen's attention on himself; and Allen's back was now toward the door.

"We are not asking you to betray your friends, but if you will lead us to them, we will pay you well." The explanation was even more offensive than the original statement.

"Yuh aimin' to get me mad?" Allen asked. He grinned at Bill Anderson and shook his head. "Mister, I never get mad, 'cause things might happen if I did, and me not notice 'em. I let yuh talk 'cause I wasn't sure—now I'm certain."

Only one of the bystanders, Powers, understood the significance of Allen's words. The others glanced curiously from Allen to Anderson. The politician's face flushed, and he shot a quick glance at Ace Cutts, who had reached the door, then he glanced over his shoulder into the mirror behind him. At once he understood that Allen had been watching Ace Cutts reflected there, and was fully aware of the foreman's attempt to gain the outside, where he could give the alarm to the Yuma Kid and the others waiting there.

"Yuh gents gave me yuhr promise no one was to leave the room while I was here," Allen reminded.

"We sure did," Jim Hogg cried.

"Get away from that door, Ace," Tim Lynch snapped.

"Ace, don't leave this room," the judge commanded.

Ace Cutts had his hand on the doorknob. Now he paused.

"If he turns that knob I'll drop him," Allen said.

All expression had left the little gunman's voice. It was flat, toneless. But its very flatness made Ace hesitate. He glanced at Anderson, who nodded to him to go. Then realization came to him that Allen had been watching him in the mirror and that Anderson knew it. Even if he failed to get clear of the door before Allen fired, Anderson would have gained his objective, for a shot in that room would bring the Toad's killers on the run. Anderson was deliberately trying to sacrifice Ace. He dropped the doorknob as if it had suddenly grown red-hot, threw himself into a chair, and stared fixedly at his neat boots.

"I am given to understand that you know the members of the Lava Gang," the judge said.

"Yeah, I knows them," Allen replied softly.

"You can trust everyone here. Will you give me their

names?"

"I came here to tell yuh, but I've changed my mind."

"But why?" the judge insisted.

"Judge, if yuh'll have the sheriff leave town after dinner tomorrow night and ride straight toward Jaw Tooth Mountain, I'll pick yuh up and show yuh where yuhr cattle is," Allen said.

Argument was vain. Allen refused to mention even one member of the Lava Gang.

Slowly the little outlaw backed toward the door by which he had entered.

"Good night, gents," he called. Then his eyes caught and held those of Snippets for a moment. "So long, kid," he said softly. The door was empty and he was gone.

Allen had said that his enemies had learned he was to come there that night and were waiting for him outside. For a long moment those in the room waited, waited for the shot that would announce he had been discovered. Bill Anderson was the first to move. He picked up his hat and walked toward the front door, but Tom Powers reached it ahead of him. The sheriff shook his head.

"We promised before he came, that no one was to leave until he had been gone for ten minutes," the sheriff explained.

For the fraction of a second Anderson held his ground before the sheriff. The impulse came to him to shout, then discretion gained the upper hand; he shrugged and returned to his place by the fireplace.

"He's certainly a careful little cuss and doesn't trust people," he said with a laugh.

"Maybe if yuhr carcass was worth ten thousand you wouldn't neither," Sam Hogg snorted.

Slowly the minutes ticked away. When the time was

up Anderson was the first to leave. The moment the door had closed behind him, Tom Powers seized Sam Hogg by the shoulder and, whispered:

"Follow him and see where he goes."

To Sam Hogg it seemed impossible that the good-natured, affable politician could be mixed up with the Lava Gang, but his training in the Rangers had taught him that all things were possible, so he nodded and slipped out after Anderson.

THE LAVA GANG IN ACTION

ANDERSON WENT TO MARIA'S *CANTINA*, GAVE SOME directions to Mac Kennedy, and seated himself at a table with a Mexican girl. He had noted Sam Hogg's rather unskillful trailing. A few minutes later he saw Hogg peer in for an instant.

As soon as the cattleman's head disappeared, Anderson went out the rear door. He, who always claimed he went unarmed, now slipped his hand beneath his armpit and withdrew a short-barreled Colt. He tiptoed warily along the alley to the corral behind the Red Queen. At the small door in the barn he stood listening for a moment before he unlocked it and entered. He climbed to the loft and unlocked the second door which led to the short passage. With this door locked behind him he lost his air of caution. The third door—that same door behind which Allen had listened—opened into a room comfortably furnished with table, chairs, and a bed. Anderson lit a lamp and pressed a button near its other door.

Down in the Red Queen a big game progressed at the faro table. Francisco Garcia sat in his usual place on the platform. The Yuma Kid lounged near him, and Baldy sprawled on the platform at his feet.

Garcia leaned forward, his protruding eyes fixed on the dealer's hands. A mining man had just placed a large bet, and the dealer was about to flip the cards. Behind them a buzzer sounded. The Toad frowned impatiently and shrugged his massive shoulders. The dealer turned the cards and the mining man won.

Again the buzzer sounded imperiously. The mining

man doubled his bet, and the dealer glanced over his shoulder for mute instructions. The Toad shook his head. He never allowed a dealer to turn a crooked card unless he was present, and now he had to obey the summons of that buzzer.

He heaved himself to his feet and waddled toward the rear door. Grunting at each step, he climbed the stairs and made his way to the secret room in the barn.

"You took your time," Anderson said coldly in Spanish.

"Big game," the Toad replied. "What was your hurry?"

"A big game! Let me tell you, brother mine, that big game may be your last," Anderson snapped. Brothers! One was heavy-set, with the swarthy features of a Mexican; the other was blond, well formed, with the features of a Nordic. Yet they were brothers.

"I saw the Wolf tonight," Anderson said slowly.

"You killed him?" the big man asked eagerly. Anderson shook his head.

The Toad's swarthy face flushed, his eyes bulged more prominently than ever, and his features contorted with furious rage.

"You saw the Wolf—the man who killed our father— and he *lives?*"

Anderson's soft brown eyes became coldly contemptuous. Here lay the reason for Anderson's dominance over his brother. He never lost his temper and he possessed a cold, calculating ruthlessness. He never made a move unless he had thought out the consequences in advance. The Toad was given to quick rages in which he acted without thought.

"Stop glaring at me! You are like Pete! If he had not lost his temper we would not be in this mess now. He had to go savage and kill a man instead of waiting and

59

having him killed outside."

With an effort the Toad recovered his composure and dropped into a chair.

"Let me tell you, brother mine, you also have seen the Wolf many times," Anderson said.

The Toad shook his heavy head and growled a denial.

"Jim Anson is the Wolf!"

Francisco Garcia stared in unbelief. The color drained from his face.

"*Dios!*" he muttered. "Then it was he who was in the barn that night?"

Anderson nodded and related the events of that evening.

"He knows or suspects a lot, but he has no proof, or the sheriff would have acted. We have got to get Allen and get him quick," Anderson added.

"How?"

"That girl—Snippets McPherson, the judge's niece. She's in love with him, and he with her. She knows where he has been holing out for the last few days. Get her and make her tell. If she won't we'll get him when he trails her. That will be the Yuma Kid's job," Anderson said rapidly.

The Toad closed his eyes and thought for a moment. "We'll do it tonight," he said.

He leaned forward and lowered his voice as he explained his plan. When the Toad had finished, Anderson nodded.

"That should work. Have the Yuma Kid and Baldy cover them. And you had better start having the others cleaned up. Sam Hogg and the judge must be 'accidents.' The others, any way you can get them. Good night, my brother, I am off."

Anderson slipped out the rear door and left the Toad

brooding. Ten minutes later he arose and pressed the buzzer.

Sam Hogg had been reporting the result of his trailing. The sheriff stared through the window at the bright lights of the Red Queen Saloon. Suddenly he fell flat on the floor as a windowpane splintered and a bullet thudded into the inner wall. He leaped to his feet and yanked the shade down.

"That was a fool thing to do, and he warned me to watch out," the sheriff said ruefully as he eyed the bullet hole in the wall.

"Ain't no good chasin' that fellow; he's a mile away by this time," Sam Hogg advised. "Who tole yuh to watch out?"

"Jim Allen."

"When did yuh see him?" the cattleman asked in surprise. "Yuh seen him afore or since tonight?"

"Both," the sheriff replied shortly. He seemed to be pondering something, then he threw himself in a chair opposite the ex-Ranger.

"Seein' you're on the list marked for slaughter, I figure you got a right to know," he began. "Right after this Jim Anson turned up I knowed he was Jim-twin Allen. Toothpick comes here the first night and tells me about it. Allen tells me to trust no one but Dutchy and Snippets. He says Toothpick is all right but talks too much. He left here now, just a minute before you got here. He tells me he don't know where they got the judge's cows and not to bother to meet him tomorrow. He sends Toothpick ridin' off somewhere, then he goes out hisself, and he don't tell me one dang thing he's doin'," the sheriff cried in disgust.

"Does he know who the Lava Gang is?" Sam Hogg

61

asked eagerly.

"Yeah, but he only tol' me a couple. The Toad and his killers, the Yuma Kid, and Baldy Flynn; then there's that greaser Pedro, who bought Pete Cable's *cantina*."

"The Toad! Let's go get him!" The little cattle-man yanked out his Colt and whirled the cylinder. His eyes were snapping with excitement.

The sheriff shook his head. "We got to wait until we line up the rest—we got to catch the big boss."

"Well, I don't like this slaughter list," Sam Hogg complained.

"I guess the Toad's behind it. Me and you is on it, the judge, Dutchy, Toothpick, your brother, an' Tim Lynch. Doc Robinson was, and they got him. The Lava Gang figures if they downs us they can elect a new sheriff and judge and run things to suit themselves. Allen went to the judge's tonight deliberate, to sorta let them know he was onto them. He figures they'll get nervous and give themselves away. I got to raise about twenty men right quick and keep 'em handy," the sheriff concluded.

"Leave that to me. I got about thirty of the best boys along the border out at the Frying Pan what's just spoiling for a fight," Sam Hogg said with enthusiasm.

"They'll do fine," the sheriff agreed.

The ex-Ranger thought for a moment. "The Wolf goes to the judge's deliberate! Then he figures someone what was there tonight is playing with the Lava Gang?"

"Yeah," the sheriff muttered miserably.

"Yuh mean Ace Cutts!"

The sheriff nodded.

"Why, the judge brought him up, the dirty coyote!" The cattleman was bristling with anger. "An' he tips off the Toad to have Allen killed."

"He's a bad one," Tom Powers said heavily.

"I'm goin' to hunt up 'Big Dick,' my foreman, and have him tip off the boys to stay sober," the ranchman cried, starting for the door.'

The sheriff stopped him. "You better go out the back way."

At this reminder that he was on the "slaughter list," Sam Hogg smiled grimly.

The sheriff let him out on a vacant lot behind the courthouse, and a few minutes later he was on brightly lighted Main Street. He knew that no attempt against his life would be made in public, for the man who brought him down would have every puncher on the Frying Pan to deal with later. Still, he was in danger, and a very real danger, for a warning from Jim-twin Allen was something no man could disregard.

"Bein' him," Sam Hogg mused, "he wouldn't think a gent was in danger until he had both feet in a grave."

The Lone Star Saloon stood at the corner, and he paused in the shadow of its walls and glanced up and down Main Street. Tim Lynch, the owner of the Lone Star, was one of the men on the Toad's list, and Sam Hogg decided to drop a warning to him to be on the lookout. As he stepped up on the board sidewalk he saw the Yuma Kid and Baldy saunter out of the Red Queen.

"I ain't hankerin' to meet them jaspers," he grunted and hastily slid through the doors of the saloon. He waited a moment and peered out. The two killers were standing on the corner opposite the judge's house. They made no effort to conceal their presence. Obviously they were waiting for something.

As he watched he saw two figures, followed by a third, come out of the judge's gate and head toward the outskirts of the town.

"Darn it, why do they let Snippets go roamin' with

63

that Kennedy dude fer? Reckon they is all right, 'cause Dutchy is followin' 'em. Huh! For a minute I thinks them killers was waitin' for the gal," he grumbled.

The Lone Star was empty, and Tim Lynch, acting as bartender, watched Sam Hogg peer through the door for a time, then rounded the bar and suddenly clapped his hand on his shoulder.

"You playin' detective?" he asked, grinning. "Who you watchin'?"

"Them two jaspers standin' on the corner," Sam replied.

"They're plumb dangerous. It ain't safe to even watch them two killers. Come have a drink."

Sam Hogg tossed down a drink, then leaning forward, whispered: "Tim, I can't tell yuh how I know, but yuh been talkin' loud agin' a certain gent, and he's out for your blood."

Tim grinned and, reaching beneath the bar, brought up a sawed-off shotgun.

"Reckon I know who you mean, and the Toad don't work in the open, but this scatters some, an' I'm keepin' it darned close to me."

Before either could say more the screen doors swung open and two men entered. Both were strangers. One was drunk and the other was attempting to pacify him.

"If I lets yuh have one more drink, will yuh promise to go to bed?" the sober one demanded. "Positively," the other replied.

From somewhere outside there came a shot, followed by a shrill scream, then another shot. Sam Hogg ran to the door. As he emerged on the street it struck him as queer that the strangers' curiosity was not strong enough to make them follow him.

Several men were running and pointing up Main

64

Street beyond the judge's house. The ex-Ranger saw the Yuma Kid and Baldy a block away. The running men also noticed the two killers and instantly dropped to a walk. It wasn't safe to approach them at a run. The men halted for a moment, then edged across the road to circle them.

"That's what they was waitin' for, tryin' to delay pursuit!" Sam Hogg growled.

Rage overcame him and he yanked out his gun, leaped off the board walk and charged down the road. For a moment he thought Baldy was going to intercept him, but the Yuma Kid spat out a sentence in Spanish and Baldy stepped aside.

As Sam Hogg ran, followed by several other men, he heard the pounding of hoofs slowly receding on the plain. They found Dutchy on the outskirts of town, lying face downward in the dust of the trail.

A brief examination by the light of a match convinced Sam Hogg that the grizzled puncher was dead. He had been shot through the head from behind. Even as death was upon him he had drawn one gun and fired. The little cattleman cursed with sorrow and rage.

A little later one of the crowd discovered the prone figure of Kennedy, the dude, at the side of the trail. Examination disclosed he had been stunned by the butt of a gun. He groaned and opened his eyes.

Sam Hogg seized him.

"Where's the gal? Who downed Dutchy? What happened? Come alive and spill it."

At each question the ex-Ranger shook the half-conscious man. Finally a lanky cow-puncher interfered.

"Hell, Sam, if yuh knock the breath out of the darned dude, how can he talk?"

At last Mac Kennedy told his story. He had called on

Snippets and suggested they take a walk. He had done that many times before. Dutchy accompanied them. Just as they reached the fork in the trail he had heard a shot, and swung about in time to see Dutchy fall. Then something hit him on the head, and that was all he knew. He had seen none of the men who had attacked them. Sam Hogg was convinced that Kennedy was not trying to conceal anything, not even his own cowardice.

Sheriff Tom Powers arrived on the scene; without delay he formed a posse and started in pursuit. The crowd drifted back to town. Here they found more excitement. Tim Lynch had been knifed and killed by an unknown man. His body was discovered behind the bar of the Lone Star by one of the first excited men to return from the crossroads.

Sam Hogg walked slowly to his brother's store. The two talked in whispers for a time, then Sam called in a passing cowboy and sent him across the street to the Red Queen to fetch Big Dick, his foreman.

A few minutes later, Big Dick was dusting it straight for the Frying Pan Ranch. He was to bring back Sam Hogg's best fighters.

THE SENTENCE

A LITTLE AFTER DAWN THE FOLLOWING MORNING, eighteen heavily armed riders from the Frying Pan Ranch clattered into town. They dismounted before the Hogg Hardware Store, and Sam Hogg, followed by Tad Hicks, Windy Sam, and Kansas Jones, stepped from the store and greeted them.

The ex-Ranger's eyes lit with enthusiasm as he looked them over. Clean limbed, hardy, eager faced, reckless eyed, each one of them was willing to fight at the drop of a hat. He snapped out his orders; half of them were to be on duty at all times at the store; those not on duty were free to do as they pleased—with one exception—the Red Queen Saloon was barred to all.

Tom Powers and his posse returned to town with long faces and jaded horses. The sheriff dismounted before the hardware store. He shook his head at a question from Sam Hogg.

"The trail was plain until we struck Snake Canyon, halfway between the lava fields and the Frying Pan, but we lost it there. Cattle had been driven across the trail, and we couldn't find nothin'."

He threw himself into a chair and rolled a cigarette while Sam Hogg told him of the murder of Tim Lynch, and why he had sent for his riders. Suddenly the sheriff looked up and asked hopefully:

"You seen Allen?"

Sam Hogg shook his head.

The sheriff got up wearily. He left the store and headed for the jail. He attempted to snatch a few minutes' sleep before time to conduct Pete Cable to the

67

court to be sentenced, but sleep refused to come.

Where was Allen? Had he proof about the men he accused? Could he get it? The Lava Gang had struck twice. Who would be the third victim? The sheriff cursed when he thought of Snippets McPherson in the power of such men as the sons of *le Diable à Cheval*. He felt helpless. He suddenly realized how much he had come to depend on the outlaw, Jim Allen.

At eleven o'clock he led the prisoner, Pete Cable, into the crowded courtroom. A hush settled on the spectators as they entered. All eyes were fixed on the prisoner. His assurance had left him completely. He seemed crushed by fear.

The formalities were gone through.

"And there hanged by the neck until dead."

The judge pronounced the fatal sentence. For a moment there was silence as people craned their necks to see the condemned man. The judge walked slowly from the court, the sheriff half carried, half led, Pete Cable back to his cell.

The people filed from the courtroom. As far as they were concerned the affair was over.

Waiting is the most trying ordeal for the active man, and as the day passed and night came, and still nothing happened, the Frying Pan riders became restless.

The men within the store were fully as impatient as those without. Toothpick paced the floor; every few minutes he would stop and listen, then recommence his pacing. On his return, when he had been told of Dutchy and Snippets, the men had barely been able to keep him from immediate violence.

Jim Hogg was fuming for action. The sheriff stared at the ceiling. Tad Hicks and Windy sat on the floor close to the stove and grumbled their impatience.

"Hey, Sam," Windy pleaded, "tell a gent why for yuh're delayin' the battle?"

"An' who the devil are we goin' to fight?" Tad Hicks added.

Sam Hogg threw up his hands and shook his head. What were they waiting for? Allen? He might be dead.

Time passed, and all but Toothpick were dozing. He continued his endless pacing. Suddenly he stopped and listened for a moment, then sprang to the back door and threw it open. Sam Hogg and the sheriff jerked to sudden life and crowded after him. Someone was coming.

"It's him," Toothpick said exultantly.

They heard a faint whistle. With hands on guns they stepped outside. A black blotch materialized from the darkness and Jim-twin Allen hailed them.

"That yuh, Toothpick? Who's with yuh?"

"Tom Powers and Sam Hogg?"

The black blotch crept nearer.

"Where can I stable these old bags of bones?"

"Is them yuhr grays?" Sam Hogg asked.

"Yeah," Allen replied.

"Yuh go on in and get warm. I'll rub 'em down, feed 'em, and fix 'em pretty," Sam Hogg said eagerly.

For a fraction of a second Allen hesitated, then he spoke to the grays.

"Thanks," he said as he passed Sam Hogg.

Unceremoniously Allen sauntered into the store, sank into a chair near the fire, and called a greeting to Jim Hogg. The sheriff looked at Toothpick, and the latter shook his head; both hesitated to tell him the bad news. They served him a thick sandwich, which he munched in silence, then drank two cups of black coffee.

"Well?" he asked when he had finished.

69

Toothpick, Jim Hogg, and the sheriff stirred uneasily. Sam Hogg returned to the room just as the sheriff began to tell his story.

Sam Hogg stared at the little outlaw as he listened. This was not the boy he had seen the night before in the judge's house. The freckled face was the same, but it was older. Allen was no longer a laughing youth, but a man whom all respected and, deep down in their hearts, feared. Allen's expression never changed at the faltering accounts of the death of Dutchy and the kidnapping of Snippets. The ex-Ranger got the idea Allen had heard the story before and for some reason was concealing the fact.

Tad Hicks opened his sleepy eyes and stared at the little man by the stove. He took one look, rubbed his eyes, and looked again. He nudged Windy, and the plump puncher ceased his snores and sat up.

When the sheriff had finished, Toothpick stepped forward with clenched hands.

"Jim, Dutchy was my friend, and I want yuh to promise—" he began.

Allen interrupted.

"I get yuh, but it can't be did. Dutchy was downed by a couple of skunks what was called 'Left Steve' and Bill Rance—"

Sam Hogg now interrupted in his turn.

"Did yuh say *was* called?" he asked.

"Yeah," Allen said indifferently. "Tom, I hears yuh fellows talkin' last night where yuh lost the trail. I hears that Dutchy was downed, but don't hear nothin' about Snippets being run off. So I takes after the killers an' downs 'em."

They glanced from the little outlaw in the chair to one another, then back again. Windy Sam dug Tad Hicks in

70

the ribs.

"Yuh know him?" he whispered.

"The Wolf," Tad replied.

"I knows that, but take a look at them pants," Windy muttered.

"The hobo! He talks of downin' gents like yuh does prairie hens, an' we come near beatin' hell out of him," Tad Hicks exclaimed in an awe-struck whisper.

"But the girl! Snippets! What are you going to do about her?" Jim Hogg demanded impatiently.

"I thinks I knows where she is," Allen replied wearily.

"Let's get goin' then!" The choleric little storekeeper seized his hat.

"It can't be did. They got her over in the lava fields. I got to trail 'em. I found where they went in and I've got to pick the rest out," Allen said flatly.

"We got twenty men out there and a hundred more scattered about. We'll comb them hills and find her," Jim Hogg insisted.

Allen shook his head.

Sam Hogg and the sheriff looked at each other. They knew Allen was lying. For if there had been a single chance of Snippets being taken over the border he would be wasting no time in words. They could not fathom why he was lying.

"Looka here, there ain't no use being stubborn," Jim Hogg growled at Allen. "We *got* to do something."

"Go ahead," Allen replied. He looked at Sam Hogg and added: "I'm goin' now. Where's them hosses of mine?"

"Don't yuh go 'way, sheriff," Jim Hogg cried as his brother and Allen started toward the rear door. "I'm goin' to see the judge and make him order yuh to hunt

71

for that gal."

As the furious storekeeper stormed out of the room Allen winked at Sam Hogg and the sheriff.

Outside, while he was saddling his horses, he explained. "The Toad's got the Yuma Kid and Baldy and them two brothers watchin' the girl. What happens if we go chargin' in there? Do yuh think them four will give her up? And if we kill 'em they'll sure enough take her with them."

"What yuh goin' to do?" the sheriff asked.

"I'm hopin' Jim, your brother'll do it for me. The Toad plumb hates me, an' if he could down me he'd be willin' to cut and run for Mexico after. When he hears I'm goin' to try and pick out the trail through the lava fields I sorta figure he'll tell his killers to hike it over there and get me; then I'll get the girl."

"And yuh lied deliberate to fool Jim?" Sam Hogg asked.

"Jim is right convincin' when he's got his mad up, an' I don't think he's a good liar. I figure there'll be someone who will be plumb anxious to pass the news on to the Toad." Then Allen talked rapidly for a few minutes and the others listened in silence.

After Allen had vanished into the night the sheriff said admiringly: "Gosh, ain't he a hellion?"

Sam Hogg nodded and hurried through the store. Outside he found Tad Hicks. He ordered him to follow and hurried down the dark, deserted street. He explained a little to Tad, and the two crouched down in some bushes opposite the judge's and settled themselves to watch.

Jim Hogg was still spluttering with wrath when he burst into the judge's house. Although the hour was late he found the judge's family still up. Ace Cutts and Kennedy were with them.

"We got news of Snippets!" roared the storekeeper. "An' I want yuh to order Tom Powers to gather every blessed man in town and search them lava hills, 'cause that's where they got her."

"What do you mean? How do you know? Is she hurt?" The judge fired rapid questions.

"Jim Allen tole me. He says they got her over there and that he knows part of the trail and is goin' to pick out the rest tomorrow, but by that time the gal will be over the border," Jim attempted to explain.

"Wait a minute, Mr. Hogg," Kennedy spoke quietly. "Let's get this straight. You say that Allen insists that Snippets is being held captive in the lava beds? And he's going by himself to trail her?"

"That's exactly what I said. The darn little runt—"

"It's sense to me," Ace Cutts interrupted. "Three men in those lava beds can hold off a hundred. Allen has a better chance by himself," he insisted.

The judge, Mrs. Ransom, and even Mary, joined in the discussion as to the best way to rescue Snippets.

"I think Allen is right," Kennedy said. "But then I'm an Eastern dude and don't know anything about it. Good night, folks. I'm riding out to my ranch tonight, so I won't see you tomorrow."

"I'm going with yuh," Ace Cutts stated.

The two went out and hurried toward the Red Queen.

Sam Hogg arose from his hiding place and growled: "The dirty skunk!"

"Who? Him or tother?" Tad asked.

Ten minutes later Kennedy and Ace Cutts rode down the street. The moment they had passed the judge's house they put their horses into a wild, scrambling run.

Sam Hogg smiled grimly, then, drawing his gun from his holster, he fired three times in the air.

73

KIDNAPPED

THE ATTACK HAD COME SO SUDDENLY THAT SNIPPETS McPherson hardly realized what was happening before she was roughly seized and hoisted to a horse in front of a masked man. She had uttered only one shrill scream, for common sense told her it was better to obey her captor than to risk his carrying out his threat of choking her. She realized that the single shot—the one which hit Dutchy—would raise the alarm.

So she remained passive. The thing that worried her more than her own situation was Dutchy's fate. She was sure he had been badly hurt, for she knew the old gunman would never cease firing as long as he had strength to pull a trigger.

She marked the course they were traveling. It was almost due east. They followed the trail to the Frying Pan and Bar X for about five miles, then left it to take a course south. They twisted in and out of the brush, slid down banks and scrambled up sheer slides.

Snippets estimated that they were about ten miles from town when she was transferred to a waiting buckboard. As she was driven away in this, she heard the mooing of cattle and the shouts of men, and she knew that the cattle were being driven across their trail to hide it. There were two men in the buckboard with her. She sat on the driver's seat with one, while another knelt in the rear. Suddenly the man behind her dropped a sack over her head which blinded her completely. Even breathing was difficult.

A half hour later she was lifted from the buckboard and carried into a house. The sack was removed and she found herself in a perfectly bare room. One of the men carried a flickering lantern; by its light she sized up her two captors. She had never seen either of them before. One was tall and thin, with a drooping mustache, and the other was a short, powerfully built Mexican.

"Yuh stay quiet and yuh won't get hurted," the one with the mustache said.

"If yuh don't, I'll—" the Mexican began.

She could not resist saying: "You know who will come after me, don't you? The Wolf!"

It amused her and gave her courage to see how they jumped. The Mexican snarled as, followed by the other, he left the room.

They took the lamp and left her in total darkness. She satisfied herself that the blinds on the windows were securely fastened, then tried to figure out where she was. She puzzled on this until her head nodded and she fell asleep.

She was awakened by the opening of the door. Sun streamed through the cracks in the blinds. A man entered. He was of medium height; his hat was pulled down over his eyes and a handkerchief covered his face.

"I'm not going to beat about the bush. You know where the Wolf holes out and you might as well tell me now as later," the man said.

There was something about the voice that was vaguely familiar, but the handkerchief muffled the tones so that she could not place it.

"I don't know where he is," she faltered.

"Spill it," repeated the man roughly. "I'm not going to stand here all day. I'm asking you where the Wolf holes out. You have only a little time. If yuh don't tell I'll turn you over to the Mexican out there. I'm comin' back."

He went out and locked the door after him. Snippets

tried to pull herself together. Again and again she told herself that Allen would come, yet in spite of herself the fear grew. She ran to the blinds and beat against them with her hands; then she paced the room like a trapped animal. At last, worn out, she dropped on the floor.

In the late afternoon she heard voices outside. She flashed to the window and listened. There was one voice she knew—a high, cackling voice. That was Baldy. No doubt the Yuma Kid was with him. She heard harsh Mexican voices and caught scraps of conversation. The Toad had sent his killers here to wait for Allen. They knew he would trail her. Now she dropped on her knees and prayed that he would stay away.

Time passed and she crouched against the wall and listened—fearful for the shot which would tell her that Allen had come on his last mission. Daylight faded, and night came.

It must have been past midnight when the door opened with a jerk and the same man who had faced her that morning stood before her.

"You going to tell?" he snarled.

She faced him with the courage of despair.

"How can I tell when I don't know where he is?"

He laughed harshly, leaped forward, caught one wrist in an iron grip, and twisted her arm cruelly.

"Spill it or I'll twist your arm off," he rasped.

She gritted her teeth and tried to suppress a scream. From outside came the noise of a horse at a hard gallop. The thought flashed into her mind that Jim Allen had arrived. The man threw her aside and ran from the room. She heard excited voices, the confusion of men running about. A few minutes later there came the sound of horses ridden rapidly away. The sounds ceased. She stole to the door, which the man had forgotten to lock, opened it, and glanced out. Her two captors were out there. Maybe they would go to bed soon. She must wait; she closed the door and sat on the floor near it, so she could hear them.

Hours later she sat up with a start and realized she had been asleep. The light of another gray dawn was seeping into the room. Again she opened the door. The men were still there. Their backs were toward her. She decided to chance it, to try to slip by them and out of the building. She must get away before the other man returned.

She moved softly, slowly. She was halfway there, when a board creaked, and the men turned. She leaped forward, but before she could reach the outer door the Mexican had her by the hair. She screamed and kicked at him.

"Yuh leetle fury," he growled. "I theenk I'll tame yuh."

He buried both hands in her hair and shook her, yanked her about. He shifted his hands to her throat. Tighter and tighter he gripped.

Suddenly a terrific uproar rocked the room. The man released her, and she fell back against the wall. The air was filled with smoke. Slowly it cleared, and she saw Jim-twin Allen standing close to the door she had tried to reach. There was a smoking gun in his hand. Against the farther wall stood the tall man with the long mustache, his hands upraised. On the floor at her feet sprawled the Mexican, flat on his face, his arms and legs twisted grotesquely.

Snippets crossed to Allen. "I knew you would come," she said simply.

He smiled at her. "Get back in there," he snapped to the tall man who had been her captor. The man quailed in fright and backed, hands still raised, into the room where Snippets had been a prisoner.

"Come on, kid," said Allen. "We got to get out of here."

The two grays were waiting close to the house. A rifle hung on Honey Boy's saddle.

"Do yuh think Princess will know yuh?" Allen asked.

Snippets placed her fingers to her lips and whistled. Princess cocked her ears, then, followed by her mate, dashed toward the girl. Snippets, undismayed by the snapping teeth, rubbed the mare's soft muzzle.

"Hop on her, kid, 'cause those gents will be tearin' mad," he urged.

After they were mounted, Snippets glanced about in bewildered recognition of the landscape. "Why, this is the Bar X—uncle's ranch!" she gasped. "What does it mean?"

Allen hesitated. "Reckon you'll learn some time, so I might as well tell yuh, kid, that Ace Cutts is a bad actor."

She thought of her uncle, of his fondness for the boy, and grew silent. Side by side they rode toward town in the bright morning sunlight.

Five riders approached out of a draw to the north of the lava fields. They were heading fast for the Bar X Ranch. Anderson, their leader, jerked his horse to a sudden, sliding stop. He pointed to the two figures on a smooth meadow a mile before them.

"Who the hell is that down there?" he cried. Quick suspicion fired the Yuma Kid. "Two grays!" he rasped.

Baldy's thin lips drew back in a toothless snarl. "The Wolf!"

"He tricked us!" As Anderson made the admission,

78

his face grew rigid, and the veins on the back of his neck expanded.

The other two riders were Mexicans, José and Pedro Gonzalez, two of the Toad's men. Both were killers. They were used on raids where it was bad policy to leave any survivors.

"*Madre de Dios!*" José swore. "He has the girl!"

"We hang if—" his brother began.

"We don't stop him," Anderson snapped. He gave his orders rapidly. The Mexicans swung their horses to cut in behind Allen, while Anderson, Baldy, and the Yuma Kid turned to their right to head him off. Anderson shouted with exultation when he saw Ace Cutts and several riders top the rise on the farther side of the valley. They had Allen in a trap.

Bill Anderson and the other two were within a half mile of Allen before he saw them. At a glance he understood that they would head him off. He grinned confidently at Snippets.

"Kid, we're in a jam. Don't try tuh guide Princess, she savvies how tuh follow," he called cheerfully.

Allen swung Honey Boy straight up the northern rise toward several mushroomlike buttes. Princess followed some fifteen yards in the rear. He was within a few hundred yards of the crest when Ace Cutts and his men topped the rise. Ace shouted, and three of his men threw themselves off their horses and began to fire, while he and two other men continued to race along the crest.

Allen whirled his horse and sent it in a scrambling run along the treacherous slope. Without a touch of the reins from Snippets, Princess turned and followed. The range was long for accurate shooting, but some of the shots fired by the dismounted men sang uncomfortably close to Allen's ears.

"Ain't it funny how folks always shoot over, when shootin' down a slope?" he called over his shoulder to Snippets, who waved her hand in return. Strangely, she felt excitement, but no fear.

Anderson was directly below them and riding hard. Baldy and the Yuma Kid had stuck to the smooth floor of the meadow and were a good hundred yards ahead of him. The men on the crest were also traveling faster, and they were soon ahead of him. A minute later Ace Cutts and his men headed down the slope, while the Yuma Kid and Baldy swung their horses up it. They gave an exultant whoop when they saw they had Allen surrounded.

Allen gave them an answering yell, swung Honey Boy on "a ten-cent piece," and headed down the slope straight for Anderson. Anderson yanked on his horse's bit and brought him to a standstill, then snatched out his rifle. The horse reared. Allen was within three hundred yards and coming fast. To make sure of his shot Anderson slid off his pony. The moment his feet touched the ground, Allen checked Honey Boy's wild progress down the slope and swung him parallel with it again.

Anderson threw himself on his now frightened horse and looked up. He swore bitterly; for, the moment he was in the saddle, Allen had again switched his direction and was once more headed straight for him.

The Yuma Kid and Baldy had joined Ace Cutts and his men, but all were some fifty yards higher up the slope and four hundred yards in advance of Allen.

Anderson struggled to master his plunging horse. Allen dropped his reins over the pommel and seized his Winchester. His horse covered the distance between the two in great scrambling leaps. Allen fired as rapidly as he could pump his lever.

"Damn him, he's outguessed me," Anderson growled.

It was impossible for him to fire from his frightened horse, so he swung his foot over its rump to dismount again. The horse plunged, reared high on its hind legs and fell with a crash. Anderson, in attempting to leap clear of the falling animal, dropped his rifle. A slug whipped his hat from his head, and he dived for cover behind his dead horse.

Allen again swung Honey Boy, this time away from the Yuma Kid, and tore down the slope at a slant. He passed Anderson, out of pistol range, flew down to the meadow and raced straight for the willows that bordered Stone Creek.

He gave a shrill whistle. Princess lengthened her stride and drew abreast of Honey Boy.

"Oh, Jim!" Snippets called enthusiastically. "What a wonderful horse! I closed my eyes on that slope. I thought she would surely stumble and fall."

Allen laughed aloud, as he shoved new cartridges in his rifle.

"She's part cat. Keep goin'—'cause those gents is comin' fast."

The two Mexican gunmen, who had gone to intercept Allen, if he tried to backtrack, were whipping and spurring to head him off from the creek.

Up on the slope Anderson was cursing. One of Ace Cutts' men gave him a horse. He glanced down across the meadow, in time to see Allen and Snippets vanish among the willows.

"Them hosses of hisn is wonders," cried the Yuma Kid.

"Them greasers is plumb foolish to follow him in there," Baldy cackled. The two Mexicans headed straight for the willows. They were within fifty yards

81

of where Allen had vanished, when two muffled reports came to the watchers' ears, and two fleecy puffs of smoke appeared above the thicket. The leading Mexican fell from his pony, limp as a sack of flour; the other wheeled his horse and headed back. But he had not gone twenty yards before he started to sway and, a moment later, he crashed to the ground.

"Tole yuh they was fools," Baldy stated without emotion.

Anderson cursed again. With the others at his heels, he crossed the meadow and plunged among the willows some four hundred yards upstream from the spot where Allen had entered. They splashed across the shallow stream and emerged from the undergrowth on the farther side. From there they could see Allen and Snippets fully half a mile ahead. Anderson realized that pursuit was almost useless, but it would be disastrous for them if Allen reached town; so they spurred their horses and started after the distant grays.

Two miles farther on a group of twenty riders appeared from a hollow and galloped forward to intercept them. With muttered curses, Anderson and his killers checked their horses, swung about and raced for the lava fields.

Jim Hogg's continued raving had at last borne fruit. That morning Tom Powers had been forced to form a posse to hunt for Snippets.

Now Allen and Snippets spurred onward to join their friends, while their baffled enemies beat a hasty retreat. Hogg, Powers and the others bombarded them with eager questions, but Allen slurred lightly over his rescue of the girl. Already his mind was busy with the important task still before him—to clean up the Lava Gang.

THE MINE FORTRESS

JUDGE RANSOM WATCHED WITH HEAVY HEART, AS SAM Hogg, at the head of the Frying Pan riders, and Tom Powers, with a hastily formed posse, rode away. He held no hope for their success. He felt that Snippets was lost. And he blamed himself. Though he believed he was ruined, financially and politically now, his thoughts were only for the girl. He condemned himself for not having taken better care of his sister's child.

He paced the porch back and forth hour after hour. Better that ten thousand murderers escape the rope than that Snippets be harmed. Perhaps it was not yet too late. He might bargain Pete Cable's life for Snippets' safety. Obviously her kidnapping had been an effort to force him into doing that. He would treat with the enemy, bear the white flag of surrender at last, for the girl's sake.

It was now close to lunch time; he might find Anderson at the Red Queen. Though that was the hangout of his enemies, the judge did not hesitate. He walked quickly down Main Street.

The loungers gaped with astonishment when the judge turned resolutely into the big saloon. He asked a question of the bartender and was told that Francisco Garcia might know when Anderson would return. The Toad was eating at a small table in the gambling room.

Head held high, the judge marched forward.

"I am told that you might tell me when Mr. Anderson will return," the judge said.

The Toad's protruding eyes fixed on the judge with a fishlike stare. Here was the man whom the Toad considered the cause of all his troubles. The big hand on

83

the table closed convulsively. Slowly the Toad controlled his passion.

"What do you want him for?" he asked heavily. The judge hesitated. "That must remain between him and me. But I must see him—at once."

"So?" the swarthy Mexican rumbled. "Is it something to do with Pete Cable?"

The judge nodded.

"Then I will take you to him—I think I know where he is, and I think I know where your niece is."

"You do? Thank Heaven for that," the judge cried fervently.

"You would exchange Pete Cable for your niece?"

"Yes! Yes!"

"Then we must go quickly and stop them before they take her across the border." The Toad looked crafty.

The judge shuddered. He knew the man before him was not to be trusted, but he must take the chance.

Ten minutes later, the two were bowling along in a buckboard, headed for the lava fields.

Tom Powers and his posse had followed Anderson, Ace Cutts and the others to the border of the lava fields, where Allen insisted they stop.

"Yuh got to walk yuhr hosses, an' besides, two men could pick yuh-all off like chickens," he explained.

A rider was sent to gather in Sam Hogg and his men; then Allen led the others in the direction of Kennedy's ranch.

"Why for yuh goin' there?" Tom Powers asked.

"To catch a gent called Cupid Dart." Allen grinned at the sheriff's astonishment.

"Yuh mean that Texas gunman?" Toothpick queried.

"Yea. The gent yuh saw learnin' Spanish," said Allen

with a laugh.

"Not that dude, Mac Kennedy?" Toothpick was incredulous, and the others added their grunts of astonishment.

"That same. He ain't a dude. Not any," Allen told them.

They surrounded the ranch. Sam Hogg and his men joined them. Slowly they closed in upon the silent building as dusk was obscuring the land. But no firing greeted them. The building was empty; that wary bird, Cupid Dart, alias Mac Kennedy, had flown to safer parts.

"Musta made his get-away to the gang's stronghold," Allen commented.

He led the others up a narrow trail into the lava fields. Here, in a cuplike depression, they found the judge's cows, as well as several hundred other stolen animals. All had been rebranded and were being held there until the new brands healed. Of the men guarding the cattle all had escaped. The place was totally deserted, and they prepared to make camp for the night.

It was then that Allen discovered Snippets was still with them; he thought she had gone on into town long before. He stared at her, open-mouthed.

"What yuh doin' here?" he asked.

"No one told me to go anywhere else." Snippets smiled demurely and mischievously.

"Yuh wanted to be along in the ruckus, kid?" Allen accused. "Yuh should've gone home an' told folks you wus all right."

Snippets hung her head meekly. She knew that he knew why she had lingered. She had wanted to remain by his side as long as possible.

A shelter of blankets was rigged for her; they could not send her home now before morning.

After the others were asleep, Allen slipped out alone and followed the outlaws' trail for several miles. It climbed rapidly to the remains of an old mine shaft. Suddenly there loomed before him a low, one-story adobe house. He realized that he was looking at the real stronghold of the outlaws.

"Huh, they could stand off an army in that place," he told himself after he had scouted about it. Quietly he returned and rejoined the campers.

With day they considered the possibility of an attack. Tom Powers, Sam Hogg, and Jim Allen looked over the situation carefully through strong glasses. All three decided that it would not only be costly in lives, but completely hopeless. The place had been built to serve as a fortress against the Apache, in the days when the mine had been worked. Over the crest of the hill there were several roofless buildings and a huge weather-stained derrick that had been used to hoist ore from the mine.

"Hello! There's a gent with a white flag," Tom Powers said, pointing.

The heavy metal-studded door of the adobe house had been opened a crack, and a man stood waving a white shirt. Sam Hogg arose from the concealment of the bushes behind which he had been crouching and waved his hat. The door opened wider, and Mac Kennedy, still holding the shirt, stepped out into the sunlight. He advanced twenty yards and beckoned the ex-Ranger forward.

"Makin' believe he was a dude!" Tom Powers growled.

"Like I did pretendin' to be a hobo," Allen replied with a grin.

"Sam, don't go to meet him. Make him come to you. I've heard stories about Cupid Dart—he's treacherous as a snake," the sheriff advised.

"Don't worry none, Mr. Hogg. If he bats an eye, I'll drop him," Allen said confidently.

Sam Hogg advanced to meet Cupid Dart, and they talked for several minutes. When Sam returned to Powers and Allen, after the outlaw reentered the fortress, his face was white and drawn.

"There's hell to pay!" he exclaimed. "They has the judge in there with 'em. And unless we gives up Pete Cable, they promises to hang him high and proper."

"But we can't do that, 'cause Pete Cable is now in the State Prison, an' they wouldn't give him to us, unless the judge signed an order," Tom Powers sputtered.

"And the judge won't sign nothin'," Allen said.

"Yea. That damn fake dude tells me, the judge refuses flat. They want us to sorta persuade him," Sam Hogg added.

"I figures yuh might as well try and persuade a mountain." Allen shook his head. "Does he savvy we got Snippets?"

"Yep. He heard 'em talkin' and knows we got her, otherwise they might have him sign the paper by using her," Sam Hogg said.

"Damn 'em! If they touches the judge, we'll stick here until we starves 'em out," Powers declared wrathfully.

"Not any. Yuh savvy we are in Mexico? He tells me the soldiers is comin' along, 'cause they sent for 'em. Tomorrow they'll dust in here and chase us away," Sam Hogg explained.

The sheriff and the cattleman entered into a heated discussion of various plans to rescue the judge. Their men would follow them if they attacked, but the attack would be foredoomed to defeat. Allen, his face thoughtful, slipped away. At last the two brought their discussion to a close, for they realized they were wasting words.

There was nothing to do except wait until the Mexican soldiers arrived, then scurry back across the border.

A ROMAN BATTERING RAM

IT WAS NOON. A MOLTEN SUN LOOKED DOWN FROM A copper sky. The rocks reflected the terrific glare. What little shade there was brought no ease from the furnacelike heat. As one man expressed it: "You roast in the sun and stew in the shade." The water was gone, and there would be no more until evening; the men's suffering from thirst was intense. All thought themselves beaten.

"Reckon the judge is due to get his neck stretched," Toothpick Jarrick confided dolorously to Silent Moore.

The two were sprawled behind a boulder in the thin shade cast by a cactus. The taciturn deputy thrust out his jaw and growled:

"We sticks just the same."

Sam Hogg wormed his way between the blistering rocks and joined them. He nudged Toothpick and pointed up toward the valley wall behind them.

"What's the Wolf doin' up there? He's been lookin' through those glasses of his for an hour and shiftin' his position constant. Yuh reckon he's figurin' up somethin'?" the cattleman asked eagerly.

Allen was lying flat on a high shelf of rock. They watched him for a time. Now he vanished. A little later they saw him again, fifty yards farther along the shelf. From the shelter of some brush he focused his glasses on the long adobe building. Toothpick was puzzled as to what Allen was studying. He decided that it must be the lone window that broke the surface of the western wall in the outlaws' fortress. The window was little more than a porthole, about three feet by two. Toothpick

89

knew that a real purpose lay behind all of Allen's actions; that many of his surprising victories were the result of carefully thought-out plans. But what did the little outlaw hope to gain by studying that window? Allen closed his glasses and looked down at the three watching him. He waved his hand and wiggled out of sight.

"What's he aimin' to do?" Sam Hogg addressed Toothpick.

The lanky cow-puncher considered a moment and shook his head.

"I dunno. But the little hellion has sure got somethin' in his head," he said thoughtfully.

"If he's aimin' to go through that window, the gents in there will shoot him in two," the cattleman protested.

"Sure would," Silent agreed.

"I don't know what he's aimin' to do, but I'm sayin' positive, whatever it is, I'm backin' his play," Toothpick stated emphatically.

"Hey, Toothpick, come over here," Allen called from his hidden perch.

Toothpick, followed by Sam Hogg, wiggled toward the depression from which he knew the voice came. A rifle cracked from within the adobe building, and Toothpick's hat flew from his head. He flattened out and wiggled the faster. A few seconds later he slid down the side of the small basin to Allen. He was closely followed by Sam Hogg, who had retrieved the hat. Toothpick looked at it ruefully for a moment and poked his finger through the hole in the crown.

"Huh! That gent sure parted my hair."

"Jim, yuh figured out a way we can get at them hombres?" Sam Hogg demanded.

"I ain't sure she works," Allen replied. "Yuh gather

Tom Powers and yuhr brother over the hill by that ore wagon—if she works, I'll come and tell yuh about it."

The cattleman told himself that Allen deliberately tried to be mysterious. However, he went to collect his brother and Tom Powers.

Allen and Toothpick sought out Tad Hicks. The three passed along a deep gully to a ledge some ten feet high. Here Allen explained to them the first part of his plan and the part they were to play in it. A half hour later, when they approached the ore wagon, all three were grinning like schoolboys.

"Yuh two is sure baseball players—yuh tossed me at that mark and hit it every time," Allen said to them.

Tad Hicks halted to explain to his bosom friends, Windy Sam and Kansas.

"The Wolf is goin' to have us toss him through that window, an' he makes us practice tossin' him at a rock an' keeps us doin' it, until we hit it three time runnin' with his head."

Sheriff Tom Powers, the Hogg brothers, and several men of the posse listened in silence until Allen had finished telling his plan. For a moment its sheer audacity held them silent, then they shook their heads. The thing was impossible. Sam Hogg glanced wonderingly at Allen's freckled, youthful face. He could discern nothing but the spirit of youthful adventure there, like that of a schoolboy planning to rob an orchard. He sighed and again shook his head. Courage such as Allen's was too precious to be wasted. There wasn't a chance in a thousand of success.

"Yuh can't do it," the sheriff objected.

"Hell, there's thirteen men in there," the little cattleman added.

"A darned unlucky number for them," remarked

Allen.

"And five of the best gun fighters on the border," Toothpick pointed out.

"I ain't aimin' to wipe out all them gents. I'm aimin' to sorta keep 'em busy, while you bust the door down," Allen explained.

"You're loco! Bust that door down? It would take an hour to do it," Jim Hogg protested.

"Yuh ever see a Roman batterin' ram?" Allen asked.

"Roman batterin' ram?" the sheriff queried in return.

"He's funnin' us," the storekeeper insisted.

But one glance at the little outlaw's face convinced him Allen was serious.

"Waggle yuhr ears, gents, and I'll learn yuh what erudition, as Toothpick calls it, does for an hombre." Allen grinned at the tall cow-puncher, then told them of his scheme to break in the door.

"She sure works!" Sam Hogg cried, a few minutes later. He gave a whoop and sent his Stetson sailing into the air. Then all at once he grew silent and stared at Allen. A sinister thought had come to him.

"I figure we'll get in, but they'll shoot yuh to bits," he said.

"Not any. I'm so darn small I ain't easy to hit, an' I'll keep moving constantly," Allen said cheerfully.

He stepped up to the ore wagon, which was just over the crest of the hill, and out of sight of those in the fortress.

"Yuh take the box off, take that boom off the derrick by the mouth of the mine and rig her up, and yuh'll have a Roman batterin' ram that'll bust that there door to splinters," he said.

Sam Hogg dashed off to bring in some of his men. Tom Powers went to the roofless tool house to see what he could find. He returned a little later with a couple of rusty picks, a battered saw, and an ax that had seen better days.

When the Frying Pan punchers arrived, they fell to work with a will. The box on the freight wagon was dumped off, and on the frame they lashed two cross bars. They had no nails, but plenty of rope which served the same purpose. After much cursing, sweating, and heaving, the arm of the derrick was pushed in between the crossbars. It then hung in such a way that it would swing back and forth. It was a little wabbly when finished, but, after an examination, both Tom Powers and Sam Hogg admitted it would serve its purpose.

It was close to five o'clock before the battering ram was finished. The men scattered to seek rest in the shade. The deputation which had been sent for water and provisions arrived. Fires were built, and preparations made for the evening meal. The cowpunchers cast curious glances at Allen, as he sat and talked to Sam Hogg, Toothpick, and Snippets. They shook their heads, wonderingly.

"He ain't got no chance of comin' out of that place, unless he's carried, yet look at him over there. The others who ain't riskin' nothin' a-tall is plumb gloomy and gravelike, while he is happy as a kid," pronounced one admirer.

The sun hung low over the western hills; then went down with a rush, and its farewell painted the sky in a thousand brilliant colors. Dusk softened the flaming canvas to soft pastels, and then darkness fell over them swiftly, like a velvet, all-concealing mantle.

The men talked in hushed whispers, cleaned and oiled their guns and paced up and down nervously.

It had been decided to make the attack at midnight;

the men were impatient. Hogg and Toothpick wandered away, and Snippets and Allen were left alone before the fire. They chattered and laughed. He told her of that valley of his in the Painted Desert where he had other and younger gray horses.

"I got two colts up there—twins. Yuh never see their like. They ain't nothin' but legs and nerve. Do yuh know what they do—them little jaspers? Walk right into my house an' help theirselves. I can't cook me a dinner, they don't eat it up. Huh, if I didn't chase 'em out, they'd get in bed with me."

He went on, painting that valley of his as a veritable paradise.

Snippets laughed. "Jim, I never know when you stop tellin' the truth and start lying."

Toothpick, Sam Hogg, and Tom Powers watched the two by the fire.

"Look at that runt," Sam Hogg said. "Laughin' his head off, an' in an hour he's goin' to pull a stunt that he ain't got a Chinaman's chance in."

"He's sure got nerve," Tom Powers agreed.

"He's darned sure to cash in, an' he's laughin'." Sam Hogg shook his head.

"That's why he's laughin'," Toothpick said heavily.

"Yuh mean—"

"I know the little cuss. He tole me once, if yuh sit in a game and is dealt two-spots, yuh can't quit until the Lord cashes yuh in."

"I dunno," Tom Powers said thoughtfully. "If I'd been on the dodge for ten years, maybe I'd feel the same."

"And the gal?" Sam Hogg asked.

"She knows," Toothpick said. "She knows everything. She's plumb bright. That day he gets

94

throwed off the train she knows him pronto, and he has me fooled complete."

"She's in love with him an'—" Tom Powers left his sentence unfinished.

"Knows he's goin' to cash pronto an' keeps laughin'," Sam Hogg finished for him.

"She's got nerve, even if she is only a gal," Toothpick stated. "

"It's a shame. Ain't there a chance of gettin' the little cuss a pardon?" Tom Powers asked.

"Not any, an' that's positive. The United States wants him, an' every State west of Mississippi has a price on him," Toothpick replied.

"I'm tellin' yuh he'll get a pardon in Texas if he comes out of this," Sam Hogg cried.

"Yea, *if*—!" Tom Powers said softly.

The two they watched continued their laughter. "Tell me where this valley of yours is," Snippets pleaded.

"Yuh start from Wilton in Arizona. Yuh follow the sun until yuh come to the Three Widows. They is Black Buttes what looks sorrowful. The trail goes up Paintbox Canyon. An' when yuh can't go no farther, yuh start climbing to the moon, and pretty soon yuh see it. It ain't very big, but there's surprising trees an' grass an' plumb gorgeous flowers, an' there's a house an' hosses— regular maneaters. An' there's a gal cooking pies fer 'em an'—Shucks!" Allen interrupted his dreaming. "They's everything yuh want, when yuh get to the moon."

He leaped to his feet and looked down at her. Suddenly she seemed to have grown very small and childish. Her dark eyes glistened with unshed tears.

"Shucks, kid. I was usin' plumb-loose language," he said, with an effort at lightness. He turned abruptly and walked to the men beside the other fire. Snippets watched him; his shoulders sagged, as if they were drawn down by the weight of the two big guns he wore. But a few minutes later he was laughing again and making the others laugh with him.

The men examined their weapons and gathered about the battering ram. It was pushed to the top of the crest. There, only a slight shove would be needed to send it rolling toward the fortress. Ropes were attached to the front axle, and mounted men held their ends.

"Yuh stays put, until I lights the match. Then yuh comes a-hoppin' straight for the light. An' Toothpick an' Tad tosses Allen in through the window," Sam Hogg explained.

The ex-Ranger had insisted that it was his right to give the signal. He was to creep down to the fortress, and his lighted match would mark the position of the door as well as give a signal.

He removed his boots and crept through the darkness toward the black blotch which was the fortress. Allen, followed by Toothpick and Tad Hicks, walked past the fire beside which Snippets was sitting. The little outlaw did not speak to her, but as the firelight caught his eyes, she saw they glinted with yellow, and she knew the boy who had talked to her a short time before was gone. He had given way to the Wolf.

"Yuh remember, if yuh gents don't toss me straight, the judge will sure enough stretch rope," Allen warned.

Tad and Toothpick nodded. They knew that, not only would the judge be lost, but that, if Allen failed to clear the window at the first attempt, the gunmen within would make a sieve of him before he could struggle clear.

96

THE ATTACK

THE INTERIOR OF THE FORTRESS WAS LIGHTED BY three big ceiling lamps. The portholes by the door were shielded from the light by screens. Four men, each with two rifles, stood guard there. That door was the only entrance to the fortress. It was formidable in its metal-studded oak. The Lava Gang were convinced that, before the attackers could batter it down, they could annihilate them by pouring a stream of lead through the portholes. They were supremely confident in their impregnable position.

Three men sat at a table and faced judge Ransom. The Yuma Kid, Baldy, and several other men lounged against a nearby wall. One of these wore his hat pulled down over his eyes and a handkerchief over his face. He kept to the shadows and did not speak. The judge wondered why he wanted to conceal his identity.

The man in the center of the trio at the table laughed heavily, but there was no mirth in his laughter; it sounded more like the snarl of an animal than anything human.

"Judge, maybe I better explain, so you'll understand just how serious we are. Did you ever hear of Jean Napoleon? He was a direct descendant of the great Napoleon. He called himself *le Diable à Cheval*."

The judge had heard of him, and heard of his terrible cruelty. He nodded.

"Then let me start with myself. You have known me as Francisco Garcia. My real name is Francisco Napoleon. He was my father. The gentleman here on my right, you have known as Bill Anderson, is my

97

brother, Richard Napoleon. On my left you have Mac Kennedy, otherwise Cupid Dart; he also is my brother— Thomas Napoleon. We have a fourth brother; can you guess who he is?" the big, toadlike man asked.

Puzzled, wondering, the judge shook his head. "You sentenced him to be hung—Pete Cable." The Toad's face was mottled with fury; his large, protruding eyes were bloodshot. The judge recoiled from the hate he saw there.

"You understand now we are serious. We will go to any length to save our brother and to avenge him," the Toad growled.

Bewildered by these revelations, the judge remained silent for a moment, but when he spoke his voice was steady.

"I have nothing more to say. Pete Cable was a murderer, tried and convicted as such. To save my own life, I will certainly not turn him loose," he said quietly.

"Judge, be sensible. We will surely hang you, if you refuse, and there are some things worse than death. Things that make a man want to die, make him beg for death," Bill Anderson said calmly.

The judge shuddered. Anderson's very calmness was far more terrifying than the Toad's animallike rage. He knew these men were not bluffing, and he had no hope that his friends outside would be able to save him. Yet never for a moment did he consider weakening. He would not turn a beast like Pete Cable loose on the world, in order to save his own life. He summoned his courage to face the ordeal and remained silent.

The three at the table waited, while the judge could hear his own heart pound. At last the Toad beckoned to two men leaning against the wall.

"Sam, suppose you show the judge what the Apaches

do to prisoners. Don't hurt his right hand; he'll need that to sign a release. Start easy, but show what you can do," the Toad said.

One of the men, with a pockmarked face, started around the table toward the judge. In spite of himself the judge shivered, then he clenched his hands and waited for what was to come.

"*Dios!*" one of the guards at the door cried. Every one swung about to face the door.

Outside there came a chorus of shrill cries, the thumping of horses' hoofs, and the rumbling of a loaded wagon running wild downhill. For a fraction of a second the men at the table were still; they started to rise, then—

Straight through the window there shot a figure. At first it looked to the judge like some huge cat, for its eyes were flaming pools of fire. For an instant it seemed to remain suspended in the air. As it started to fall toward the floor, jagged streams of fire leaped from two big Colts. One of the guards at the door cried out and toppled from his platform.

The hurtling figure struck the floor, somersaulted, and, with its guns spitting fire, bounced to its feet. The Yuma Kid's guns came into play first, then Baldy's and Cupid Dart's. The room was filled with a continuous bellow of hellish noise, clouds of acrid smoke, and streams of fire. Then, above the boom of guns, came a grinding smash, overwhelming all the other noises by its volume.

Every man in the room now had his gun out, firing at that bounding figure. Allen was in lightning action; he leaped by one man, spun about, and used him for a shield. His guns empty, he snatched out another pair from his holsters. The Yuma Kid fired at him. Flame

99

from the gun burned his cheek, but the shot missed. As he ducked by the Kid, Allen fired in turn. The gunman stood for a moment with a startled look on his face, took two or three tottering steps, and fell straight forward on his face.

Smash! Smash!

The heavy battering ram beat at the door. The thick oak splintered, hung by one hinge.

The room was full of smoke cut by lightning, and through it the judge saw Allen leaping, ducking, and dodging. He was slower now; but always red flame poured in continuous streams from his two guns.

Cupid Dart was down, sprawled across the table. The Toad, one hand clutching his chest, was trying to bring his wavering gun on Allen.

Another crash, the door came down. Led by Sam Hogg, men poured into the room. A few more shots, and it was over.

The judge had not moved from his position before the table. Scarcely a minute had passed since Allen came flying through the window. Yet death had struck on all hands.

"Yuh all right, judge?" Sam Hogg bawled hoarsely.

The judge was speechless. Tom Powers ran through the swirling smoke and threw his arm around Ransom's shoulders. Slowly the dense, blue-white fog melted away and revealed the wreckage.

The Yuma Kid lay dead, almost at the judge's feet. Cupid Dart was sprawled on the table, and even as the judge watched, his body fell in a heap to the floor. Baldy was dead against the wall. Three others lay sprawled on the floor. The Toad was dying, breathing curses through the bloody froth on his lips. The rest of the outlaws were prisoners, their faces full of terror and their hands upraised.

The judge saw Jim-twin Allen leaning weakly against the farther wall. Each hand still held a Colt; smoke gently curled from the barrels. Tom Powers sprang toward Allen, but before he reached him Snippets dodged through the door and was by his side.

"Jim!"

"I done it!" he said, grinning at her.

One side of his face was burned black; a little trickle of blood ran from the corner of his mouth to stain his chin. He stood on one leg; the other hung limp and twisted.

"Ace Cutts—cover him—so the judge—won't—know," he whispered.

His guns slipped from his hands and fell to the floor. He smiled at Snippets.

Tom Powers caught him as he swayed forward. Sam Hogg pushed the sheriff away, almost fiercely. "Let me tend to him!" he cried.

After an examination he arose to his feet, and there were tears in his eyes.

"He was hit six times—once through the chest, twice in the leg—and got a rib smashed. The others don't count. But the little runt is going to live!"

Two riders were sent to town for a doctor. With the first streak of dawn Allen was carried in a litter across the border, where, five hours later, the doctor confirmed Sam Hogg's opinion. Allen had a chance.

Later that day, when the Mexican soldiers arrived, they found six men dangling from beams in the adobe house, and seven others laid in a row and covered with blankets. Anderson had been one of the unlucky ones to die at the end of a rope.

Tom Powers started a collection to pay a famous

101

bonesetter to come from San Francisco and set Allen's leg, but Sam Hogg insisted on bearing the expense himself.

"The little cuss aggravates yuh, 'cause he won't tell what he's doin', but I'm tellin' yuh he's a seven-eyed wonder for guts, so I'm payin' to have his leg fixed," he explained.

Anderson's power being broken, the judge's dreams appeared destined to come true.

One night, six weeks after the battle, when the nurse entered Allen's room, she found him gone. He and his grays had started on their return trip home—home to that valley of his in the Painted Desert.

THE WAMPUS ON STILTS

AS IN SO MANY OTHER MINING TOWNS, KILLERS AND robbers walked the streets of Goldville, and the authorities tacitly agreed to forget their pasts unless they committed some fresh crime within the town. So wanted men, with huge rewards offered for them by other States, drank, ate, and slept and had no other worry than to keep a wary eye out for an enemy.

Real law would come later, and the enforcement of it, but now, while many of the decent citizens of the town disliked and feared the roughs who hung out in the Ace High Saloon, few had the nerve to interfere, if the rowdies attempted to ride a stranger.

"Gents, I'm tellin' yuh it's the only lollygaholopus that ain't in captivity," a big, florid-faced man said with mock gravity as he pointed to one of the passengers who had arrived on the stage. There had been five in all—three hard-rock miners, "Pop" Howes, a leathery-faced old prospector, and the man who was the object of the rough's joke.

He was a small, undersized man of about twenty-eight. His hat, with its extra high crown, was the finest grade of Stetson; his boots, custom-made patent leather, had abnormally high heels; his shirt was of silk and knotted with a loose black tie, and his suit was black, and silk-faced lapels adorned his longtailed frock coat. If he heard the rough's pleasantry he made no move to resent it. He pulled at his heavy black beard and gazed indifferently about the town.

"Anderson, yuh is plumb mixed in your animology. That ain't no lollygaholopus; it's a wampus on stilts!" a tall, gawky, hook-nosed man cried.

The bums roared at this allusion to the little man's high heels. Even the other spectators who disliked Anderson and his cronies smiled, but still the little man in the frock coat paid no attention to the remarks.

A small, undersized young fellow, dressed in ragged, faded jeans, who was standing on the outer fringe of the watchers, stared at the little man as if he were a ghost. Then suddenly the youth's freckled face split in a wide, loose-mouthed grin.

"Gosh, it's him!" he cried excitedly.

Pop Howes, the old prospector who had arrived on the stage, raised himself on tiptoe and peered over the heads of the crowd.

"Who's 'him'?" he asked, then added regretfully "Darn them big bullies! Why don't they take a gent their own size?"

"Jack ain't used to being made fun of, so he don't savvy they're talkin' about him," said the ragged fellow. "But don't yuh worry none. When he does, he'll swell up and get darned big in them gents' eyes."

"Big" Anderson, the florid-faced bully, took several steps toward the little man, cocked his head on one side, and carefully surveyed the stranger from his patent-leather boots to his high-crowned Stetson. Then Anderson nodded his head decisively.

"Yep, 'Hi,' yuh is plumb correct! It's the most perfect specimen of a wampus on stilts I ever seen. What do yuh say we capture it an' sell it to some museum?"

The little man suddenly realized that these remarks were directed toward himself and, very slowly, he turned and glanced at Big Anderson and Hi Stevens, the other rough. They met his eyes with broad, taunting

104

grins.

The little man stood there, quietly watching them for a moment, then walked briskly across the road toward them. Because of his high heels, he seemed to strut like a bantam rooster. His eyes were steady and bored into those of the two crude jesters, who were taken aback at his sudden advance.

"Was yuh gents talkin' about me?" he asked coldly.

The two recovered from their surprise and grinned mockingly, then prepared to have further fun with the "wampus."

"We sure was. I was remarkin' yuh is the most perfect specimen of—"

Big Anderson's grin vanished, and his words came to an abrupt halt, for the little man's coat opened like two doors on springs, and two big black guns seemed to leap from his belt into his hands. The bullies' mouths grew slack, as they stared pop-eyed into the big, round barrels of those Colts.

"Yuh was sayin'?" the little man inquired.

"Put them guns away or—or—" Hi Stevens attempted to bluster, but he could not bring himself to finish the sentence. While the stranger was small, those two guns were big, the hands that held them steady, and the eyes behind them very hard.

"Yuh was sayin' I was a wampus?"

The voice was gentle, but it sounded to the two bullies like a death knell. Their courage oozed away visibly, and their hands fell limply from the butts of their guns. Hi Stevens choked and stammered, then spoke hesitatingly

"Naw, I never said that."

"Then it was your friend. Now, mister, yuh'll have to teach him manners. Yuh'll have to show him it ain't nice to go callin' strangers names. Just so he won't forget it, yuh pull his ear with one hand an' slap him good with the other."

The spectators gathered closer; this was good—the bullies being bullied. The two roughs' friends near the door of the Ace High moved restlessly, and one or two of them handled their guns; but the boy in the tattered jeans ran across the road and whispered something to them, and their desire to interfere seemed to vanish.

Anderson and Stevens stared at the little stranger as if they had suddenly become half-witted and did not understand his words. He repeated them again more sharply this time, and when Hi Stevens made no move to obey, his right-hand gun roared, and the bully, white-faced, hopped about on one foot and stared at his left boot, the heel of which had vanished.

"Hey, mister, don't do that," he whined.

"Do what I tole yuh to, or I'll take one of your toes off next," the little man warned.

Instinctively Hi Stevens knew that the threat was no bluff. Moved by resentment toward Big Anderson, who had started this ill-fated horseplay, Stevens suddenly reached over and, before his astonished friend could recover from his stupor, yanked one of Anderson's ears and clouted him across the cheek with his other hand.

Big Anderson roared with anger and glared at Stevens; but, while he rubbed the red mark on his cheek, he made no move that the frock-coated stranger might have interpreted as hostile.

"Now, mister, it's your turn to teach him not to go callin' names."

Big Anderson stepped toward Stevens with blood in his eyes.

"Mister, yuh stand still an' take it or I'll—" The

106

stranger had no need to voice his threat, for Hi Stevens stopped in his tracks and waited. Anderson yanked Stevens' ear, raised a big, hairy paw, and clouted him on the side of the head with such force that Stevens reeled backward.

"Now get the hell out of here!" the stranger snapped.

The two bullies, murderous with rage, both at each other and at the stranger, whirled about and hurried into the Ace High Saloon. The little man waited until they disappeared. Then he returned his guns to their holsters, with a movement as swift as that with which he had drawn them, whirled on his heel, and stalked toward the hotel.

"Baldy" Kane, a slender man of forty whose face and head were as guiltless of hair as an egg and whose gray eyes and long, sallow face were entirely devoid of expression, watched the black-coated stranger enter the hotel, then turned to a friend and asked:

"Who's the little rooster?"

His friend nodded toward the ragged boy, who was now walking down the dusty street by the side of Pop Howes.

"Jim-twin Allen horned in suddenlike when the boys was thinkin' of stoppin' the little man, so I figger the little runt with the whiskers is Jim's brother—'Jack-twin' Allen."

Kane shrugged, turned on his heel, and followed Big Anderson and Hi Stevens into the Ace High. A miner leaped down and whispered to a companion.

"If that there rip-snortin' hellion of a Wyoming sheriff is here, hell is sure goin' to pop, an' Baldy is thinkin' fast an' hard!"

" 'Tain't safe to talk!" the other mumbled out of the corner of his mouth and turned away.

THE MINERS' MEETING

POP HOWES' MINE, THE AMERICAN BEAUTY, WAS about a mile from town on the south side of the mining gulch where the walls became sheer and closed in. At the foot of the slope he had built a small three-room shack where he and his wife lived. Back of this were the barns, a donkey engine, and a narrow building where his Mexican workers formerly ate and slept. But the bunk house was now deserted, the engine silent. No work was going on in the shaft.

For thirty years Pop Howes had worked and saved; now he had been robbed and was broke. He had exhausted his credit at the bank. His eyes were bitter as they stared at the empty buildings.

The gulch had been formed by a cataclysm that had split a mountain when the world was young. On the north side of the gulch was the El Dorado Mine that was making a fortune for its owners. Pop Howes believed that the El Dorado lode extended through the whole mountain, on the south as well as the north side of the gulch, and that if he could run his shaft down another hundred feet, to the same level as the El Dorado shaft, he, too, would strike a rich, ore-bearing vein.

Jim Allen, who had accompanied Pop from town, glanced with ready sympathy at the old man's brooding face. "So the bank wouldn't give yuh a nickel?" he asked.

"Not a nickel, darn 'em! They was only too glad to loan me five thousand last year, but now they acts as if I was wantin' to steal money from 'em!" Pop cried wrathfully.

"Maybe they figger if they don't lend yuh no money

they'll get the mine an' a fortune on the mortgage," the ragged one said thoughtfully.

"Of course that's it. That young fellow that they sent here knew his onions; he spent a week measurin' an' clippin' rock from this side an' then goin' over yonder an' doin' the same thing," Pop sputtered. "An' if it hadn't been for them darned quartz thieves what cleaned me out last week, I'd never have had to ask the bank for no money!"

The two reached the house and entered a long, low room where they found Mrs. Howes waiting for them. She was a thin, frail woman of fifty. Her face was lined and her hair snow-white, but her eyes still had the cheerful courage of the woman who has been taught by life to take the good with the bad. One look at her husband's face and she knew his trip to the county seat had been unsuccessful.

Experience had taught her that disappointment is easier to bear on a full stomach, so she bustled into the kitchen and returned a few minutes later with a dish of venison stew. She placed this on the table and added a plate of hot biscuits and a pot of coffee.

When the men returned from washing up she had already piled their plates high with the steaming stew. Pop Howes slumped into his chair and gloomily told himself he was to lose the chance of a fortune, after thirty years' labor, for the lack of only a few dollars.

It was not that he minded so much for himself, but his wife, who had stood by him through all sorts of hardships, loneliness, and the bitterest poverty, deserved some reward. Not that she had ever complained, though he had noticed at times a wistful look in her eyes and even the traces of tears. He knew that she wanted to visit again those relatives of hers in the East whom she had not seen since the days of her marriage. And recently, when they had thought they would soon strike the lode, soon have money, she had looked forward to it with a new longing.

Hardly had the two men finished their dinner when a messenger arrived with the news that a miners' meeting was to be held that evening at the hotel.

"Bill Tucker sent up north an' asked one of them gun-slingin' sheriffs to come an' help ketch the quartz thieves," the messenger explained.

"Never knew Bill Tucker had enough sense to do that. Always figgered him as the dumbest town marshal I ever see," Pop Howes grunted.

He arose, buckled on his gun, took his coat and hat from the peg behind the door, and filled his pipe. After he had lighted it he turned to the messenger and asked thoughtfully:

"Who's this gun-slingin' hombre?"

"Jack-twin Allen, the Wyoming sheriff."

Pop Howes glanced at the small figure sitting by the fire, started to speak, thought better of it, and clumped from the room. The messenger followed.

The woman glanced curiously at Jim Allen, but her curiosity was tinged by sympathy and understanding. After a moment she asked falteringly:

"He's your brother?"

"Yeh. Twin brother." The voice was toneless, flat.

"An'—have you spoken to him?" she asked. At the sight of his face she instantly regretted her words.

"Naw, an' I don't reckon I will. 'Cause, yuh see, Jack's here on business, an' he can't go cavortin' about with a disreputable gent like me. Reckon I'll pull out pronto."

Jim Allen was grinning now and he spoke with

110

assumed indifference, but the woman saw behind the mask.

"Let me tell yuh somethin', ma'am. Jack Allen is the darnedest, fightingest gent I ever see. Let me tell yuh what he done now."

Enthusiastically Allen poured out praises of his brother's courage, his skill, and the wonderful things he had accomplished. But the more he praised his brother, the more the woman understood his grief. Jim-twin Allen was an outlaw, with a fortune on his head; his brother was an officer of the law—the gulf between the two was insurmountable.

When Pop Howes arrived at the hotel he found "Hard-rock" Hogan and Bill Tucker, the town marshal, waiting for him. Tucker was a powerfully built man with a round, red face, a large mouth, and small gray eyes.

"Howdy, Pop!" he cried jovially. "We sent for Baldy Kane, Steven Brandon, 'Two-finger' Smith, and some of the other boys. Bill Tucker sent up North and asked Jack-twin Allen—yuh've heard of him, yes?—well, Bill asked him to come on down here to help ketch these here quartz robbers. Well, he's here now, feedin' his face, an' he'll be in here pronto."

Bill Tucker cultivated a hearty, jovial manner, and, as the different owners and managers of mines in the gulch arrived, he greeted each one like a long-lost brother. Steve Brandon, the manager of the El Dorado, was one of the last to arrive.

He was a short, heavy man with gray hair and a close-cropped mustache. When he spoke he snapped out his words like pistol shots. Shortly after Steve Brandon arrived, Baldy Kane slid into the room. He nodded to those present, and then his face became an

111

expressionless, claylike mask. He silently drifted into a dark corner.

"I hears tell that this here Jack Allen is faster than his brother Jim," Bill Tucker boomed.

"Not any," Pop declared shortly but emphatically.

"Wonder if the two speak? It's darn funny—Jack comes here to clean up this town, an' here is Jim, his brother, the best of all the jailbirds." The marshal chuckled as if he found the situation amusing.

Hard-rock Hogan was one of the men who had worked in and about mines since early childhood; he had lived all his life among rough, violent men, and his experience with human nature was vast. He had discovered that many men used words to hide their thoughts, while others cultivated a masklike face after the manner of Baldy Kane. He glanced curiously at Bill Tucker.

Now he saw only the tragedy that lay beneath the meeting of two brothers in such circumstances, and he wondered if the town marshal had been aware the two would meet when he sent his invitation to Jack Allen. He was curious as to that, but he was more curious as to the reason behind the invitation; he was reasonably sure Tucker had some hidden motive. Hogan was still pondering the matter when the door opened and Jack Allen entered.

The famous Wyoming sheriff and United States marshal was cool and collected. His eyes swept the room and rested on each man in turn. Most of the miners met his searching gaze unflinchingly. But there were one or two men there who hastily looked away, for they had a feeling that Allen's rather hard brown eyes might read more than they cared to tell. Bill Tucker stepped forward and introduced Allen to the assembly.

"Howdy, gents!" Jack greeted them.

They murmured a reply, then all grew silent.

"Suppose yuh give me a line on what's been goin' on here," the little man suggested.

"It's this way," Bill Tucker explained. "The placers has been givin' out an' there ain't nothin' but quartz mining hereabouts now. About eight mines are workin' sinkin' shafts. The veins are darned thin but mighty rich. About four months ago some gang started stealin' quartz, an' since then every darn mine has been robbed."

"On the quiet or with guns?" Allen interrupted.

"Sometimes one, sometimes the other. The last time this here gang worked they held up the American Beauty—about a week ago—shot one guard, locked up the workers, and made off with about four thousand dollars in quartz," the town marshal explained.

"When did you find out about it?" Jack Allen asked.

Pop Howes cut into the conversation. "I was stayin' in town that night with my wife an' went out to the mine about daylight. I find a young Mex kid I left in the house, gunned proper, an' the rest locked up, so I come into town an' fetched Bill Tucker."

"Yuh track 'em? Where did they go?"

"Yeh, I follered them clear to the head of the canyon an' then come back. Yuh see, I'm town marshal, an' we got a tough bunch of hombres hangin' aroun' here, so I got to sorter stick close to town an' not go trackin' across the mountains." Bill Tucker flushed beneath Allen's direct appraisal and floundered in his explanation.

"Why for d'yuh let these here tough hombres hang aroun'?" Allen asked quickly.

"Why for? 'Cause—why, there's a bunch of 'em, an'

113

I sorta figgered to let the past slide, so long as the boys behaved," Bill Tucker said uneasily. His eyes refused to meet Jack Allen's direct gaze and glanced furtively about the room.

"All right. The first thing to do, then, is to make a list of all the gents what is not workin', an' all them who have a reward on 'em or are known to be bad ones, an' tell 'em to get out of town," the Wyoming sheriff said quietly.

"Would yuh put your brother, Jim Allen, on that list?" Steve Brandon barked.

"Yes!" Jack Allen snapped.

The miners regarded Allen curiously. Instinctively they knew he spoke the truth and would lock his own brother in jail if called upon to do so in the line of duty. Here was a man who made a fetish of honesty. Some of them had heard of him by reputation. Honest, hard, relentless in his pursuit of outlaws, he was known to be just. He cared nothing about the rewards for the outlaws he sought; having cleaned up a town or county, he would silently fade away, none the richer for his work.

After a general discussion, it was agreed that Jack Allen was to be given a free hand in the gulch. For a long while Bill Tucker insisted he should have authority within the town limits, but at length he was forced to give way and to agree to take orders from Allen.

Later, as Hard-rock Hogan and Pop Howes were walking up the starlit gulch toward their homes, they both chuckled as they recalled Bill Tucker's expression when Jack Allen questioned him.

"Bill sorta showed up as a windbag, didn't he?" the old prospector remarked.

"Yeh, Jack Allen is sure enough a little hellion on wheels." Hard-rock grinned his admiration.

"How come yuh persuaded Bill to write to him?" asked Pop.

"I ain't supposed to say, but it was Steve Brandon who got me to prod Bill to get Jack Allen," Hard-rock answered, after a moment's hesitation.

When Pop Howes entered the living room he found Jim-twin Allen waiting for him. Pop laughed as he related what had happened at the miners' meeting that night.

"An' yuh say it was Steve Brandon who started gettin' Jack down here?" Allen asked curiously.

"Yeh. Steve sure has a head on him. Reckon he don't want it known for fear these here quartz robbers will get after him."

"Listen, Pop. I've been thinkin'. That night they robbed yuh—yuh say the kid they downed was dressed in his underclothes an' wasn't armed?"

"Yeh."

"Did yuh ever think that maybe someone downed that kid, figgerin' it was you—an' done it for a purpose?" Allen asked.

Pop Howes frowned and stared thoughtfully into the fire.

"Jim, I reckon you're correct. An' that means that gang is workin' for someone who knows I'm due to strike it rich an' wants to cash me in so he can buy my claim off the old woman for almost nothin'!"

"Well, I figgers I'll bunk here, an', if they comes ag'in, I'll give 'em a surprise." Allen grinned cheerfully.

Pop Howes lay awake for a long time that night. He racked his brain despairingly, trying to think of some way by which he could raise the money to continue his operations and at the same time pay the bank its interest on the mortgage. The more he puzzled, the more hopeless it seemed. He was within a few feet of riches and, for the want of a few dollars, would be forced to watch someone else profit by his work. He thought of his wife, sleeping quietly beside him—how patient she had been, how hard working! Time after time she had been forced to work like a slave while he was in the mountains prospecting. And now what good had it done?

Pop turned back to bed. His wife tossed restlessly and moaned in her sleep.

JIM-TWIN AND JACK-TWIN

ONE DAY, TWO DAYS PASSED, AND STILL JACK-TWIN Allen made no move. He looked over the jail and had certain repairs made on it. He walked about the town, and, while he did not stroll down the center of the street, neither did he sneak about the alleys. He had a certain cold nerve that was far superior to reckless courage. He was there to catch and punish the gold robbers, and he had no intention of making a move until he was thoroughly familiar with his surroundings and the situation in general. He would stalk into various saloons, look the people over, and then draw one man aside and question him. His questions were direct and to the point, and usually the men would answer them freely, for they felt that what they said would go no farther. If a man lied, Allen would fix him with those hard, penetrating eyes of his and bluntly tell the man he lied. Yet, strangely enough, there were none who made an overt move to resent his accusations even in that town which was overrun by gunmen.

There were many who wondered why Jack Allen delayed his clean-up. The miners became impatient, but Jack knew the gang which was stealing the quartz would be getting nervous, and there is nothing so trying to the nerves as waiting.

On the third day he borrowed a horse from the livery stable and started to visit each mine in the neighborhood. Each one told him the same tale. The mine was robbed, the robbers' trail went up the gulch and was finally lost in the wooded hills. Always pack horses had been used to haul the gold away.

The Blue Sky Mine was close to the American

117

Beauty. When Jack Allen dismounted before the shack used as an office, Baldy Kane, the owner, stepped through the door and greeted him.

He was like a death's-head, with his expressionless eyes, his hairless face and head and tightly stretched, sallow skin. When he spoke, his lips scarcely moved. Jack Allen knew the man had no more fear in him than a stone. There would be no taking such a man alive.

"Yeh, I've got a hard bunch workin' for me, but I figgered that until this quartz gang is busted up I might as well have fighters as well as workers," he said softly in reply to a question from Allen.

The Wyoming sheriff nodded; this sounded like sense to him.

"I hear yuh struck it rich?" he asked, after a pause, in which each man frankly studied the other.

"One of the old-timers went broke sinkin' my shaft," Baldy explained. "His vein petered out, an' the fool killed himself. A greaser who worked for him tipped me off that by putting in a side cut I could strike a rich vein. I bought the place for taxes an' did what the greaser tol' me. An' I've struck it rich—plenty rich! I'm sorta hopin' that what that old fool Pop Howes believes about the El Dorado mother lode startin' again on this side of the gulch is true, 'cause, if it does, I've got it an' not him."

"How many men yuh got workin' for yuh?"

"Eight—an' they're all gun slingers."

Jack Allen was silent for a moment. Was this a threat, or a mere statement of fact? His eyes caught and held Baldy's.

"How did that ol'-timer kill himself?"

"Threw himself down the shaft," said the mine owner quickly.

Allen thought to himself.

"He's sure enough a cool customer, an' he'd do

118

anything—cut a man's throat without a wink. Mebbe he threw that old-timer down the shaft, himself. But if the Blue Sky is as rich as he says it is, there ain't no use tryin' to hitch him up with them quartz robbers. A man worth a million doesn't go about stealin' thousands."

It was late noon when Jack Allen turned up the path that led to the American Beauty Mine. Jim Allen, who was sitting on a bench on the shady side of the house, saw him coming and arose to his feet with the idea of vanishing, but on second thought he decided to remain and speak to his brother. Pop Howes was over visiting Hard-rock Hogan, and Mrs. Howes was asleep upstairs, so there would be no one to report that the sheriff had talked to the outlaw. But Jim was mistaken in this, for Mrs. Howes peered through the window and saw the meeting between the two brothers.

"Hello, Jack," Jim said hesitatingly.

"Hello, yuh darned ol' hoss thief," Jack responded with a grin.

"Yuh ain't changed none sense I see yuh last up in Wyoming."

"You neither—yuh don't look a day over twenty."

There was a heavy silence. Both rolled and lit cigarettes. The woman watched through the window, and her heart ached at their attempt to appear casual and indifferent. She knew that here were two men, twin brothers, who had slept together, fought side by side in a feud that had rocked the whole West, until at last they were the only ones left. They had no other kin; all had died in the feud. Yet the two had been separated by an impassable gulf since that day when Jim Allen had shot and killed a United States army captain. That the killing had been deserved and had prevented an Indian uprising made no difference. Jack was one who believed in the letter of the law.

"Yuh remember when we was kids an' pa used to hide our dinner an' make us track it or go hungry?" Jim asked.

"Yeh. Yuh was always better'n me. Guess yuh are still," Jack answered and stared down the gulch. He had less ability to hide his feelings than his twin; Jim had been forced to wear a mask so long it had become second nature to him.

Jim Allen's freckled face split in a wide grin.

"Yuh try livin' in the desert where yuh got to track lizards or go hungry an' yuh'll soon learn trackin'!"

Suddenly the restraint between the two dropped away. They were once more boys, brothers. Jim pointed at Jack's high heels and then threw back his head and laughed aloud.

"The only lollygaholopus an' wampus on stilts out of a museum! Ha-ha-ha!"

"Yuh darn little hoss thief!" Jack retorted. "Yuh still got Honey Boy, the hoss yuh stole from me? Lissen, you! Yuh want to stop laughin' or some day the top of your head will fall off."

The two stood there and thoroughly abused each other, mixing their abuse with fighting words. But in each case the fighting words were terms of endearment.

But again the twins grew silent. Jack was thinking of the day after tomorrow when he intended to post his list of undesirables. Jim headed the list.

"Listen, Jack," the little outlaw said earnestly. "I'm thinkin' that quartz gang what robbed Pop last week sure dropped that Mex kid, thinkin' it was Pop. They tried to down him deliberate. I figger some gent knows Pop is due to strike it rich and figgered on buyin' the American Beauty cheap from the widow. An' don't forget that gent is runnin' with the quartz gang!"

He lowered his voice and explained his theory, but

120

after he had finished, Jack shook his head.

"I don't blame yuh, but your life has made yuh too darn suspicious. Yuh suspect everybody."

"Mebbe so, but yuh got to set a thief to ketch a thief!" There was a touch of bitterness in Jim's voice.

It was a long while before he spoke again.

"I'm tellin' yuh, Jack, there is somethin' darned funny about how an' why them gents sent for yuh. They aim to double cross yuh, or somebody else, or mebbe both!" Jim warned.

"Why?" Jack smiled unbelievingly.

"Mebbe they got yuh down here to do somethin' they're scared to do," Jim suggested.

"What?"

"I dunno, but suppose some gents is plumb scared of their partner. Suppose this here Baldy Kane was a member of their gang, an' they was scared of him. He's hell on wheels, that bald-headed ol' jasper. They would figger out you would learn somethin', then go try for Baldy. He ain't a gent what would ever give up, so you'd sure cash him, an' he'd prob'ly cash you. They'd have got rid of him, an' anythin' you'd learnt wouldn't matter, 'cause you'd be dead!"

Later Jim-twin Allen stood there and watched his brother ride away. And the woman watching him saw Jim's face grow old, become covered with a thousand wrinkles. It was lifeless, nearly, dead like the desert that was his home. The woman turned away, ashamed that she had witnessed the baring of a man's soul.

Suddenly the outlaw's face grew young again, and he grinned.

"All right, Jack. Whether yuh like it or not, the Wolf is goin' to horn in on your play an' sorta prove to yuh that yuh don't know nothin' a-tall!"

121

THE TRAP

THE SUN HAD RUSHED BEHIND THE DISTANT mountains, and the dusk was gathering in the gulch when Pop Howes rode up to the American Beauty and dismounted. His face was worried and haggard. He had had a long talk with his friend, Hard-rock Hogan, but neither of them could think of any way by which they could raise sufficient money to save the American Beauty from the clutches of the Black Rock Bank. Another week and the bank would automatically take possession, unless Pop could raise the necessary cash to pay the interest and part of the loan.

Jim Allen was waiting for him, and before Pop entered the house, the little outlaw drew him aside and talked rapidly for several minutes.

"That would be a fool thing to do!" Pop complained. "What you got in your head now?"

"Yuh do like I say; yuh trot down to the post office an' pretend to get that letter; then yuh tell two or three people on the quiet what I just tol' yuh to. Yuh act happy an' glad—make believe you're a little drunk—an' then tell a coupla more folks. Then yuh come back here, get your ol' lady, an' sneak over to Hard-rock's place an' lay low. I'll do the rest, an' don't yuh worry none. I ain't sure she works, but if she does, mebbe yuh won't lose your mine!" Jim spoke confidently and grinned one of his broad, likable grins.

Pop grumbled and complained about being left in the dark as to just what Allen intended to do, but at length he consented to do what Allen asked. He told his wife that he had to go to town with Jim Allen. And as Jim saw the look of worry that crossed her face, he realized she must have known all the while that the Mexican boy had been killed by mistake for her husband.

"Don't worry none, ma'am. I stick close to him an' he won't get hurt none!" Allen reassured her.

The woman watched them, as the famous outlaw walked down the path beside her husband, whose tall, gaunt form made Allen seem smaller than ever. Behind them trotted Allen's two gray horses. One was saddled and the other carried a small pack. Mrs. Howes felt no fear now for her husband; those two low-hung guns that Allen wore brought her a feeling of confidence that her man would return safely.

Dusk had given way to night by the time the two arrived in Goldville. The miners were streaming into town, and the saloons were rapidly filling. Most of the miners were Mexicans, but there were a few husky, broad-shouldered Americans among them.

Allen left his grays at the hitching rack before the Ace High and followed Pop Howes through the milling crowd toward the post office. Pop entered and then reappeared a moment later with a letter in his hand. Allen watched him as he ripped it open and read it by the light cast from the office window.

"Huh! It's supposed to be good news, an' Pop acts like it was an invitation to a funeral," Jim grumbled. "He's sure a bum actor!"

After Pop had consumed a few drinks, an optimistic conviction came to him that this plan of Allen's, although he did not know just what it was, would work and the little outlaw would save his mine. So he no longer *acted* the part of a man who has just been saved from disaster, but in reality *felt* like one.

"Hello, Pop!" Bill Tucker greeted him. "Yuh look like the cat what just swallered the canary!"

"I sure feel all set up. Have a drink. I'm sorta celebrating."

The two drained their glasses, and Pop ostentatiously drew the letter from his pocket, glanced at it, and then returned it, with a self-satisfied smile. The ruse worked perfectly.

"Did yuh get good news in the mail tonight?" the marshal asked.

"You betcha!" Pop hesitated and then added in a whisper: "I ain't supposed to say nothin'—for some reason the gent wants me to keep it under my shirt—but he's goin' to buy a quarter interest in the American Beauty for five thousan' dollars!"

"Who is he? Who's the darn fool?" Bill Tucker's genial manner dropped from him like a cloak, and he snapped out the question.

"He ain't no darn fool! He's connected with the bank an' knows that the youngster that examined the American Beauty reported I'm due to hit the El Dorado lode!" Pop said aggrievedly and convincingly.

"What's this gent's name?" Tucker asked.

"I ain't tellin' that!" Pop shook his head.

"Reckon I better have a look aroun'," the marshal said as he swung around and headed toward the door. Then, as an afterthought, he called back over his shoulder: "I'm darn glad yuh got the money."

Pop Howes had another drink, then wandered across the street to the Ace High. Here he found Hard-rock Hogan and confided his good news to him in a whisper which was clearly audible to several men standing near. By the time Pop had had another two drinks and had repeated the story several more times, always in confidence, he began to believe it himself and gave it a real ring of truth.

Jim-twin Allen followed him about and watched him. Several times he chuckled to himself.

"Darn me, if Pop ain't turnin' into a real fancy liar!"

Presently Allen wandered out and started a search of the various saloons. He found the man he sought playing stud poker in the back room of the Red Blood Saloon at the far edge of town. Allen whispered to him and went out again; he walked out of town a short distance, seated himself on a rock, and started whistling.

"Slivers" Hart, the young card player, waited several minutes and then cashed in his chips and left the bar. He was very slender and but a few inches taller than Allen. He had straw-colored hair and laughing, reckless eyes, but his mouth was hard and bitter.

"Hello, Slivers! I want yuh to do me a favor," Allen greeted him a few moments later.

"Yuh saved me from wearin' a necktie once, so shoot," the other said quietly.

" 'Tain't much. I want yuh to go to the other end of the town an' sorta watch an' see if any one leaves in a hurry," directed Allen. "Then, if someone comes a-runnin' back, an' if he's a plumb important person, sorta foller him an' see where he goes."

"Is that all?"

"Yep, for now."

Allen suddenly remembered he had not eaten that evening. After Slivers left him, he went into a Chinese restaurant, hastily devoured a steak, and then wandered back to the Ace High. He saw Pop sitting with several friends at a table in the rear. As Jim neared a group of men standing at the bar they grew silent, and he knew they had been discussing Jack Allen. He ordered a drink.

"Yuh driftin' tonight? I see yuh got your grays all

125

packed," the bartender said genially.

"Reckon so. I hears tell that brother of mine is goin' to post his list tomorrow, so I figgers on gettin' out of town afore he tells me to get." Allen grinned.

He waited and consumed another drink before going outside. At the hitching rail he swung onto the back of his saddled horse and waved his hand toward a group of loafers.

"S'long, fellers! To hell with this town, I say!" he called back with a laugh.

And, riding slowly, Jim-twin Allen passed down the street and out of the town. A mile farther on he climbed the banks of the gulch and hid his grays in a clump of trees. Then he hurried back toward town, his rifle under one arm. He skirted Goldville and cautiously approached the trail that led to the American Beauty. Here he found Slivers Hart waiting for him.

"About an hour ago a feller went by so fast I couldn't tell who it was," Slivers informed him.

"I'm bettin' my hunch is plumb correct," said Allen, grinning, "an', if I ain't mistaken, another gent will come a-runnin' pronto."

The two men waited. Minutes passed; several hours elapsed. Drunken Mexicans singing ribald songs staggered up the trail toward the mines. At last Allen heard what he was waiting for—the drumming of a hard-ridden horse's hoofs.

"When he comes, follow him an' see who he talks to, then beat it to the American Beauty, an' don't let no one see yuh arrivin' there," Allen warned.

Slivers nodded, and the moment the horseman passed he started in pursuit. The rider had pulled his mount down to a slow trot, and Slivers was able to keep him in sight.

A short time later, Jim Allen heard Pop Howes and Hard-rock Hogan coming from the direction of town. Pop was talking loudly and joyously. Allen waited until they were a short distance away and then glided like a shadow up the trail before them. He did not expect there would be any attempt on Pop's life until later, but he dared not take chances, so he searched the trail carefully for a possible ambush.

The three arrived at the American Beauty, where Allen told Mrs. Howes that she and her husband were to spend the night with Hard-rock. Pop grumbled at not being allowed to stay to see the fun, but Allen insisted the whole scheme might fall through unless Pop obeyed orders. So the old couple departed.

It was an hour before Allen was joined by Slivers Hart, whose eyes were snapping from excitement.

"That gent on the horse was Steve Brandon!" he cried.

"Steve Brandon! Hadn't expected that!" Allen grew thoughtful. "But, of course, that's it. He would know that the El Dorado vein would be found again on this side!"

Young Hart related what he had seen. "Steve hits the steps of the Ace High two at a time. He is in a plumb big hurry. He grabs Bill Tucker, an' they goes to a corner an' whispers. I slide up, but can't hear much, only somethin' about 'double-crossin' sneak; he'll go to jail if he tries it. Things don't pan out tonight. Time to sick Jack Allen on—' I couldn't ketch the name. Then I hears Bill whisper clear: 'If things don't pan out tonight, yuh got to write to Ed to put the screws on Thornton—' Then they sees me an' sorta glares, an' I walks off innocentlike!" Slivers declared triumphantly.

Allen smiled with satisfaction.

"I figger that part about things pannin' out tonight means gun play, an' I hereby declare myself in!" Slivers said positively.

"Don't worry none. You're playin' decoy, an' decoys sometimes gets plugged plenty!" Allen assured him cheerfully.

All was still within the house an hour later. A low-turned lamp burned in the living room, and a man sat in a chair asleep. Outside, two shadows glided up the trail and carefully picked their way toward the house. A foot snapped a twig, and both shadows sank to the ground. A pause, and they again crept toward the house. They hugged the wall and slowly turned the corner and approached the lighted sitting-room window.

Behind them came another shadow, a strange thing that looked as if it were part animal and part man. A hunched beast. Yellow eyes glowed in the darkness.

The first two shadows peered through the window, and one whispered: "Yuh knock, an' I'll watch."

While one shadow remained by the window, the other knocked loudly on the door. The shadow by the window glided forward and joined the one by the door, while the third shadow moved closely behind them.

"He's comin'," came in a hoarse whisper.

"Who's there?" called a voice from inside the house.

"This is Hard-rock. Open up, Pop," the answer came.

A sound of a door being unbolted, a creak of hinges, and a shadowy figure appeared in the doorway. Two streams of red fire, the boom of two shotguns split the night. Then a long streak of jagged red flame coming from the crouching third shadow. A scream of agony, of surprise, of terror! A sound of falling bodies, and then silence.

"Come on out, Slivers! I got 'em both," Allen called, as he straightened up.

Slivers appeared at the doorway and cautiously peered down at the two sprawled figures.

"Hell! I thought I was goin' to get in on the gun play," he grumbled. Then he added: "Hey! Them fellas must have used cannon, 'cause they sure peppered ol' Pop's overcoat an' hat!"

Allen glanced at the straw-stuffed overcoat lying on the floor. It was riddled by buckshot.

"Pop would sure be in kingdom come if he had been in that coat. Take a look at them fellers, Slivers," Allen directed.

Slivers stooped and examined the two bodies by the light of a match.

"One of 'em is Ben Jones what works for Steve Brandon, an' tother is Big Anderson who works for the Blue Sky," Slivers announced.

"Anderson will know better the next time not to mix with the Allens." Jim Allen grinned at his joke, and Slivers chuckled.

"Take a look at Anderson's hands an' see if they looks like a miner's hands," suggested the little man.

"Naw, not a callous on 'em," Slivers announced a moment later. "That gent never worked none with a drill."

"Thought so. Reckon I knows now where Baldy Kane gets that there gold he is so proud about."

"Yuh mean he steals it an' then pertends to mine it?" Slivers asked. "I get you. Quartz is plumb heavy to move an' hard to market, if yuh don't have a mine."

"Correct! An' I figgers I knows why certain gents got Jack down here!"

"They're double crossin' Baldy an' plannin' to have Jack drop him, 'cause they is scared to do it themselves!" Slivers whistled softly.

"Correct again," Allen said dryly. "Darn it! I knows everythin', but Jack won't believe me, 'cause I ain't got legal proof! That's the worst of tryin to do things lawfully. Reckon I'll have to stick to outlaws' law," he grumbled.

THE MAIL ROBBER

IT WAS CLOSE TO SEVEN THE FOLLOWING MORNING when Pop Howes and his wife returned home. They found Slivers Hart and Jim-twin Allen finishing their breakfast.

"Anythin' happen last night?" Pop asked eagerly.

"Nothin' a-tall," Jim replied, with his mouth full of bacon and bread. He and Slivers had spent the night in erasing the signs of the fight.

"Then the thing didn't work?" Pop asked, and his face clouded.

"She sure did!" Allen said quickly. "I figger yuh don't have to worry none!"

Directly after breakfast Slivers Hart started for town, and Pop went out to inspect his mine. Mrs. Howes took Allen by the hand and led him into the sitting room. She pointed an accusing finger at some holes in the wall opposite the door.

"Nothin' happened last night! Then please tell me how them holes got in that wall Now don't lie. I know—yuh saved Pop an' me once before when we was in Arizona, an' yuh did it ag'in last night! They are buckshot marks, an' they was intended for Pop. Oh, Jim, Jim! Yuh are too good to go on bein' all alone!" she ended with a sigh, and there were tears in her eyes.

"Shucks, ma'am! Where did yuh get all the loose language at?" Allen asked nervously and twisted his hat in his hand.

"Will there ever come a time when I kin repay yuh for what yuh have done for Pop an' me?" she asked wistfully.

"Sure! Didn't yuh feed me pie an' let me steal some for my hosses? Ain't we even then?"

She looked at him and shook her head. "You know, Jim, I guess you really think that makes us even!"

"It sure does!" Allen said decisively, as he picked up his rifle. "Ma'am, don't yuh worry—things is comin' out pretty! I'm sayin' good-by, 'cause I don't figger on comin' back!"

"Are yuh sayin' good-by to Jack?"

"Me? Not any! After this mornin', I hopes I don't see him again for a long time!"

"Why?"

Allen hesitated.

" 'Cause if he ketches me here, he'll sure enough lock me up, an' if he sees me afore he has time to forget things, he'll paddle the stuffin' out of me!"

At the ludicrous seriousness on Allen's face the woman smiled. His expression was like that of a small boy who has been caught stealing apples. Then her heart swelled with pity. She knew him—she knew his job of saving herself and others was not yet finished. Yet he thought so little of his own life that his chief worry was of what Jack would do or think.

She watched him climb the trail that led to the shelf above the gulch and shook her head.

"Just let me ketch folks sayin' anythin' against him an' I'll empty a pan of b'ilin' dishwater on 'em!" she said aloud.

Allen had hardly rejoined his two horses at the place where he had left them the night before when Slivers topped the rim of the gulch and rode toward him.

"Steve Brandon runs into the post office just after they close the mail bag an' makes such a holler that they opens her up, an' then he insists on droppin' a

132

letter in personal!" Slivers reported.

"That there stage will be along pronto!" Jim Allen cried, as he deftly tightened his cinches and swung into the saddle.

"I'm comin' with yuh!" Slivers announced.

"Not any!" Allen said positively. "Yuh know, kid, we figgered last night that we'd sorta drift down to Texas an' square yuh so yuh could marry that gal of yours. Yuh got to remember that Uncle Sam don't never forget, if yuh monkey with his mail. So yuh ain't goin'!"

"You're goin'!" Slivers argued.

Allen grinned.

"Hell! There ain't nothin' I could do now that would make it worse!" he explained cheerfully.

Slivers watched him ride down the slope toward the trail to Black Rock.

That morning Jack Allen tacked notices about the town. They read:

The following men will leave town before sunset.

There followed a list of ten names, and the first one was Jim-twin Allen.

Those who are still in town after sunset will be held for investigation and later extradited, if wanted elsewhere.

Curious crowds collected about the notices, and friends ran to warn those whose names appeared on the list. The men named received the news in grim silence and made no threats, but the roughs who aspired to being bad and had not been mentioned blustered and

133

threatened as to what they would do if the little sheriff from Wyoming had tried to exile them. In a town full of hard men Jack Allen had unerringly selected the ten who were at all times dangerous, who believed in talking with their guns rather than with their mouths.

A short time before the stage left that morning, Jack Allen walked into the office of the jail and found Bill Tucker waiting for him.

"Yuh sent for me?" Jack Allen asked bluntly.

Bill Tucker silently handed Jack a letter. The little officer of the law read it carefully and then eyed Tucker curiously. There was something about the man that he could not place. Tucker should have been elated, and he seemed frightened.

"This gent to be relied upon?" Allen asked after a pause.

The big town marshal nodded. His face seemed to have grown suddenly flabby.

"Well," said Jack thoughtfully, "he says bluntlike that the ores shipped from the Blue Sky Mine didn't all come from out the same hole, so I reckon that means Baldy Kane is mixed up with these here quartz robbers."

Bill Tucker licked his dry lips and nodded.

"Huh!" mused the little sheriff inwardly. "That's what's the matter with him. He's scared plumb pink of Baldy! He's a hell of an officer!" Allen thought he had found the reason for Tucker's nervousness. Silently he mapped his campaign. "Baldy Kane is in town, an' mebbe if I start toward Black Rock I could circle the town an' get into the gulch an' have a look-see at his mine without any fuss!"

"Don't forget he's a killer, an' be darned sure to shoot first!" Tucker advised, as Allen strutted out the door.

After Jack had left, Tucker wiped his face with a handkerchief and sighed with relief. He buried his head in his hands and thought hard for several minutes, then called his deputy and said he would not be back until noon. Without further waste of time, the town marshal went to the livery stable, secured his horse, and headed for the El Dorado Mine.

As Jack-twin Allen left town, he pulled his horse to a walk to escape the dust of the Black Rock stage that was just ahead of him. About three miles from town he swung his horse off the trail and climbed up the bank of the gulch. Two faint reports of a Colt floated to his ears. He remained undecided for a moment. If it had been rifle fire, he would have ignored it as shots from some hunter, but this, he was sure, was a short gun.

"Some gent practicin' on rabbits, I reckon. Still, it can't be more than a mile down the trail, an' I ain't in no hurry. Won't have to be back in town afore sunset, to see if them gents has left as ordered. Guess I'll take a look!"

His horse slid down the shelving side of the gulch, and once more he trotted along the trail to Black Rock. He did not hurry—he was simply following a sort of routine duty in investigating those shots. The hill flattened and then turned sharply into a narrow cut. Jack Allen gave an oath and spurred forward. At the farther end of the cut was the stage, with several men trying to straighten out the tangled horses.

"What's up?" Jack snapped.

Old Bill and the three passengers turned and stared at him for a moment before replying.

"Holdup!" one of them explained at last.

"Did yuh recognize him?" Allen asked sharply.

135

"Which way did he go?"

He had to wait for an answer. Here was a situation altogether uncommon. Each of the men waited for the other to reply.

"It was Jim," Old Bill finally blurted. "He didn't make no attempt to disguise himself. He headed north!"

Jack-twin Allen's face went white, and he stared unbelievingly at the man. Then his face changed, grew stern, and his mouth became hard. He circled north until he found his brother's trail and began to follow it grimly.

"He's only pretendin'!" Old Bill said.

"Not any!" came a reply. "Them twins ain't human. Jack is set on law, an' Jim on justice, an' there ain't nothin' they won't do to get what they think is right!"

Jack Allen's mind was bitter, as he followed Jim's trail. Why had Jim done this thing? As a sort of dare? No, he knew that was not the answer Then why? Some fool idea of learning something from a letter? That was it. But the fool must be taught that Uncle Sam's mail is sacred. Jack Allen fought a bitter battle with himself as he rode through those winding hills. He cared more for Jim than for anything else in the world—save the law! He found his outlaw brother's trail easy to follow. No attempt had been made to throw off possible pursuit by a false scent.

"He's in a hurry now. He'll try his stuff later. He's sure enough circling back to the gulch," Jack Allen told himself.

It was well past noon when the Wyoming sheriff suddenly pulled his horse to a sliding stop and led it into the shelter of some brush. He tied it and then began to crawl between the clumps of sage. He breasted a slight hill. Not twenty yards away he saw Jim sorting the mail from an open mail bag at his feet. Jack crouched lower and crawled ten yards nearer, then sprang upright. His gun was in his hand, as he called:

"Put 'em up, Jim, or, by Heaven, I'll shoot!"

Jim Allen turned his head and stared at his brother, then slowly raised his hands. In one of them was a packet of letters.

Jack Allen picked his way through the brush toward Jim. But he was forced to keep his eyes on his brother, and one of his extra-high heels betrayed him. He slipped and nearly fell. During the second when Jack's eyes were off him, Jim's hand moved with incredible swiftness, and the little packet of letters was jammed into a fissure of the rock on which he was sitting.

"Come on, Jim, drop your belts!" Jack ordered when he had recovered his balance.

Jim loosened his belts and allowed his holstered guns to drop to the ground. While Jack was gathering the scattered letters together, Jim thought hard. Jack must not find the letters he had hidden. He was sure one of them contained the proof he needed. Suddenly the freckle-faced outlaw laughed aloud.

"Jack, yuh sure is a hell of a gun fighter. When yuh slipped, I could have potted yuh easy!" he taunted.

Jack Allen started, but made no reply.

"I was so darn sure yuh was stalkin' about town tryin' to make yourself tall that I got a bit careless," Jim continued.

"What fool idea did you have when yuh done this?" Jack said angrily.

"Hell, I was playin' a joke on yuh!" said Jim, with a taunting grin.

"Yuh won't think it a joke much longer! Damn yuh!

137

I could have let most things pass, but yuh robbed the United States mails an' you're goin' back with me!" Jack hastily closed the mail sack. He hooked Jim's two gun belts over the pommel of the outlaw's saddled gray and then swung into the saddle.

"Yuh climb onto that nag I rode," Jack ordered.

" 'Fraid I'll run for it?" his twin asked sneeringly.

Then the two started back toward town. Jim sighed with relief.

"He's sure sore an' mad at me," he muttered to himself. "But if I hadn't riled him, he would sure have seen them letters stickin' out behin' that rock! I'll tell him some day—afore they hang me! They'll sure search me in jail—so why did I bring along these here letters?"

While Jack had been busy with the horses, Jim had seized the moment to cram the letters into his pocket. But he knew he would be searched at the jail.

For want of a better hiding place, therefore, he thrust them into one of the empty saddlebags on Jack's horse!

The slanting rays of the sun hanging over the peaks of the Bear's-foot Mountains were again hitting the piles of old cans and bottles, as the two brothers rode into town. Jim's face seemed aged, and Jack's hard. People stared at them in wonder. Like a flash the news spread about the town.

"Jack Allen is locking up his brother, Jim, as a mail robber!"

Jack thrust Jim into one of the strongest cells in the Goldville jail and locked the door. He departed without a word.

THE WOLF FILLS THE JAIL

JIM-TWIN ALLEN SAT HUNCHED ON THE BENCH IN HIS cell and watched the bars of the window slowly fade, blending into the darkening sky outside. For a long while he sat without moving, then, like a caged animal, he commenced to pace back and forth, back and forth, across the floor. His bitterest thought was—that he had failed! Jack had refused to listen to him when he had attempted to explain while returning to town. He gave no heed to his own fate, though he knew what that would be! His only thought was of Jack, stubborn Jack, who was blinded by a sense of duty.

Joe Elston, the jailer, came with a light and looked at Jim through the bars.

"They tell me they is goin' to ship yuh down to Santa Fe to be hanged," he jeered.

Jim Allen stopped his restless pacing and thrust his face between the bars. Elston backed away, for there was something about Allen's face that brought fear to him.

"I was only goin' to tell yuh that there's a lady wants to see yuh!" he muttered aggrievedly.

There was no use in antagonizing the man.

"Yuh was talkin' of me gettin' hanged—not seein' a lady!" said Allen, grinning.

"It's different, ain't it?" the jailer asked good-humoredly.

"Yuh betcha!" Allen agreed and wondered who could be calling on him. Could it be some woman Slivers Hart had sent? If it were, that might mean that Slivers was planning a rescue. In the minute the jailer was gone his hope grew, sprang to life. When Elston returned with Mrs. Howes, Allen had a sense of bitter disappointment. Tears were streaming down her face.

"Oh, Jim—Jim! I know you did this tryin' to help us," she cried.

"Aw, shucks, you're talkin' large," Jim cried with acute embarrassment. He glanced at the jailer, who was smirking.

"Jim, I've brought you a pie," said the woman, still sobbing.

"Thanks, ma'am. Yuh go on home now an' don't worry none," Allen begged.

She refused to go home, but leaned against the bars and wept. Jim Allen patted her head and otherwise showed acute embarrassment of a man who is being cried over publicly. The jailer stood close by and seemed to enjoy the spectacle.

From somewhere outside the jail there came the report of two gunshots. The jailer turned and entered the office. The moment he was gone Mrs. Howes took a package from the fold of her skirt and passed it into Jim's hand.

"Slivers is waiting with your horses in the lot back of the livery stable," she said in a cool, collected voice. Then suddenly she began to cry again. "Oh, Jim—Jim Allen!" The jailer had returned. He placed a hand on her shoulder.

"Come on out of here, ma'am ," he ordered. "Yuh go on back to Pop. 'Tain't fit for you to take on like that!"

Mrs. Howes allowed herself to be led from the cell door, still pretending to weep. The moment the two disappeared Jim Allen unrolled the package. It contained a Colt .45. He grinned to himself.

"Who would have thought the ol' gal had that much

spunk? Gee, she sure can act!"

He threw himself on the bench in an attitude of abject despair. Minutes passed, precious minutes. At last Joe Elston returned. Jim's eyes searched the man, as he stood by the bars jeering at him.

"Wolf, hell! You're a hell of a wolf—cryin' with old ladies!"

Then his mouth dropped open and he took a step backward.

"Yep, the 'Killer Wolf'!" Jim Allen snapped. "An' I'll sure drill yuh if yuh don't open that door pronto!"

The jailer was only two steps from the door opening into the marshal's office. He had but to take one backward leap and he would be free. But he never took that leap—for there was a deadly warning in Jim Allen's eyes. And he knew the Wolf never missed.

With hands that trembled so that he could scarcely find the keyhole, Joe Elston hastily unlocked the door.

"She gave you—that gun?" he stammered.

"Mebbe so. But if yuh ever say it, I'll come back an' cut your throat," said Allen quietly, as he forced the jailer into the cell. The very flatness of his voice convinced Elston that he would keep his promise. Allen locked the cell door, entered the office, and secured some rope. Then he returned and securely tied and gagged the jailer.

"You stay put!" he warned. "I'm comin' back, an' if you've moved an inch, I'll sure fix yuh so yuh won't move no more."

The diminutive outlaw secured his guns and holsters from a hook in the office, then slipped out of the jail and stood in the shadow while he glanced down the street. He took the precaution of locking the outer door and then trotted toward the livery stable. Slivers Hart

141

was waiting for him in the rear.

"So yuh made it?"

"Good kid, sendin' the ol' lady," Jim praised.

"Figgered she'd get to yuh, if anybody could. She tol' me she always got her way with Pop by cryin' real tears!"

Slivers grinned.

Allen told him briefly where he could find the letters, and Slivers slid through the darkness toward the door that led to the saddle room of the livery stable. He was back again, five minutes later, with the letters.

"Come on, kid," said Allen. "We'll go over to the jail to read 'em. I figger we'll have a minute alone there."

When they reached the jail he ripped open the letters and at last found the one he sought. He read it eagerly and then looked up at Slivers. Allen's face was split in one of his broadcast grins. Young Hart was walking about impatiently. He thought it a crazy act to return to the jail one has just succeeded in breaking. Yet Jim's expression was that of a delighted schoolboy who had no other thought in the world but that he had won a prize.

"Read that," Jim said.

Slivers hastily read the letter. When he had finished, he said: "That sure puts Bill Tucker an' Steve Brandon in plenty bad." A sound outside caused him to whisper: "Some one's comin'!"

"Yeh, I heard 'em," grunted Allen. "When they knocks, yuh open the door an' stand behind it."

A knock came. Steve Brandon entered and found himself staring into a heavy .45 held by Jim Allen. Slivers again closed and locked the door. Quickly and deftly the stupefied Brandon was tied, gagged, and

142

rolled into a cell.

"Where's Jack?" Allen asked.

"Last I see of him he was eatin' in the chink joint an' talkin' to Hard-rock," Slivers replied.

"We got to find him," Allen said, as they slipped out of the jail again.

Slivers chuckled to himself, as he realized that escape was the last thought in Jim Allen's mind. Allen himself laughed recklessly, as they crept down the street, hugging the shadows.

"There goes Bill Tucker," Slivers whispered and pointed across the darkened street.

"We'll lock him up for Jack," Jim decided and swung about after the town marshal.

Bill Tucker was trying the outer door of the jail when something hard was poked against his ribs and someone cried warningly:

"Don't move!"

After a moment Allen added: "All right, open the door."

Too paralyzed from fear and surprise to think, Tucker staggered into the jail and stared open mouthed at Jim and Slivers. They disarmed him quickly. While Slivers was binding and gagging him, Allen spoke.

"Yuh skunk, I know why yuh brought Jack down here. Yuh was scared of Baldy Kane an' wanted Jack to rub him out. I got the letter yuh wrote to the gent in Black Rock, an' when I gives it to the miners, I reckon they'll come an' hang you an' Steve Brandon. It's darn lucky for you that your little double cross on Jack hasn't worked, 'cause I'd sure enough string yuh up, if it had. I'm goin' now an' tell Jack somethin'. What yuh lookin' at me like that for? Yuh got somethin' on your mind?"

Jim Allen looked down at the trembling, pale-faced man. Then suddenly a fear flashed through his mind. Jack! Was he too late? Allen's face changed, grew old. His eyes were smoldering sparks of yellow flame, as he stooped to stare into the marshal's glassy ones.

"Yuh set a trap for Jack? Yuh skunk—tell me where he is! I'm tellin' yuh true—if he's downed this night— I'll sure cut your throat."

Allen's voice was lifeless, flat, again. His soft tones gave greater force to his threat.

Bill Tucker shuddered. When first he attempted to speak, no sound came from his lips; then a flood of disjointed words poured forth:

"Ace High—Baldy Kane—to get him—men he warned to leave—hurry—hurry!"

The words were still pouring forth when Jim Allen bounded out of the jail and ran toward the Ace High Saloon. He had heard enough to know that the trap was set and that Jack had walked into it. Slivers came after him and cursed at the cans that caught his feet. Fast as Slivers ran, Allen had reached the Ace High and was pushing through the crowd about the entrance before his companion had covered half the distance from the jail.

A group of spectators had gathered in the street before the saloon. Some had left the Ace High at the first sign of trouble. Like carrion crows, others had gathered to witness a killing.

"The Wolf!"

Like a startled band of sheep, they opened a path to allow him to pass. Far better to try to block an avalanche than Jim-twin Allen. He was a relentless force of destruction. His face was drawn into a thousand tiny wrinkles; the corners of his lips were

144

drawn up; his eyes were great pools of yellow flame. Walking stiff-legged like a wolf, yellow eyes flaring, body loose and swaying, hands hanging close to his big guns, he stalked through the crowd into the saloon.

Jack Allen stood in a far corner, with his back to the wall. Before him stood Baldy Kane. A little to Baldy's right stood a group of five men—five of the ten who had been ordered out of town that day. The Wolf saw it all now. Jack had been sent there to arrest Baldy. Even if he got Baldy, those five men would get him.

As Jim-twin Allen stalked by the bar toward the group in the rear, the bartender called out:

"Look! The Wolf!"

Jim Allen was still thirty feet away from them when he saw a flash of a hand and knew that Baldy had gone for his gun. As his hand flew down to his own weapons he knew that Jack had beaten Baldy to the draw. The hands of the five were clawing at their guns when Jim Allen opened fire on them. Surprised, the nearest ones attempted to turn their guns on the little outlaw. A continuous stream of fire came from his guns. The reports were blended into one, and the five men melted as if caught by a machine gun.

Blue smoke swirled in rings; the glasses and bottles on the bar danced and crashed to the floor from the heavy concussion of many Colts. The roar of the reports was deafening. Then, as quickly as it had commenced, it was ended.

Then silence—complete.

Jim-twin Allen stood staring through the swirling smoke—stared. With a cry he ran forward. Jack Allen lay in a crumpled heap against the wall. Swiftly Jim examined him and gave a cry of relief when he saw that his brother was only creased. A bullet had made a

145

slight furrow across the top of the sheriff's head.

Slowly the Wolf rose to his feet and faced the men who were crawling out from behind the bar, from beneath tables. As he stood there he pressed fresh shells into his guns and then dropped them back into their holsters.

"Jack ain't hurt bad. When he comes to, I want you gents to tell him somethin'. The Blue Sky Mine ain't no good—Baldy was gettin' his ore by stealin' from other mines. Steve Brandon was in it; so was Bill Tucker an' a gent in Black Rock, called Ed Tucker—reckon he was Bill's brother. Tucker an' Brandon gets scared of Baldy an' sends for Jack. They fixes things so that Jack will tackle Baldy an' rub him out. They has men waitin' to get Jack, so he can't dig no deeper an' mebbe go after them!"

Murmurs swept the crowd—a surge of resentment against such treachery. Then the murmurs died away and the men stared past Jim Allen. He turned and saw that Jack had struggled to his feet and was leaning weakly against the wall.

"These here folks will tell yuh all about it. So long, Jack!" Jim Allen cried and moved slowly toward the door.

"Come back here! Yuh're goin' to jail for robbin' the United States mail!"

Jack was covering Jim with a big Colt. Jim stared at him and then shook his head and laughed.

"Yuh're sure game, darn yuh! I've purty near filled your jail with crooks, an' left the evidence on the office desk, so everythin' is legal and plumb accordin' to law!" Jim laughed and took a step backward.

"Darn yuh! Stop!" Jack ordered. Then he added "Hell! what's the use? Yuh know my gun is empty!"

146

Jim Allen turned, and the crowd opened to let him pass.

Several hours later that night two riders were traveling across the desert, headed due south. As they went they sang:

> "He's neither rich nor handsome,
> Unlike the city dude—"

Suddenly one of them broke off and laughed. "Slivers, I'm sure glad to have met yuh—'cause you're the first man I ever knowed what sings worse than me!"

"If I does, yuh can shoot me!"

"Kid, we'll sure fix up that mess of yours down in Texas. Yuh figger that gal is still waitin' for yuh?"

"Yeh."

The two rode for a while in silence.

"Yuh know Jack is sure strong for the law. Hell, I wish I knew if that gun of his was really empty!"

THE LONG TRAIL

JIM ALLEN AND HIS COMPANION KEPT THEIR HORSES AT a gallop for a mile or so, then realizing there was no pursuit, they pulled them down to a fast walk.

"That's the seventh town, since we hit New Mex, that we had to leave suddenlike," Slivers growled.

Jim-twin Allen started singing:

> "Oh, I'm a Texas cowboy,
> Far away from home.
> I longed to be an outlaw
> And—"

Slivers interrupted Allen's song with an oath, and putting spurs to his horse, galloped on ahead. Allen watched him and then shook his head.

"Reckon the kid's plumb cured of hankerin' to be the bad boy from Bitter Creek," he commented to himself. "Guess he's thinkin' more of how to clear himself of the charge agin' him now than to make it definite by bustin' into Little Deadman's Branch an' shootin' up the gents what double crossed him. Reckon I showed him just in time what it means to ride the long trail."

Allen had deliberately taken Slivers through the small towns to give him a taste of what it meant to be hunted.

That night the two camped in a thicket close to the Pecos. After they had finished their frugal meal, Slivers smoked several cigarettes and stared silently into the fire.

"Jim, yuh win," he said at last.

"Meanin'?"

"Meanin' yuh can boss things when we get to Little Deadman's. I ain't sayin' that 'Spur' Treadwell, the gent what planted the killin' of 'Iky' Small on me, ain't due to die. But I figger on runnin' with the law instead of agin' it from now on, so we'll get Spur legal."

"Yuh ain't hankerin' to be my partner no more an' ride the long trail with me?" Allen bantered. Slivers flushed and moved uncomfortably.

"Shucks, I ain't desertin' yuh, 'cause yuh'd never took me along no way. But I'm plumb sick of bein' chased ragged. Hell, I dream of sheriffs sneakin' upon me," Slivers said slowly and a little shamefacedly.

Suddenly Allens' face was old, lined with countless wrinkles. His eyes grew somber, as he stared at Slivers' face. When he spoke again, it was like a father speaking to a son.

"Kid, remember them words. No matter how rotten yore cards, play them straight. It sounds excitin', this outlaw stuff, but the end of the long trail is sartin sure. Yuh get so yuh can't trust no one. Friends try to pot yuh in the back, an' excuse themselves by sayin' it's their civic duty, while they're thinkin' of the blood money on your carcass. No, kid, there ain't nothin' in ridin' the long trail." Allen's voice had been serious when he began, but it was flat, expressionless, as he finished.

Slivers glanced at Allen's face and then looked hastily away.

When Slivers next glanced at Allen, the outlaw's face was once more young. There was a broad grin on his face, as he stuffed some brown sugar in his pockets.

"How long yuh been hidin' out, Jim?" Slivers asked.

"Since I was eighteen. I'm twenty-eight now," Allen replied cheerfully, as he stepped into the brush to feed sugar to his two grays.

Ten years. Ten long, lonely years. Betrayed by friends, pursued by the law, constantly on the move. Yet there was no bitterness against his fate, only a great fatigue. Slivers cursed himself for a weakling and a baby.

He stood up and shook his shoulders, and his growing hatred of the world fell from him like a cloak. From now on he would fight like a man, fight to clear his name and confine his hatred to the man who had framed him.

Before dawn the following day, they crossed the Pecos a little above Pilgrim's Crossing and started on their long ride across the Staked Plains. On the third day, they turned northeast and headed toward Wichita Falls and then, little by little, they swung about until they were traveling almost due north.

They traveled slowly, for it was necessary to keep their horses fresh in case it became necessary to run for it. It was ten days after they crossed the Pecos that they struck the rolling hills and dense thickets that marked the country to the south of the Nations, hangout of hunted men.

One morning they looked down from the top of a heavily wooded hill into the smooth cuplike valley through which flowed the Little Deadman's Creek. At the farther end, doll-like buildings marked the site of the Double R Ranch.

"There she is," Slivers cried.

"I'm bettin' yuh can pick out that gal of yourn settin' on the porch," Allen grinned.

Slivers did not reply, but continued to stare out across the valley to the ranch buildings. Allen's words were true, for he saw, even if it were in his imagination, Dot Reed sitting on the front porch, just as he had last seen her on that day he had had to flee from the mob which was intent on lynching him.

DOT REED

THE TWO WENT OVER THEIR PLANS, ARRANGING CAMP. Slivers was to remain there while Allen went on to the ranch to ascertain if the feeling against Slivers was still vindictive. Jim Allen knew that the fame of his grays had traveled all over the West and that if he took both with him, it would make the chances of his being recognized that much greater, so he hobbled Honeyboy and saddled Princess. The stallion uttered shrill neighs of protest at being left behind, and Princess balked at leaving her constant companion.

Allen circled to the east, for he did not wish to leave a direct trail from Slivers' camp to the ranch. After an hour's ride, he struck the road that ran south to Wichita Falls, where he turned to the north. It was close to sundown when he arrived at the small town of Malboro. This was the typical cow town of the region. It consisted of a few stores, a combination hotel and bar, a post office, and three or four saloons.

There were but a few people about the streets as he rode into town and these gave him but a casual glance. If they classified him at all, they put him down as some kid from a distant ranch. He wore no gun that could be seen, his shirt and jeans were tattered and torn. Princess was the personification of a tired, worked-out old horse. Her head drooped, her feet shuffled up little clouds of dust as she ambled along. No one would have taken her for one of the most famous horses in the West, nor her rider as the most famous outlaw of all time.

Allen swung from his horse before the Wichita Hotel, dropped the reins over the hitch rack and stood for a

151

moment gazing about like a gawky country boy on his first visit to town.

He wandered aimlessly along the street. Spying a store that displayed candy bars in its window, he entered and reappeared a moment later sucking at a brightly colored candy bar. Munching the candy, he slipped through the doors of the hotel and entered the bar. There was no one there, so he walked briskly toward the wall where they had posted the bills for the men who were wanted. He found one for himself, but he gave a sigh of relief when he noted it was an old one and did not have his picture. He also found one for Slivers Joe Hart, which offered a reward of five hundred dollars for that young man, dead or alive. He was reading this when someone entered the room. He glanced over his shoulder and saw a stout, one-armed man, of about fifty, whom he surmised to be "One-wing" McCann, the owner of the hotel.

"Hello, bub! Lookin' for your own picture or figgerin' on nabbin' some of them gents?" McCann asked genially.

"Naw, I was just lookin'," Allen said awkwardly.

"Where did yuh come from an' where yuh goin'?"

"I come from down Fort Worth way an' I'm driftin' aroun' lookin' for a job," Allen replied.

"I'm goin' out to the Double R tomorrow. Spur Treadwell, the manager, is a friend of mine. Want to go along an' ast him for a job?" One-wing asked.

"Sure—but I don't want no job peeling potatoes," Allen complained.

"Yuh be aroun' at seven tomorrow, an' I'll take yuh out an' make Spur give yuh a job as top hand," the older man chuckled.

One-wing McCann was the sort who would do a

favor for someone if it did not cost him effort or money, but his generosity did not run to staking a ragged, homeless boy to a dinner and bed. He walked behind the bar and helped himself to a drink.

Allen wandered out into the street. It was dark now, and he made for a small restaurant he had seen when he entered the town. Having tucked away a beefsteak and some coffee, he wandered forth again and peered into the various saloons. He carefully studied each man he saw, but found none whom he knew or who might know him.

The following morning, when One-wing McCann came from the hotel and climbed into his buckboard, he found Allen waiting for him. He stared; his invitation of the evening before had been carelessly given and forgotten ten minutes after.

"Yuh said yuh'd take me with yuh," Allen said with assumed ignorance.

"That so. Yuh want to ride with me, or are yuh goin' to fork that of bag of bones?" McCann asked, and jerked a contemptuous thumb toward Princess.

"She ain't much to look at, but I've had her ever since I was a kid, so I reckon I'll ride her," Allen said aggrievedly, seeming to resent One-wing's abuse of his horse.

"Suit yourself," McCann said indifferently.

He climbed into the buckboard and picked up the reins. He spoke to the horses, and they started out of town at a fast trot. Allen held the indignant Princess down to an awkward gait that was half trot and half gallop.

Allen was well pleased with his good luck. His arriving with McCann would lessen the chances of his being recognized. He had felt that he would run a great

153

risk of this, for the Double R was not many miles from the Nations, the refuge of many a hunted man. And most outlaws and gunmen hated and feared him far more than many an honest citizen

The road wound in and out between hills and followed the course of the Little Deadman's Creek.

It was close to thirty miles from Malboro to the Double R, and it was well past noon before the road dipped into the valley and the ranch buildings appeared before them. The scene took Allen back to his boyhood, for he had been raised in just such a place. He marked the place where the old stockade had stood, for these buildings had been built in the days when the savage Comanche had laid claim to all this part of the country. Within the old stockade, the eight or ten houses had been built in the form of a rough square, with the main ranch building forming the southern side. Where once there had been only loopholes, there were now windows. All the houses were of one story, built of heavy logs and roofed with sod.

One-wing McCann brought his sweating horses to a sliding stop before the front porch. A puncher ran around the corner to take the horses, and as One-wing climbed from the buckboard, a man came out of the front door.

"Hello, One-wing."

He was a powerfully built man, fully six feet three in height, with a large mouth, a pair of china-blue eyes and close-cut straw-colored hair.

" 'Lo, Spur," McCann replied.

Allen twisted in his saddle and studied Spur Treadwell, the man who, in Slivers' opinion, had killed Iky Small and then placed the guilt on Slivers. Allen had the uncanny gift of being able to look at any man

154

and shrewdly estimate that man's real character. The little outlaw utterly disregarded the outer signs that influence most men. He was not to be fooled by a genial manner, a straight-looking eye or any of the other outer attributes which are usually worn by men to hide their real thoughts and selves.

So now, after studying Spur Treadwell, he knew him to be a man of great force, a dominating character, yet one who was utterly unscrupulous, who would fight with the brutality of a bull and the savageness of a tiger. He shrewdly surmised that the man's weakness was his vanity. Here was a man who possessed the force to make other people carry out his wishes, but would fail because of his pride.

"Who's the kid?" Spur Treadwell asked, as he cast a searching glance at Allen.

"A kid from down Fort Worth way—he's lookin' for a job."

Allen chuckled to himself. One-wing's words implied that he knew for a fact that Allen had come from Fort Worth. It was a little thing, but it might some day serve to throw some suspicious person off the scent.

"All right, kid, yuh go aroun' back an' ask cooky to get yuh some chuck, an' I'll see yuh later," Spur Treadwell said.

"Yuh know right well, Spur, that 'Arizona' won't give him nothin' at this time of the day," a young girl cried, as she stepped out of the door onto the porch.

"All right, Dot, yuh're great at carin' for ol' animals, hobos, an' kids—go, feed him yourself." Spur Treadwell laughed and shrugged his great shoulders.

Dot Reed was a young girl of about nineteen, with dark, curling hair and vivid blue eyes. Bidding Allen to

155

follow her, she reentered the house and led the way to the kitchen. She cut some cold meat and placed a platter of it on the oilcloth-covered table with some bread and butter. Quickly she stirred up the embers in the kitchen stove, built a fire, and placed a coffeepot on to boil. Allen followed her with his eyes as she prepared the meal.

"Gosh, I don't blame Slivers none at all, yuh sure are a real girl," he told himself.

"I'm bettin' yuh're Dot Reed," Allen told her, with his mouth full of meat.

"How did yuh know? What is your name?" she asked with a smile.

"A gent tol' me about yuh. He said yuh was the best-lookin' gal in seven States," he said, grinning. "My handle is Jim Ashton."

She decided she liked this boy and she smiled again with the condescension of a girl of nineteen looking down at a mere boy of eighteen.

"An' your dad, John Reed, owns this outfit?" he asked.

Her face clouded and her lip trembled. She was silent and looked away.

"He was killed a month ago," she said at last.

This was news to Allen and came to him as a shock. Slivers had hoped that John Reed would help clear his name. It meant they had lost a powerful ally. Allen now understood the lines of worry he had noticed in the girl's face. He waited for her to go on.

Dot Reed looked at Allen and saw something in his face that inspired her with confidence. There was a look of understanding that was unusual for one of his age.

"Dad surprised two rustlers over near Hard Pan, an' they shot him," she faltered.

"Did they get the coyotes?"

"Yeh, Spur Treadwell an' the twins come along an' shot them both. They—they—" She faltered, and the tears sprang to her eyes.

"They?" he urged her gently.

"They said there was another man with the rustlers, but he got away. They said it was a friend of mine. Oh—oh—I won't believe it of him!" she ended passionately.

Allen swore to himself. Without being told, he knew whom Spur Treadwell had said the third man was. Spur Treadwell was both deep and thorough. Allen had come to Little Deadman's to help clear a boy's name, and he now believed he had stumbled into a dark conspiracy that had a deeper motive than just the removal of a rival.

"That's right, ma'am, don't believe it of him, 'cause it ain't true," Allen said earnestly.

The girl looked at him with big, round eyes. Something of hope, of fear, sprang into them.

"What do you mean? Do you know him?"

Allen saw that he had stepped out of character. In order to gain time for thought, he busied himself with his food for a moment. After he had swallowed his meat, he looked up at her and grinned.

"I don't mean nothin'. Only the way yuh spoke, I sorta thought yuh liked him, an' it ain't right to believe nothin' of nobody unless yuh give them a chance to tell their side," he blundered.

"But—the rustlers were blottin' the Double R to Double B, an' that's his brand. He—he—Someone said he killed a man an' he had to hide out. Spur said he came back an' tried rustlin' to get even."

"Did yuh see your dad after he was shot?" Allen

asked quickly, as thought materialized in his brain.

"No."

"Then he didn't live to say nothin'?"

"Yeh, he talked to Spur an' wrote a—a—" She broke off, as a heavy tread sounded in the next room.

A moment later, the door opened and Spur Treadwell entered. Allen noticed he was so tall that he had to stoop as he came through the door. He glanced swiftly at Allen and then to the girl. His eyes were penetrating, inquiring, and Allen saw a glint of suspicion in them.

"If yuh're goin' to work for me, yuh have to hustle down your grub faster than that," he said with a touch of harshness in his voice.

"It was my fault, an' it is *my* ranch, an' if I want to talk to one of my men, I will." The girl was quick to spring to Allen's defense.

"Let's not go into that again, Dot. It's your ranch all right, but don't forget I'm your guardian until yuh are of age an' that I do the hirin' an' firin'," Spur said tolerantly with the touch of authority in his voice that one uses to an unruly child.

The girl flushed. Allen rose to his feet and picked up his hat. A moment before, he had been irritated that Spur Treadwell had entered before the girl had time to tell him what her father wrote before he died, but he now felt that it made no difference, for he was certain that he knew what John Reed had written, or at least what Spur Treadwell had said was written.

"Well, anyway, it was my fault the boy stayed here to talk," Dot said after a pause.

"Talk?" Again Spur glanced from the girl to Allen.

"He was tellin' me about his home," she said. She cast a quick glance at Allen as if to beg him not to contradict her lie.

SHORTY TALKS

LATER, WHILE THE OUTLAW WAS WATERING AND feeding his horse, he went over his talk with the girl. He knew from her last lie that she feared Spur and that for some reason all talk to strangers about her father's death was taboo. He decided he would like to see that last note written by John Reed. The whole thing sounded natural enough, for two of the rustlers had been killed—yet he felt there was something wrong. He believed in Slivers, believed the boy had been framed by some one; and the fact that Spur Treadwell had taken trouble to fasten on Slivers this second killing and rustling went to prove that perhaps the boy was right in his belief that the big manager of the Double R was the one who had framed him. If he had not known Slivers, Allen would have unquestionably accepted, as others had apparently done, Spur Treadwell's story of the killing of John Reed.

Two of the rustlers had been killed, and if a murder is committed and you produce the bodies of the murderers, people will usually accept your story and not inquire further. Allen told himself grimly that he had known other men who had double crossed their tools. Perhaps these two rustlers knew too much, and Spur Treadwell had killed two birds with one stone, shut their mouths and got rid of John Reed.

"Shucks, it's plumb easy to talk an' figger out things for yourself, but it's a cow of another color makin' other folks see along with yuh. An', Mr. Jim-twin Allen, if that there hombre, Spur, gets one little suspicion yuh're snoopin', you'll take a ride one day an' never come back," he told himself seriously.

Later, Spur Treadwell turned Allen over to Bill

159

McAllister, the boss horse wrangler, and told him to put the boy to work with the cavvy. The Double R was a large outfit and employed between twenty to forty men, depending on the season, so there were always two or three hundred horses in the cavvy.

Bill McAllister was a weather-beaten man of fifty. His lined and seamed face had been tanned by wind and sun to the color of leather. His grizzled hair was thin over his temples, and his blue eyes were faded. He was a taciturn man whose jaws got their exercise from chewing, not talking. His greeting to Allen was short but friendly enough.

The little outlaw decided McAllister was honest and could be trusted. This bothered him for a time. He could not see how McAllister could be honest and yet be a sort of foreman for Spur Treadwell; especially as the few punchers he had seen loafing about the ranch were obviously more used to handling their Colts than their ropes. Their smooth hands, free of callouses, marked them as gunmen rather than cowpunchers.

"I'm sure in luck to get a job like this," Allen said, grinning. "I've worked aroun' hosses since I was a kid, but I never been on such a big outfit as this before. Yep, I'm sure in luck."

The old horse wrangler's reply was only a grunt. Allen refused to be discouraged by this and continued to prattle like a schoolboy on vacation. Bill McAllister listened to him for a time in a disgruntled silence, but little by little his reserve fell away, and before he knew it, he was chuckling at the boy's remarks and answering his apparently pointless question without reserve.

"I betcha when ol' man Reed first come here he had to be right smart in watchin' for Comanches," Allen said.

"Yuh betcha! More than once I high-tailed into the corral one jump ahead of a dozen of them devils," the old wrangler said reminiscently.

That settled one thing in Allen's mind. Bill McAllister had worked for John Reed long before Spur Treadwell appeared on the scene. Spur Treadwell either did not find it necessary to fire him, or was afraid to do so for fear of comment.

"I betcha yuh have fights aplenty with rustlers," Allen said and then added eagerly: "I'm goin' to get me a gun so I can help fight them."

"Son, don't yuh do no such thing. Yuh're a whole lot safer naked than if yuh packed a gun," the old-timer warned.

"But suppose I met a rustler?" the boy insisted.

"I ain't talkin' about rustlers, but some of the gents what has come to work on this outfit since the ol' man died," Bill McAllister said gruffly.

Allen allowed the subject to drop. He had learned enough for the present. The horse herd was pastured to the south of the ranch in a large meadow which was partly fenced in by dense thickets and partly by wire. Here he met "Maverick Ed" Stone, the other day herder.

Maverick was a lantern-jawed, stoop-shouldered, lanky man of forty, and Allen found him almost as taciturn as his boss. The herder's job was an easy one. It consisted in riding along the boundaries of the meadow and watching to see that none of the horses escaped through the brush.

That night at chow, Allen glanced along the long table in the cookhouse at the score of punchers present. The riders were of all ages. The seven men who sat at the far end of the table were as different from the others as sheep from goats. They were quiet-spoken men and all wore their holsters tied down. The others were cow-punchers pure and simple, who, while they would all fight at the drop of a hat, were not professional fighters. To Allen these gunmen were one more point against Spur Treadwell. He knew they could be explained satisfactorily to others by the fact that the ranch was close to the Nations and that several raids had been made on the Double R stock. Every ranch in such a situation would keep a gang of fighters on its payrolls.

By keeping his ears open and asking a few judicious questions that night in the bunk house, Allen learned that the gunmen worked the northern end of the ranges, as this was considered the danger point. It was near the Hard Pan country which led to the Nations.

"That's plumb natural, but if a gent was lootin' the ranch, it would make it plumb easy," he told himself.

Yet he was convinced that Spur Treadwell had a deeper game than the looting of the ranch. Sooner or later, Treadwell would be sure to be discovered if he tried that—yet it was hard for Allen to decide what his game was. It would take time to burrow deep enough to uncover the mystery and it might necessitate several trips into the Hard Pan country.

The little outlaw was talking, laughing, and adroitly questioning a short squat puncher named "Shorty" when two men entered the bunk house. Allen's eyes flicked yellow for a moment as they rested on the newcomers, then he turned so that his back was against the light. He knew them, but would they remember him? If they did—He worked the gun he wore in a shoulder holster a little more forward.

The bunk house was lined on either side with a double row of bunks, with wooden pegs on either side for the occupants' clothing. The place was lighted by two big lamps, one at each end of the long room. Here, as in the cookhouse, there was the same sharply drawn demarcation between the gunmen and the cow-punchers.

The newcomers stalked down the room and took their places at the table at the farther end among their own kind.

Both were gunmen-killers. They were twins, "Sandy" and "Mac" McGill. There was Indian mixed with their Scotch blood. From the first they had inherited their killing propensity, from the second a cool, deadly nerve.

Mac had a scar on his left cheek, and it was only from this mark that one of the twins could be distinguished from the other. Both were of medium height, rather slender and wiry of build. Their eyes were like blue marbles, their hair sandy in color. Their faces were rather long, and their jaws heavy, which contrasted strangely with their thin and cruel mouths.

Covertly, from beneath the brim of his hat, Allen watched them while pretending to listen to a long-winded story by Shorty. If they recognized him, it would be the end, for no matter whether he won the gun fight or not, it would mean his quitting the ranch. Perhaps he could keep out of their way for a few days, but sooner or later, he would come face to face with them. As long as the crisis had to come, it might as well come that night. He would play his part—and the ragged boy from Fort Worth should not be found packing a gun in a shoulder holster. That was a risk he would have to take, for if he took off his gun and they recognized him, they would shoot him down like a dog.

A little later, he slipped out of the bunk house, unfastened his shoulder holster and gun, hid them beneath the bunk house, and then returned to the long room.

"Yuh was tellin' me about this here Hard Pan country," he said to Shorty, when he returned.

"Yeh, I was tellin' yuh to stay clear of it 'cause it ain't nothin' but a lot of buttes with hard pan between them. Yuh can get lost there easy. Yuh could drive a hundred cows over this here hard pan and never leave no trail a-tall 'cause it's just like stone. An' there's a thousan' trails windin' about in there. Some of 'em is blind ones an' they twist about scandalously. Then, besides, 'Boston Jack' don't like folks wanderin' about the buttes."

From the corner of his eye, Allen saw that both the McGills were watching him and whispering to each other. He saw them slowly arise to their feet and move toward him. Mac came directly toward him and Sandy circled the table to take him in the rear. It was coming.

"Who's this here Boston Jack?" he asked, and there was no quiver in his voice—nothing to show that he knew he might be dead in sixty seconds. His voice was eager, curious.

"He's the gent what bought the ol' Double B Ranch after the bank foreclosed. It's about twenty mile from here, tother side of the Hard Pan. He's runnin' hosses, but folks figger he's runnin' cows on the side—other folks' cows—but they never can catch him." The garrulous Shorty paused to yank off a chew from a piece of black plug.

"Stay put!" Mac snapped.

Shorty looked up, saw Mac with his gun out, and then promptly fell over sideways to be out of the way. At the same time Mac spoke, Allen's arms were seized by Sandy from behind.

"I ain't done nothin'," Allen cried.

164

He struggled to his feet and tried to free himself from Sandy's iron grip. As he struggled, he ducked his head to shield his face with his hat brim and blinked his eyes. He knew that they were what would be most likely to give him completely away.

"Dang yuh, I ain't done nothin', let me be!" he again cried in a perfect imitation of an angry boy.

"Stay still. What's your name an' where do yuh come from?" Mac asked coolly.

Allen felt Sandy's hands exploring beneath his arms and every other place where it would be possible to conceal a gun.

"My name's Ashton, from down Fort Worth way. Mr. McCann brought me out here," he replied.

"Yuh know One-wing?" Mac asked sharply.

"Sure, I see them arrive together, an' One-wing tol' Spur he knew him," one of the other gunmen volunteered.

"An' he ain't heeled," Sandy announced.

"Guess we made a mistake—no wolf would travel without his teeth," Mac smiled thinly.

Sandy released him, and Allen pretended to trip and fall to the floor. The shadows were deeper there.

"Who'd yuh think he was?" a gunman asked, as the two returned to their table.

"One of them Allen twins," Mac replied shortly.

"Ha-ha-ha!" Shortly laughed. "That's a hell of a joke on them—they took yuh for the Killer Wolf."

"Dang fools," Allen grumbled, as he arose to his feet and ruefully rubbed his arms where they had been seized by Sandy's steellike fingers.

He grinned to himself. He had carried it off and besides he had learned one important thing. Every cowpuncher in the bunk house had cowered away from the

165

killers except Maverick Ed Stone and two punchers by the names of "Flat-foot" and "Snoots" Stevens. At least he had learned that these three had nerve and were not friends of the McGills'. He was glad of this, for he felt that before many days passed, he would have need of men with nerve to help him.

Spur Treadwell looked through the bunk house door and said shortly: "Time for yuh boys who is ridin' tonight to get started."

Several riders, among whom was Shorty, arose grumblingly to their feet and, taking coats and hats from pegs, went outside. Allen drifted out after them. He saw that four of the gunmen were also assigned to night herding.

"Where yuh goin'?" he asked, as he watched Shorty and three other riders as they saddled their horses.

"The Double R cows is shrinkin' like snowballs in hell—so a dozen of the boys is put ridin' the range to keep the herd from shrinkin' complete," Shorty explained.

"Spur is sure gettin' ready to go on the prod," another rider said with a laugh.

"Yuh let me go with yuh?" Allen asked.

After a moment's protest, Shorty agreed to allow the boy to accompany him. After Allen had retrieved his gun and shoulder holster, he saddled his gray and he and Shorty rode south from the ranch.

There was a quarter moon, and the whole plain was covered with a deceptive light.

"Why for don't Spur go an' talk personal with this Boston Jack?" Allen asked.

"He done it just after ol' man Reed was downed, but didn't find nothin' a-tall. Boston just laughed at him— but one of his riders gets hot under the collar an' talks

166

war to Sandy McGill, who drops him pronto. Just the same, I'm plumb curious an' I figger on amblin' some night into the Hard Pan an' havin' a look. Spur puts them gunmen of hisn over that way—but I don't trust them gents none a-tall!"

"Spur gets 'em after the old man is downed?" Allen asked.

"Naw, the old man gets 'em up from the border a couple of weeks afore he stops lead. Funny how he was wanderin' about by hisself when he runs into them rustlers what downed him. Yep, it's sure funny, 'cause I hears he hires them McGills as personal bodyguards. It would a' been positively ludicrous if Spur hadn't been there," Shorty said reflectively.

"What yuh mean—Spur bein' there?" Allen encouraged.

" 'Cause I don't trust them McGills a-tall. But Spur is white an' ain't the sort to have no truck with rustlers. Then, besides, he's got money. An' ain't he goin' to marry Dot Reed? So he ain't goin' to steal what will be hisn some day," Shorty explained, as he deftly rolled a cigarette.

Their horses slid into a deep wash floored with boulders. After they had picked their way across and climbed the opposite bank, Allen started to ply Shorty with questions again.

"I hears Dot was goin' to marry this Slivers person?" he said.

"Yeh, mebbe she was, but Slivers is wanted bad for two murders, among which is her old man, so I reckon she forgot him."

"Mebbe she don't believe he's guilty," Allen volunteered.

"Mebbe so. I sorta liked Slivers myself an' never

167

figgered him the sort of gent what would dry-gulch a man. Yeh, there's somethin' sorta funny about that too an' I'm a-gettin' plumb curious."

Allen decided that Shorty was altogether too talkative for a man who had such a broad, curious streak. Under the present circumstances to have either was dangerous, but to have both was suicidal.

CONFERENCE WITH SLIVERS

HE RODE WITH SHORTY A SHORT DISTANCE FARTHER and then announced that his gray had gone lame and that he intended to return to the ranch. Shorty gave a few brief directions as to the trail back to the ranch and then rode on alone. Allen waited until the glow of Shorty's cigarette had faded in the faint light from the moon and then swung Princess about and headed across the plain almost due north to where he had left Slivers earlier that day. He put his horse into a long, space-devouring lope and headed straight toward the tall, wooded mountain that stood out against the starlit sky.

As he rode on and on, he tried to piece together the bits of information he had gathered. From Shorty's talk he knew that if Spur were guilty, it was going to be hard to trap him, for Spur had covered his tracks well.

The stars told him it was past midnight when he started to climb the knoll on which Slivers had his camp. He dismounted and cautiously made his way upward on foot. Once, twice, three times he gave the wolf call. This was the agreed signal. A few seconds later, he heard Slivers' answer.

" 'Lo, kid," Allen said, when he at last stood beside his friend. "How about some java?"

"How are things? What did yuh find out? Did yuh see her?" Slivers eagerly fired out his questions, as he made a small fire and put the coffeepot on to boil.

"I'll give yuh the best first. The girl is fine an' still thinkin' of yuh plenty. But the rest is plumb rotten bad. John Reed is dead an—"

"John Reed dead?" Slivers cried in dismay.

169

"Yeh. Now, yuh hold tight while I tell yuh about it. He was downed by a couple rustlers that he caught blottin' brands. Spur Treadwell an' the McGill twins downed the rustlers. Afore ol' man Reed cashed, he made Spur Dot's guardian—"

"I don't believe it," Slivers interrupted positively.

"Me, neither—but just the same Spur's got a paper, an' folks figger said paper is genuine." Allen grinned sardonically.

Slivers considered this news. Then an idea flashed into his head.

"Them rustlers—they was blottin' the Double R brand to the Double B?" he demanded.

"Yep, yuh can go up to the head of the class. Now then, kid, keep cool!" Allen paused for a moment and then grinned cheerfully at Slivers. "Spur says one rustler got away an' that feller was yuh!"

"The dirty coyote!" Slivers' face whitened, then flushed to an angry red, as he leaped to his feet. "I'll kill him!"

"Keep cool, kid. Spur sure made a mistake when he tried to fasten that killin' on yuh, 'cause yuh can easy prove yuh warn't within five hundred mile of the Little Deadman's when the killin' was done. An' let me tell yuh now, your gal don't believe it a-tall!"

"Damn it, yuh can grin, but it—I—"

"Shucks, there ain't no use gettin' her up," Allen interrupted. "Didn't I just tell yuh Spur overplayed his hand when he tried to fasten that second killin' on yuh?"

Slivers regained his composure with an effort and once more sat down by the fire.

"Now, what's to be done?" he asked.

"Yuh can't do nothin' in a hurry—we got to sorta

170

wait for Spur to bungle another play. What I want of yuh is this—first, the names of the gents yuh figger yuh can trust, then I wants yuh to tell me all over again just what happened the night Iky Small got gunned," Allen replied, as he poured out a cup of steaming black coffee.

"There's Bill McAllister, the foreman—" Slivers commenced.

"Ex-foreman," Allen corrected.

Slivers Hart mentioned name after name, but the only ones who were still at the ranch were Maverick Ed Stone, Flat-foot, Shorty, Snoots Stevens, and Arizona, the cook. The rest had been replaced since Slivers left the country.

"Spur is stackin' the deck with his own men," Slivers commented.

"Sure. What do yuh suppose he'd do?" Allen said cheerfully. "Now, tell me about that killin'."

"Iky Small worked for me, an' he was so blamed lazy I kicked him off the place. I had supper with Dot Reed an' her pa. I was goin' to Malboro the next day to try an' wrangle some money out of ol' 'Miser' Jimpson, so I decides to cut for town an' stay there for the night. It's close to thirty mile from the Double R to town an' it's near midnight when I gets to the crossroads, where the trail branches off to my outfit, the Double B. I meets 'Squint' Lane, an' he tells me 'Doc' Hollis has hotfooted it out to see my ma, who is plumb sick. His cayuse is fresh an' mine is tuckered, so he offers to swap. We changes saddles, an' I hotfoot it to my place—it's about twenty-five mile from there.

"When I gets there, I find my ma sleepin' peaceful an' not sick a-tall. I gets hot under the collar at that, for I figger Squint done it as a joke. Makin' a hombre ride

171

fifty mile ain't no joke, an' so I gets mad. I throws Squint's hoss in the corral, forks another, an' hits for town to give Squint a drubbin'. It was close to ten in the morning when I gets near town. I meets Snoots Stevens, an' he tells me that Iky Small was gunned, shot through the back of the head, an' that a bunch of stranglers is lookin' for me.

"So I hits out for the Double R, 'cause of John Reed is a friend of mine, an' I figgers he'll tell me what to do. When I gets to the Double R, I finds Spur Treadwell an' Dot settin' on the front porch, an' they tells me ol' John ain't home. Dot sees I'm plumb worried, so she sorta hints to Spur he ain't wanted. Spur gets up an' grins at me an' says 'Every dog has his day.' "

"An' because he said that yuh figger he knows what's comin'?" Allen interrupted.

"Yep, that an' one other thing. Every puncher was away from the ranch that day, an' Spur turned all the hosses out of the corral, so when I see the stranglers comin', I has to light out on a tired horse, an' they damn near catch me." Slivers ended his story and rolled a cigarette.

"So on the night of the killin' yuh ain't got no alibi whatsoever, 'cause yuh was ridin' about the range all by your lonesome all night?"

"An' the next day, when John Reed looks for Squint, they tells him Squint left town a week afore, an' One-wing McCann says he got a letter from Squint postmarked up in Utah, so everybody figgers I never seen Squint an' am lyin'. An' that darn hoss Squint trades to me was the one Iky Small was ridin' that night, an' they finds it in my corral. An' my hoss is found lame on the range, so they figgers after I kills

172

Iky I trades hosses. If yuh can see a way out of that mess for me, I'll say yuh ain't only a wolf, but a whole pack of 'em." Slivers spoke gloomily.

"An' they say yuh first fired him an' then killed him to close his mouth."

"Of course, Spur would spread that aroun'—he's so darn complete," Slivers answered.

"Yeh, it's so darn complete that there's sure a hole in it somewhere," Allen said paradoxically. "Yuh got a real good friend in town?"

"Yeh, Doc Hollis—he'd swear I was innocent if I was guilty as hell. He's courtin' my ma," Slivers ended with a faint smile.

"Well, I'm goin'. Yuh sit tight an' don't go off half cocked," Allen warned.

He saddled Honeyboy and left Princess behind. He knew there was a risk in changing mounts, but this had to be taken, as Princess had been ridden far that day, and it would be necessary to ride fast if he wished to return to the ranch before daylight.

He had just finished rubbing the sweat marks off Honeyboy on his return to the ranch, and had just slipped into the bunk house, when the ranch began to waken.

As Allen stepped out of the cookhouse after breakfast that morning, his face was swathed in a flannel bandage. He saw that both the twins were watching him. He slipped through the bar of the corral and headed toward Bill McAllister, who was preparing to rope his mount for that day.

"Say, mister, can I have another cayuse to ride today?" Allen asked. He did not want the twins to see him mounted on a gray horse.

"Yeh, fork that roan mare," McAllister said shortly,

as he glanced shrewdly from beneath his shaggy eyebrows at the boy.

"I got me a terrible toothache," Allen volunteered to several punchers, as he was saddling the roan. They glanced at his bandaged face and offered various sure cures.

"Shucks! I think I'll go to town an' have the darn thing yanked out," the little outlaw told them.

Bill McAllister and Allen skillfully cut some twenty horses from the milling crowd in the corral, drove them through the gate, and started them toward the cavvy. Among them was the gray.

As Allen swept by the twins and Spur Treadwell, Mac McGill watched him and then shook his head.

"He sure rides like him," he said thoughtfully.

"He sure does," Sandy agreed.

"Who's that?" Spur Treadwell asked.

"Last night, in the bunk house, I was certain that kid was Jim Allen, but we jumped him an' finds him naked like a baby," Sandy explained.

"Yuh thought he was the Wolf?" Spur Treadwell asked. His eyes followed Allen.

"Yeh, but I reckon we was wrong," Mac said indifferently.

"Mebbe so, but I aims to talk turkey to that kid when I next sees him an' make plumb certain," Sandy said flatly.

"One-wing knows him," Spur Treadwell announced.

His mind was occupied with other things. He frowned and then rolled a cigarette.

"Why don't yuh marry the gal an' save all this bother?" Mac asked maliciously.

The cords tighened in Spur's neck at this taunt, but his eyes showed no resentment when they met Mack's. Though he had sufficient courage, he was not foolish

174

enough to quarrel with either of the twins. They were too deadly with a gun. He knew their type—knew their blood lust—knew that if he pressed them, they would drop him as quickly as they would some hobo puncher. No, he would never place himself in a position where he would be forced to draw against them. Later, after they had outgrown their usefulness—that was different. They would pay then for any taunts they threw at him now.

"Mebbe I will marry the gal—but I don't hanker none to have no rich wife—they get bossy," he said coldly.

The twins grinned at each other, then the three strolled slowly toward the house.

About a mile from the ranch house, Bill McAllister pulled his horse over close to Allen, and the two rode on side by side in silence. The bunch of horses trotted on ahead.

"Kid, I hears about the ruction yuh had in the bunk house last night with the twins. I'm askin' yuh, who are yuh?" the old horse wrangler said keenly.

"What yuh mean?" Allen said innocently.

"Yuh was out ridin' last night—I see the saddle marks on that gray of yourn—an' what's more, it ain't the same one yuh was ridin' yesterday. That was a mare. Figgered mebbe yuh didn't want folks to notice, so I brung him along," McAllister said bluntly.

Allen cast one quick glance at the honest, rugged face of the old-timer and made up his mind to trust him.

"All right—I'm Jim-twin Allen," he said soberly.

Bill McAllister's jaws worked rhythmically for a minute as he studied Allen. He touched his pony with his spurs and dashed forward to head off several horses that were breaking away from the bunch. When the horses were again bunched, he dropped back to the outlaw's side. He skillfully hit a distant stone with tobacco juice and then took up the conversation where he had left it.

"I've heard tell of yuh. What's your game?"

Allen briefly told him how he had met Slivers and of his belief that the boy had been framed by Spur Treadwell. Bill McAllister listened in silence.

"Always thought there was something funny about that killin'. So Slivers figgers Spur framed him. I ain't sayin' Slivers wasn't jobbed, but yuh an' he is plumb mistook if yuh figgers Spur done it. He ain't that kind of a feller—he ain't enough of a fool to do anythin' raw."

"I ain't sayin' he's a fool an' I don't figger he done anythin' raw, 'cause the job was planned by a gent with a head on him," Allen grinned.

Bill McAllister chewed reflectively for a moment and then nodded his head.

"An' don't be forgettin' that Spur turned the hosses out of the corral when he sees the posse comin', an' Slivers says he acted like he expected 'em," Allen argued.

"Mebbe so. But, son, yuh're runnin' agin' somethin' that's big an' hard when yuh tackle Spur," Bill warned.

"Sure—but a wolf can drag down a bull moose," Allen replied and smiled. After they had turned the horses into the big pasture, he added: "This bein' Saturday, the bunch will be headin' for town. I'm goin' to have Doc pull a tooth for me. Yuh want to meet me there?"

"So that's why yuh got a toothache so suddenlike?" the old-timer asked.

"Them twins is darn suspicious, so I figgered it would cover my face likewise."

"Yuh watch them twins. Arizona says yuh is quick like a snake, but there is two of 'em," the old man warned.

"Arizona—he knows me?"

"Not him, but his brother down in Cannondale knows yuh plenty. He wrote how yuh had yourself tossed through the window and cleaned out a bunch of woman stealers across the border. If half what he wrote's the truth, I'm sayin' yuh've got nerve aplenty," Bill McAllister said admiringly.

"Shucks! Yuh're too ol' to talk such loose language," Allen answered irritably.

ON SQUINT'S TRAIL

DOC HOLLIS' HOUSE WAS AT THE FAR END OF TOWN. IT was small and set quite a way back from the street. Shortly after dark that night, Allen pushed open the gate and walked up the path. On the porch he stood and listened for a moment. He had no reason to fear a trap, but his life had taught him the cautiousness of a wolf. He waited for a moment and then knocked on the door. Doc Hollis opened it, and Allen entered the small living room where he found Bill McAllister before him.

"Doc, this is the gent I tol' yuh about," the old horse wrangler said bluntly.

Allen shook hands with Doc and grinned a greeting. Doc Hollis was a small, rotund man with a smooth, bald head. He stared in puzzled wonder at the outlaw. It seemed impossible that this smiling, freckle-faced boy could be the most notorious gunman of all time.

Allen seemed to read his thoughts, for he said with broad, loose grin: "I'm sure me."

The doctor chuckled, and Bill McAllister's leathery face broke into a fleeting smile.

"What yuh aimin' to do?" Doc asked curiously.

"Postmaster a friend of yourn?" Allen countered.

"Frank Cragg? He sure is," Doc answered.

"Do yuh figger he'd fake a letter—postmarks an' the whole thing—an' make believe it just arrived from New Mex for Squint Lane?" Allen asked.

"Reckon he would. Why?"

"Well, if he tol' folks he had a letter which looked important for Squint, mebbe one of Squint's friends

178

would put a new address on it, an' then we'd know where to look for Squint," Allen said, grinning.

"I'm bettin' there's three or four of Spur's gunmen who knows where Squint's holdin' out," Doc cried excitedly.

In case the letter was opened by some friends, they carefully wrote a long epistle from a supposed friend of Squint's in New Mexico.

"Now, Doc, there's one other thing yuh can do. Did yuh ever stop to figger that if Slivers was blottin' Double R cows to Double B, it's darn funny that after he lights out there wasn't enough cows to sell an' pay off a measly eight hundred what he owed to ol' Miser Jimpson."

"Darn me—that's true," Bill McAllister growled.

"Sure is—an' I never thought about it," Doc commented.

"Then yuh start other folks a-thinkin'. Sorta hints that the gent what framed Slivers was the one what ran off his Double B cows."

Doc persuaded Allen to wait for them; there was no use for him to run the risk of being recognized on the streets. Doc Hollis and McAllister would visit the post office and arrange about the letter, and then they would all have supper with Mrs. Hart, Slivers' mother.

As the two walked toward the door, Allen stopped them.

"When did this rustlin' start?" he asked.

"About six-seven months ago. Old man Reed began to suspect someone was makin' free with his cows. He started the boys ridin' night herd. Pretty soon a bunch of 'em runs into a gang of rustlers, an' two of 'em, Bill Steel an' 'Big-foot' gets downed. The old man knows then the rustlers is strong an' workin' hard, so he sends

179

down to the border for a bunch of gunmen. But the rustlin' goes right on—we has several night battles. Then Slivers is supposed to down Iky Small an' lights for the hills." McAllister concluded and cut off a large piece of black plug, which he thrust into his mouth.

"But the rustlin' goes right on?" Allen asked.

"Correct. Then the ol' man gets plumb crazy, 'cause his cows is bein' run off wholesale. A little later he gets downed," Doc cut in.

"Any rustlin' since then?"

"The boys ain't reported nothin' suspicious, but there ain't a hell of a lot of Double R cows left," Bill McAllister said, after a moment's thought.

"When did this here Spur Treadwell person turn up?" Allen asked.

"Now, look here, Jim, yuh're barkin' up the wrong tree," Bill said warmly. "Spur ain't got nothin' to do with this rustlin'. 'Cause why? 'Cause didn't he down them rustlers what gunned the old man? No gent could get away with a thing like that, 'cause tother gents workin' for him would sure quit."

"That's sure correct," Doc said gravely. "An' didn't Spur, after John Reed was killed, go tearin' over to Boston Jack's outfit ready to tear it apart. An' he sure would have if he'd found anythin' wrong. An' Sandy McGill dropped one of Boston's men. No, sir, Spur ain't in cahoots with Boston or he could never get away with a thing like that."

"Jim, yuh're sure wrong about Spur," Bill insisted. "I ain't sayin' he didn't frame Slivers 'cause of Dot, but he ain't no rustler," Bill insisted.

Jim Allen had far more knowledge of the duplicity of which some men are capable than the other two. It was hard for him to understand how any men could be so

180

blind. He looked at them quizzically for a moment.

"Yuh see ol' man Reed after he was shot?" he asked unexpectedly.

"Sure—we both see him," Doc replied. "They sent for me when he was shot, but when I reached the ranch Spur tol' me he was dead. I was goin' to look at him, but Spur says I couldn't do no good an' for me to tend to Dot."

"Then yuh didn't see him?" Allen asked sharply, with a touch of acute disappointment in his voice.

"Yeh, I did. Me an' Bill, here, was his oldest friends, so we sneaked in to sorta say good-by all by ourselves, late that night," Doc said sadly.

"An' I'm bettin' yuh both was mad when yuh see how he was shot to pieces."

"We sure swore loud and plenty," McAllister growled.

Doc Hollis stared at the outlaw, and then took two quick steps toward him.

"Most folks don't know he was shot up bad. How'd yuh know?" he asked, as a quick suspicion entered his mind.

Allen's face held a hopeless expression as he met the angry eyes of the older man.

"Yuh thinkin', 'cause I claims to be a friend of Slivers—an' as Spur says he was there, mebbe I was, too, when the old man got his?" he asked sarcastically. "That sorta proves yuh can think, but if yuh'll recollect that Spur is now Dot's guardian, mebbe yuh'll see what I see."

Doc Hollis looked from Allen to Bill McAllister. His face wore a puzzled expression. Slowly this changed to one of startled wonder and then to furious anger.

"The thing was so complete I never thinks. Damn the

181

skulkin' coyote! Don't yuh see, Bill? Think! The old man couldn't write that will after he was downed!" Doc cried excitedly.

"Hell! I sure does now—but them dead rustlers—the thing was so pat," McAllister mumbled.

The moment when full realization of how their old friend had been foully murdered reached their minds, Allen had all he could do to keep them from dashing out and trying to exact a summary revenge. He pointed out that a hasty move would spoil everything and, little by little, calmed the two older men.

A few minutes later, the two walked out and headed toward the post office. Arriving there, they told the postmaster everything. They got an envelope and addressed it to Squint Lane. The mail came in on the stage at seven that night, and the postmaster promised to show the letter to all who came for their mail.

"Bill, yuh an' me an' the rest of the folks in this town is plumb blind," Doc said sadly.

"We sure is, but Jim Allen ain't. Do yuh know, Doc, I bet there's a dozen men in this town what would give an arm to get a shot at his back, an' he goes roun' grinning like a schoolboy," Bill remarked.

They stopped and picked up Allen at Doc's house and continued on to Mrs. Hart's little cottage.

She was a short, motherly looking woman with bright-blue eyes and graying sandy hair. "Lands sake, what's the matter with the boy?" she asked.

"I got a toothache," Allen replied.

At that she bustled about him like a hen with a lone chick. Allen played the part of the suffering boy until he caught sight of two large, brown pies on the kitchen table, when he instantly lost all interest in everything but those works of art.

"Pies! Well, I'm jiggered if it ain't pies!" He added greedily: "Yuh aimin' to give us a piece of that?"

"After yuh eat, yes," Mrs. Hart replied with a smile.

"I hate to waste space," Allen said regretfully. The two other men chuckled, and the woman shook her head.

"Yuh're just like my boy—he was always crazy for sweets." Her words brought bitter memories to her, and her eyes clouded.

Allen pecked at his food, and his unabashed greediness, as he cast longing glances at the pies, made the woman momentarily forget her grief at being separated from her son. At last, she could no longer stand his wistful, greedy eyes, and arose and cut him a big piece of pie. He gobbled it down before she could regain her seat. With a laugh, she cut him a second piece. As she handed it to him, there came a knock on the door. The others started, but Allen continued to eat his pie.

Mrs. Hart opened the door, and the postmaster entered at a run, bubbling with excitement.

"It sure worked. 'Lefty' Simms takes that letter an' sticks it into another envelope an' addresses it. I fishes it out. Shucks, I suppose I robbed the mails, but here she is," he cried, as he held out the letter triumphantly.

Bill McAllister grabbed the letter, glanced at it, and then handed it to Allen, who read the address and grinned gleefully.

"Shucks! He's way down at Brushtown, along the border," McAllister said in disappointment.

"But Brushtown ain't far from Cannondale, an' I got—"

"Whoopee, I get yuh! Yuh got friends down there," Bill McAllister interrupted, "I betcha yuh do have, after what yuh done—"

183

At Allen's warning glance, the old-timer brought his sentence to a close with a series of coughs.

"What yuh goin' to do?" Doc asked.

"Me? I'm aimin' to eat another piece of pie, if Mrs. Hart will give it to me, then I'm goin' to ride to Three Roads junction an' send a telegram," Allen said carelessly.

Mrs. Hart hastily arose and cut Allen a double portion of pie. The postmaster stared at Allen with protruding eyes. He was too overcome to speak. He nudged Bill McAllister and pointed to Allen. The old horse wrangler nodded in reply.

Doc Hollis volunteered to furnish Allen with a fast horse and then hastened away to saddle it. Five minutes later, he was back again. Allen finished the pie, thanked Mrs. Hart, walked outside, mounted the waiting horse, and rode away into the night.

"He sure does things casuallike," the doctor said admiringly.

"It's sure him," the postmaster said in awe.

"Yeh, but don't go talkin' loud," Bill McAllister warned.

"What is it? Who is that boy?" Ma Hart asked.

"Never yuh mind that," Doc told her seriously. "Yuh get down on your knees this night an' pray if yuh want to see that boy of yourn again—pray as yuh never prayed afore that nothin' happens to the White Wolf tonight."

"Who is he? The White Wolf? What could happen to him?" the woman asked, bewildered.

Doc pointed to a picture of a man on a white horse that hung over the mantelpiece.

"Read me that there title!" he said.

Wondering, the woman read: "I saw a man on a

white horse, and his name was Death!"

"That's him!"

The other two gravely nodded their heads. The woman glanced from the picture to the three solemn faces and then back to the picture again.

Late that night Bill McAllister and Doc Hollis laughed softly to themselves. The rumor they had started was spreading like wildfire. On their way home, at least three friends stopped them and said practically the same thing:

"Yuh know, I been thinkin'. If Slivers Hart was rustlin' cows, how come there warn't no cows on the ranch when the sheriff seized it? It's funny about the killin' of John Reed—" They all would go that far and then nod as if they could say more if they were so inclined.

"Folks is sure startin' to think," McAllister chuckled.

The following morning Bill McAllister was with the cavvy when Allen trotted down a slope and rode toward him.

"Yuh send it all right?" the old man asked eagerly.

"Yeh." Allen slipped to the ground and unsaddled his horse, which was drooping from fatigue. "There is two things I wants yuh to do. Don't tell her any more than yuh have to—'cause she might act hopeful an' give her hand away—but tell Dot to insult Spur Treadwell—call him names, say he ain't nothin' but a bull of a man an' that she's plumb disgusted with him. Then I wants yuh to make me night wrangler."

With that, even before Bill McAllister could ask the reason for these requests, Allen curled up beneath a clump of brush and was asleep.

185

AN OLD FRIEND

BILL WATCHED HIM FOR A FEW MINUTES, THEN SWUNG into his saddle and started to ride the pasture. He had reached the lower end when he saw a horseman galloping toward him from the direction of the ranch. A few minutes later, he recognized the rider as Snoots Stevens, a tall, gawky man of thirty with a long, thin face.

"Why for yuh out here?" McAllister asked after Stevens had brought his horse to a sliding stop.

"Nothin'—only—" Snoots broke off and then added: "Where's that kid?"

"The kid—why?"

"Nothin'—only I hears them two twins talkin' about him plenty—I hears them say they wasn't goin' to take no chances, but was goin' to drop him," Snoots blurted out.

Bill McAllister had no reply for this. He chewed reflectively and tried to decide what this would lead to. It might be talk and then, again, it might mean that their suspicions had hardened to certainty.

"Yuh better tell that kid to high-tail it out of here. Where is he?" Snoots demanded.

"I'll go tell him. He's over by them cottonwoods," Bill McAllister replied.

The two walked their horses toward the trees. They were no nearer than two hundred yards before Allen awoke. A swift glance told him they were friends. He glanced at the sun, calculated the time, and decided he had napped long enough. He took a thick sandwich of bacon and bread from his pocket and was contentedly gnawing at this when the two slipped from their horses.

McAllister had Snoots repeat his story. Allen frowned thoughtfully as he leisurely finished his frugal meal. Having swallowed the last crumb, he negligently lit a cigarette.

"Yuh act as if them twins ain't nothin' a-tall," McAllister snapped. "I'm tellin' yuh them hombres is hell on wheels, an' if they starts throwin' lead at yuh, every one of the killers will join pronto."

"What yuh figger I better do—cut out an' run?" Allen asked with a grin.

McAllister had no suggestion to make, so he grew silent and shook his head. Snoots looked curiously from the older to the younger man. He recalled the scene in the bunk house the first night Allen arrived, and his eyes popped out as he began to understand the truth.

Allen looked at McAllister with a broad grin.

"There ain't no use growlin'. I knows them twins is plumb homicidous, but I got to stay an' try to fool 'em, 'cause there ain't nothin' else to do. So it won't do no good to fuss about it."

The old-timer realized that this was Allen's simple philosophy. There was no use worrying about a bridge until you came to it. As McAllister watched Allen saddle Honeyboy, he knew that all thought of the twins had been dismissed from the boy's mind.

Snoots was about to speak, when a peremptory gesture of Allen's hand held him silent.

The little outlaw's head was cocked sideways like that of an animal who has heard something and is unable to place it. He rose in his stirrups and gazed across the brush, then a second later he relaxed.

"Two gents comin' with a dead man," he announced.

The other two strained their ears, but could hear nothing. It was several minutes later before they heard the clink of a horse's hoof against a stone. Then, from out of the brush, two riders appeared, leading a third horse on which there dangled a strange pack.

The faces of the three watchers grew white and then hard. They instantly recognized the two riders, as well as the man who was taking his last ride. It was the garrulous Shorty who was tied across the saddle. The two riders were both newcomers to the ranch.

"Where'd yuh find him? Who downed him?" Bill asked.

"Reckon he was dry-gulched," one said.

"We finds him over to Sunk Creek in that wash by them big white stones," the other added.

"He had his gun in his hand, three shells empty, so I reckon he made a fight for it," the first continued. "We scouted around an' finds where the killers lay behind some brush."

McAllister and Snoots stared at poor Shorty, but Allen's eyes were on the men's faces as they told their story.

"Why don't yuh go track them killers?" Allen said, with apparent excitement, to McAllister.

"Reckon I will."

The two riders headed toward the ranch. McAllister ordered Snoots to stay with the remuda until he returned, and then he and Allen headed toward Sunk Creek.

"What did yuh want me to come out here for?" McAllister asked after they had ridden in silence for a time.

" 'Cause Shorty wasn't killed where they found him," Allen explained. "There was blood on his off-stirrup leather, and he was tied on with his head on the near side, so I figger he was packed twice. Reckon he got too curious—he tells me the other night he was plumb curious naturally."

A short time later, they were in the wash near the big white stones where Shorty's body had been found. Allen circled around and found the tracks of three horses. He followed them with the sureness and cunning of the desert wolf, up the wash, across the range, and twisting among the brush. There were times when Bill McAllister could see no sign at all and believed that the outlaw had lost the trail. Then, after they had twisted about for a mile, he would see bent blades of grass or scuffled stones, proving that Allen had been following the trail with the sureness of death itself.

The trail twisted this way and that, but always came nearer and nearer to the Hard Pan country.

"Yep, Shorty was tellin' me he was plumb curious to visit over there. Reckon he did an' gets cashed," Allen said. "Reckon if they kills a gent for gettin' curious about this here Hard Pan country, I figgers I better amble in there myself."

He warned Bill McAllister to say nothing about their having followed the trail, and then he swung Honeyboy about and headed toward the wooded country that lay to the left of the Hard Pan. His companion rode soberly back to the Double R Ranch.

It was not until the following morning that McAllister saw Allen again. The boy was sitting in the sun against the wall of the bunk house, laughing and talking with two of the Double R riders. Bill McAllister tried to signal that he wished to talk to him, but Allen ignored him completely. The old wrangler edged up close to the group by the bunk house.

"Yuh take that old mossback—I once heard if a gent

chews regular the tobacco works up in his brain an' makes it solid," he heard Allen say.

Then the boy went on and added a ribald joke. Although his name had not been mentioned, Bill McAllister knew that he was the butt at whom Allen was poking his fun, and the laughter that followed made the old wrangler's cheeks burn. He took one step forward with the intention of chastising the grinning kid. Then realization came to him—that grinning kid was Jim-twin Allen. For some reason of his own, Allen was giving the impression of disliking the old wrangler.

Just the same, Allen's joke had been a cruel one, and Bill McAllister's face was flushed as he walked away. He was anything but in a good humor when he passed around the front of the ranch house and climbed into the buckboard waiting there. He was to drive Dot Reed into town that day.

A few minutes later, Dot ran from the house and stepped into the buckboard. She shot a flashing smile at McAllister as she announced she wanted to drive into town. The two half-broken horses hitched to the wagon were fresh, rearing to go and trying to break loose from the two men who held them firmly by the bits. But Dot was an accomplished horsewoman, so McAllister changed places with her without any protest. She gave the word, the two men holding the reins sprang back, and the horses leaped forward at a wild gallop and went tearing down the lane. With a shout she swung them through the gate and deftly sent them dashing down the trail toward Malboro. They covered several miles before the team allowed itself to be pulled down from its headlong gait.

"Yuh're lookin' real perky this mornin'," Bill

McAllister said curiously.

"I am—I got some good news this morning," she smiled. She studied the weather-beaten face of the man beside her. "Do yuh think Slivers was guilty of the murder?"

He stiffened and thought quickly for a moment, then said cautiously, "I always figgered as Slivers wasn't the kind of man to dry-gulch a gent."

"He wasn't," she cried warmly. Then, after a moment, she added: "I got a letter from him this morning. He is coming back and is now trying to prove his innocence. Do yuh know that letter just appeared out of nowhere? I don't know who brought it. It said I was to trust anyone who came to me an' said: 'My name's Allen; I come from Slivers Hart.' "

"I wouldn't go tellin' that to everybody," Bill McAllister warned.

"Isn't it exciting? I think Slivers has a friend working on the ranch."

"Look here, Dot. Mebbe Slivers has a friend in our outfit, mebbe Slivers is right close—but yuh got to remember that if yuh tol' the wrong person, mebbe that friend an' Slivers would die pronto. So don't yuh go talkin' to nobody—nobody a-tall!" McAllister warned her.

The gravity of his expression made her eyes cloud with fear. She thought for a moment and then nodded. "I won't tell anyone," she agreed.

It was close to noon when they arrived in Malboro. As they turned into the livery stable, a rider swung from a big dun horse and addressed the hostler.

"Feller, don't be skimpin' the oats. Gents call me Toothpick Jarrick, 'cause I sure whittle hombres, what rile me, to the size of toothpicks." He removed one of those implements from the corner of his mouth and held it up for the holster's inspection. "Yuh see that? That's all what's left of the gent what last annoyed me. Now, on the contrary, if I likes a gent, I buys him plenty of drinks."

The hostler grinned at him, then both became conscious of Dot Reed and Bill McAllister.

The hostler ran forward to take the horses, while Toothpick stared in frank admiration at Dot Reed and regretted his own travel-stained and dusty appearance. He watched the old man and the girl walk down the street.

"Who's she?" he asked.

"That's Dot Reed, the owner of the Double R. That gent what is crossin' over to her is Spur Treadwell, her sweetie," the hostler explained as he deftly unhitched the sweating horses from the buckboard.

Spur Treadwell walked across the road with an arrogant grace. He swept off his hat as he neared the girl, and then the three of them entered McCann's hotel.

"Yep, I'm tellin' the worl' that gent is the first gent I ever see what is handsomer than me, an' I don't blame that gal none," Toothpick said.

"Shucks!" The hostler looked him up and down and then shook his head. "Feller, yuh ain't never looked into a lookin'-glass, I'm bettin' plenty on that, 'cause my eyesight is plumb good an' I finds yuh about as handsome as a chuckwalla horned toad."

The two watered and fed the horses, then headed across the street toward the Lone Star Saloon to attend to their own personal wants. The saloon was a long, low room. At the rear four men were playing pool; the bar itself was deserted, except for the McGill twins.

When the hostler saw them, he attempted to back out, but Toothpick pushed him forward.

"Barkeeper, push out a bottle. Gents, what's yourn?" The last was addressed to the McGill twins.

Like a pair of puppets worked by the same string, the twins slowly turned toward Toothpick and allowed their hard, cold eyes to wander from his dusty boots up along his worn jeans to come to rest on his face.

Toothpick's expression never changed as he met their searching gaze. The hostler fidgeted uneasily and looked everywhere excepting at the killers.

At last, Sandy McGill broke the silence.

"Yuh a stranger?"

Toothpick remarked easily: "I sure am—an' I'm hopin' yuh gents will join me in a little liquor."

The twins made no answer to this request. Their expressions grew bleaker, their eyes colder. In spite of Toothpick's laughing eyes, they read the challenge that lay within them. It was not the challenge of a gunman—simply that of a brave man who would die rather than back down, even if faced by a thousand enemies. Simultaneously, remembrance came to both the twins of something that had happened the night before. It was too soon to kill again. They relaxed.

Mac McGill reached for the bottle and filled both their glasses. Silently they raised them to Toothpick and all drank. The twins nodded to the bartender, who refilled the four glasses and they again drank in silence. The twins then turned and commenced to talk to each other in a low voice. They thus gave notice that they wished to be alone.

Later, Toothpick and the hostler crossed the street toward the hotel dining room. As they stepped up on the raised sidewalk on the farther side, the hostler shivered and cast an admiring look at his companion.

"Feller, yuh was sure born lucky. I'm tellin' yuh them twins is worser than wolves, rattlers, an' grizzlies done all up together! An' yuh deliberately aggrify 'em. I figgers they is sure goin' to drop yuh pronto."

"Shucks! I seen plenty like them hombres," Toothpick said, as they took their places at the dining table.

"Yuh has, like Hades! Them two twins is the worst an' fastest gun slingers in this whole world," the hostler said warmly after he had ordered his meal.

"Shucks! Yuh ever heard tell of the Allen twins? Them two yuh is braggin' about ain't in the same class a-tall," Toothpick said scornfully.

"They ain't!" the hostler cried. "Yuh know what I saw last night right over there whar yuh got so darn salty? There was a young gent in there what thinks he is papa's bad boy, an' he has words with the McGill twins. This young gent was a nester, an' McGill starts talkin' to him, makes him go for his gun' an then drops him dead as a herrin'. An' yuh know he gets his gun out so fast an' puts it back faster, so nobody sees it an' nobody knows which of them McGills done the shootin' until I see smoke comin' from Sandy's holster."

"Yuh didn't know which done the shootin'? 'Cause why—'cause yuh was pushin' sawdust with your nose huntin' a hole to hide in," Toothpick said, grinning aggravatingly. After a moment, he continued: "I'm bettin' them McGills picked a fight deliberate with that kid. There's that kind what gets a rep from shootin' kids an' old men. An' wasn't there any men in this town to take that kid's part?"

"Yuh see, both them twins was there," the hostler

returned weakly, "an' they sorta got this town buffaloed. I ain't sayin' they wasn't no talk about it bein' sorta like plain murder. But the kid was a no-good nester."

"Plain no-good murder! Gunmen! Shucks! Yuh wait until they hears the Wolf howl."

"The Wolf?"

Toothpick remembered his dead friend, Dutchy's, warning about some day digging his own grave with his tongue, so he resolutely stopped it by cramming his mouth full of beefsteak.

THE WOLF CALL

DOT REED, TREADWELL, AND MCALLISTER HEADED toward old Miser Jimpson's tumble-down house.

"Yuh mean to say that I may lose my ranch?" she asked anxiously.

"No, I didn't say quite that," Spur hastened to explain. "But things are in a mess, and while I, bein' your guardian, perhaps have the right to decide without your consent, I thought it better to have it all explained to yuh an' then have both of us decide what's best."

Bill McAllister shook his head. He was floundering in deep waters. He distrusted Spur, yet apparently everything the man did was aboveboard. He could not see how Spur could be blamed for the present tangled mess of the financial affairs of the Double R Ranch. He had seemingly done what he could to straighten them out.

The three turned into the gateless fence that surrounded old Miser Jimpson's house and passed into a dingy, shabby room where they found three men— Jimpson, One-wing McCann, and a small, dapper man, named W. A. Raine, waiting for them.

"Miss Reed, this is Mr. Raine, who represents the Wilton County Bank. Yuh know the other two gents. The Double R Ranch owes them all money," Spur said to the girl.

Dot Reed smiled at One-wing and old Miser and shook hands with Raine. He was forty-five, with quick, nervous movements. He had keen blue eyes. After studying him, Bill McAllister decided that he was not only clever, but honest as well.

"Miss Reed, I may as well try to explain to you

196

briefly the bank's position," Raine said briskly, as soon as Dot had seated herself. "The bank holds a mortgage of twenty thousand dollars on the Double R. We are not pressing you for money at this time, but a sight note of twelve thousand dollars has been handed us for collection. Now, we also understand that you are indebted to Mr. McCann for ten thousand more, making a total of forty-two thousand dollars."

"But surely the buildings, the water rights, and the Double R cattle are worth that!" Dot protested.

"If you had asked me that six months ago, I would have replied that they were worth three times that, without question. But, Miss Reed, you must remember that a bank loans other people's money, so they have to take every care to protect it. And it has come to our ears that you have severely suffered from rustlers, so if the man who holds the sight note for twelve thousand insists on immediate payment, and unless you can prove that you have sufficient cattle to satisfy all claims, the bank, which has the first claim, will be forced to start foreclosure proceedings," Raine explained.

"Then what am I goin' to do?" Dot asked, bewildered.

"Don't worry, Dot. I think they'll find there's enough cows to satisfy every one," Spur Treadwell encouraged her, as he patted her shoulder.

"Who is this man who has this call note?" Bill McAllister demanded.

"Who do yuh suppose he'd be?" Spur replied, as he looked contemptuously at Miser Jimpson.

" 'Tain't me, but a client of mine back in Chicago," the old miser squealed.

"I'm bettin', like I tol' yuh the other day, that if yuh wrote to him, he would be willin' to wait, but yuh see a way of makin' a few dollars so yuh refuse," growled Spur, towering over the old man.

"Can't yuh do that?" Dot pleaded.

"No I can't. I tol' this client to lend his money to your dad when he needed it to buy them Crossbar Double A cows, because the security was good then. Now I don't think it good no more, I have to tell him to call his loan." Jimpson spoke with a touch of malice in his voice.

"If Miss Reed will supply the necessary men I will arrive at the Double R tomorrow and make an estimate of the number of cattle on her ranch. We'll hope for the best, and if these rumors are false, why, the bank will take up the note held by Mr. Jimpson's client," Raine said.

"Of course, yuh can have all the men yuh want," Dot told him. Then she faltered. "And—if—if—Then the bank will foreclose?"

It was easy to see that Raine found himself in a difficult and unpleasant position and that he disliked his task.

"I'm afraid I will have to advise them to do that," he said.

"My client is willing to buy the ranch," Jimpson sputtered.

"So that's it, yuh rat!" Bill McAllister growled as he stepped threateningly toward the leering old man. "I have a good mind to sic the twins on yuh," Spur Treadwell said coldly.

Dot Reed faced old Miser Jimpson, and he seemed more affected by the scorn in her eyes than by Spur's threat.

"An' what will this precious client of yours offer?" she asked coldly.

"He will assume all indebtedness an' pay yuh twenty thousand cash."

"He's darn generous. The ranch is worth five times that. Yuh can tell this client of yours that Miss Reed refuses his offer," Spur Treadwell cried.

"Miss Reed, I hope yuh understand that I am not pressing yuh," One-wing McCann assured her, as she moved toward the door.

Out in the street, she turned to Bill McAllister and Spur Treadwell.

"I want to thank yuh for the way yuh stood back of me," she murmured.

Bill McAllister grumbled an unintelligible reply, cast a searching look at Treadwell, and then walked slowly toward the livery stable to secure the team and buckboard. He racked his brains, but could not discover the negro in the woodpile. Nor could he in any way decide how Spur was concerned or responsible in the remotest way for the present situation.

Another problem troubled him. How were the rustlers disposing of their stolen stock? The Double R range had been robbed wholesale, and Bill McAllister had learned through the Cattlemen's Association that no large herds that were not absolutely bona fide had been sold. Yet the rustlers must get their stock out some way.

McAllister shook his head and commenced to harness the two horses. He was brought out of his meditations by a low voice close to him.

"Yuh Mr. McAllister?"

He nodded.

"My handle is Toothpick Jarrick. I got a message for Jim. Yuh tell him that me an' a couple of his friends has the jasper he wants. We camp up the dry wash tother side of Hog Butte. Tell him to come an' do his barkin'—we'll be watchin'."

Bill McAllister stared. His mind raced backward, and he realized the meaning of this strange message.

"Yuh mean yuh got Squint Lane?" His voice was husky with eagerness.

"Yep, we sure has. I gets his telegram, collects a coupla friends, an' go collect this Squint person. They thinks a lot of Jim down Cannondale way, so they arranges for a box car hitched to a train for the Three Roads Junction. We piles in, hosses an' all, an' a good time is had by all 'cept this Squint person, who is sufferin' some, both bodily an' mental torment. We gets to the junction yesterday, rides to a suitable place, an' then I comes lookin' for Jim."

Suddenly he raised his voice.

"Mister, I'm tellin' yuh I ride pronto; this here town is too dead for me," he cried, as the hostler appeared in the doorway.

Bill McAllister was in a fever of impatience to pass on the news of Squint's capture to Jim Allen, as he rode back to the Double R that afternoon with Dot Reed. He sighed with relief when he saw the diminutive outlaw trooping toward the cookhouse with the other riders to answer the supper call.

Allen had been assigned to night riding the cavvy, and it was his custom to go there each night with Snoots Stevens, change his saddle to one of the grays, and then leave for parts unknown. Bill McAllister bolted his food and then rode out to intercept Allen. It was shortly after dusk when Allen and Snoots rode up to where Bill awaited them. The old-timer drew Allen aside and hastily told him the news.

They rode forward to the pasture, and Allen whistled

for Honeyboy. The great stallion cantered up, and the outlaw swiftly changed saddles.

They gave Snoots certain orders and rode away through the night. They left behind them the most curious cow-puncher in Texas.

For the first four or five miles the two rode in complete silence, as there was danger of encountering some of the men assigned to night riding. They passed no riders, and McAllister swore to himself when he realized that they were crossing the best part of the range and that it should have been covered with bedded cattle—yet they passed scarcely a hundred head.

After they had left the danger zone behind, McAllister told Allen of what had taken place in town that afternoon. The little outlaw listened in silence.

"Yuh say this here of Miser gent didn't scare none when Spur talked of puttin' the twins on him?" he asked, when the older man had finished his tale.

"Not any—but he sure colored aplenty when Dot looked scornful at him," the other replied.

Allen made no further remark.

"A gent like him don't usually have nerve, but Spur didn't scare him worth a cent," McAllister said, after a time.

"That ain't no sign he's got nerve," Allen said carelessly.

Again they rode in silence.

"Drat him," McAllister grumbled to himself, "I ain't the kind of gent what loves to hear my own voice, but that darn little half pint never talks a-tall unless he's pryin' somethin' loose from the back of your head that yuh forgot yourself."

After they had covered some fifteen miles across the broken flats, McAllister suddenly realized that it was Allen who was doing the guiding. In that black night it

201

would have been necessary for him to stop occasionally and peer about for some landmarks, but Allen made his way across arroyos, through clumps of brush, with the sure instinct of a homing animal.

"Reckon they're here somewheres," Allen said as their horses' hoofs rang on the stones of a dry wash.

McAllister grunted, then he jumped and swore, for directly beside him a wolf mourned his lonely cry. Once, twice, three times it rang out in the night.

"Darn yuh, Jim, no wonder they calls yuh the Wolf, if yuh bark like that. Darn me, I sure thinks a big lobo is gettin' ready to jump me," McAllister complained.

He saw Allen's teeth flash in the darkness. Then ahead of them there came an answer.

"Gosh, yuh got a real wolf answerin' yuh!"

"Yuh didn't tell me Jack was with Toothpick," Allen cried.

A short time before, McAllister had complained at the matter-of-fact way Allen had taken what he thought was exciting news, but now Allen's voice quivered like that of a man who has just been reprieved from the scaffold.

"Hell, Honeyboy—get along there some—don't yuh know your ol' boss?"

In response, the scrawny gray hurled itself up the wash. McAllister urged his horse up after the gray, but was rapidly outdistanced, for Honeyboy sped up the wash, with its treacherous footing, as rapidly as most horses could have run over a smooth plain in the daylight.

McAllister was still some hundred yards from the small fire around which he saw three men standing, when Allen brought his gray to a sliding stop and sprang from the saddle and landed on top of one of them. When McAllister arrived, he saw the two engaged in what appeared a desperate struggle; and all the time both contestants hurled the most blood-curdling oaths at each other. He stared at them in amazement. They whirled this way and that. The other man was no larger than Allen, but looked years older, because of the heavy beard that covered his face. Little by little, the other bested Allen, and, finally pinning him down on his face, planted both heels in the small of Allen's back.

"Yuh got enough?" he panted.

"Yep," grunted Allen.

The two arose to their feet and stood breathing deeply for a moment. Then Allen turned to McAllister.

"That there long galoot is Toothpick; reckon yuh met him afore. The other gent by the fire is Silent Moore, who is plumb ignorant an' can't talk, an' this here is my brother, Jack, who is the dickens on hoss thieves, rustlers—"

"Hoss thieves! Ain't yuh one yourself? Didn't yuh steal Honeyboy from me?" Jack Allen interrupted Jim's flow of words.

Toothpick chuckled and Silent Moore grinned.

"Hello, Jim. Darn me, but I'm plumb glad to see yuh," Toothpick greeted.

" 'Lo, yuh little devil," Silent mumbled.

Bill McAllister knew that here were two men who would willingly die at a nod from Jim Allen.

"Where's this Squint person?" Jim Allen asked.

Toothpick led the way to where Squint Lane lay flat on his back beneath a tree. He was of medium height, with a big, loose mouth, a pug nose, and eyes like those of a Chinaman. He was snoring, and Jim Allen looked questioningly at Toothpick.

"We had to get him drunk afore he would come with us, so we figgered it would be best to keep him that way. He's been ossified for five days now," Toothpick explained joyfully.

"But he can't tell us nothin' now," Bill McAllister complained.

"I can sober him pronto," Jack Allen volunteered.

"I bet yuh could! Yuh got experience runnin' poor drunks to the hoosegow an' then maltreatin' 'em. But I figgers we better try a psy-cho-log-ical experiment on him." Allen grinned, first at his brother and then at Toothpick.

"Gents, I has erudition, so I'll elucidate what this here psy-cho-log-ical thing is. It's to do with the mind," Toothpick explained, delighted at the opportunity to use a few long words which he devoutly hoped no one else understood.

"A professor gent once tol' me that a hombre suffers a heap more from what he imagines is goin' to happen than from what does, so we'll try it on Squint," Jim Allen told them.

He quickly explained what he had in mind, and then the five retreated to the fire and brewed fresh coffee. Later, he told them what he wished to learn from Squint as to the situation at the Double R Ranch. He kept most of his suspicions to himself.

"I heard tell of 'em twins—watch 'em," Jack Allen warned.

Jim Allen hardly listened to the discussion which followed. Jack Allen occasionally volunteered a shrewd opinion; Silent emitted several grunts; but Toothpick talked continuously. That night Bill McAllister had a man who would talk and argue endlessly about Spur Treadwell's plans. Before he and McAllister returned to the ranch, Jim gave explicit directions as to where the three would find Slivers Hart. It was arranged that Jack Allen was to go for him, as the wolf call was the signal of a friend. Besides, Jack Allen had met Slivers up in Goldville.

THE WOLF MAKES HIS KILL

THE NEXT MORNING THE RAYS OF THE SUN AWAKENED Squint. He groaned and moved uneasily. His eyes fluttered open, and he stared about in bewilderment, trying to recognize his surroundings. He sat up with an effort and clasped his aching head in his hands. Once more he opened his eyes and stared about.

"What the hell?" he cried, amazed.

He buried his head in his hands again and tried to think. The last thing he remembered, he had been sitting in a back room of a saloon, and now he was in the country. He saw several things when he opened his eyes again that he had missed the first time. His foot was securely bound by several strands of wire to the trunk of a tree. From the limb of another tree, near by, there dangled a noose with a neatly and expertly made hangman's knot. Below it was a small boxlike arrangement. His jaw dropped open.

"Sorta looks as if some gent is goin' to get his neck stretched," he mumbled to himself.

He cast an uneasy glance about. There was no one in sight. Near him he saw a plate of food and some water. He drank deeply and then feverishly began to tug at the wire that fastened his foot to the tree. He soon discovered that the wire was fastened in such a way that he would need the aid of a pair of wire clippers to free himself. He cast an uneasy glance at the dangling noose. As the moments passed a conviction grew that the noose was intended for him.

Minutes slipped by, and then he saw four men approach through the trees. He opened his mouth to shout at them, but shut it with a snap when he rec-

205

ognized Slivers Hart. Again he glanced at the noose and again examined the wire.

The four walked by without speaking and seated themselves just out of earshot. They soon began to eat a hearty breakfast. Squint glanced at the plate of food near him, but his hangover and growing fears forbade his eating.

Hours slipped by, then more hours. Anything was better than this uncertainty, and Squint raised his voice and called to the four, but they gave no sign that they heard him. A little later he mouthed at them in anger.

"What yuh fellers goin' to do? Where am I?"

Again there was no answer. Apparently he did not exist for them. He shouted vile curses. Always before him was that dangling noose. One of the men arose and walked away from the others, then called over his shoulder:

"Don't worry, Slivers; the boss will be here soon."

Squint shivered and cast an apprehensive glance at the noose. The sun slowly went down behind the hills and the shadows lengthened.

The silence of those men and the sight of the dangling noose further upset Squint's already overwrought nerves. He shrieked curses and tugged at the wire until his hands were raw and bleeding. The uncertainty of the whole thing sapped his courage until he was cowering on the ground, muttering meaningless words.

"Mebbe yuh heard tell of me—I'm Jim-twin Allen."

Squint Lane looked up with a start. He saw a small man who looked as if he might be a thousand years old. The man's face was covered with wrinkles; his strange eyes were unfathomable; his voice was flat, expressionless. There was something inhuman in the small man, for his face showed neither cruelty, anger, nor hate.

Squint swallowed convulsively and then mumbled "The Killer Wolf."

"Yuh heard tell of me?" Allen repeated.

Squint nodded.

"Who paid yuh to kill Iky Small?"

The wretched man had long passed the time when he could think coherently.

"I didn't do it—he—I swear I—"

"Shut up; that's a lie. If yuh didn't, who did?"

Little by little, Allen drew the whole story from Squint. Squint had been drunk at One-wing McCann's hotel for a week before the murder. Then Boston Jack had come to him and taken him away. Squint was ordered to wait for Slivers at the crossroads and send him back to his own ranch on a wild goose chase. Squint swore he had known nothing about the murder until afterward. He had once quarreled with Iky Small, and Boston Jack had threatened to hang the murder on him unless he ran away. Lefty Simms had accompanied him part of the way on his trip. Lefty had been a friend of Iky Small's, and the two had decided, from various things they had heard and known, that Spur Treadwell was the principal in the plot against Slivers. They had discussed ways of levying blackmail on Spur after he was married to Dot.

Jim Allen was disappointed in the little information he had learned from Squint, but it added one more link in the chain of evidence against Spur Treadwell and definitely proved to him that Spur and Boston Jack were partners or at least closely associated. It also linked One-wing McCann with both Boston and Spur and made Allen at last see light in the tangled financial affairs of the ranch.

Resolving to pay a visit to Boston Jack's place that night, he briefly told the others what he had learned from Squint and then mounted one of his gray horses. With the other one following, he started toward the Hard Pan for another attempt to discover its secret.

"The aggravatin' little cuss! He don't tell no one nothin'," Slivers growled.

"Yeh, his trail is sure hard to follow," Jack Allen smiled.

All that night Jim Allen rode through the winding, twisting maze of blind passages and cul-de-sacs in the Hard Pan. But even he, skillful tracker that he was, could find no trail in the flintlike surface. Toward morning, he circled the Hard Pan and reconnoitered Boston Jack's ranch. But here, also, he drew a blank— he could find nothing that indicated rustling was going on at the ranch.

It was toward dawn when he at last turned and headed back toward the cavvy. He was sure he had reached it without being seen, but in this he was wrong. It was the two grays streaking through the pale morning light that had betrayed him and told Lefty Simms who he was. And Lefty's agile brain was busy with plans to trap the Wolf as he headed back to the Double R.

W. A. Raine, the representative of the bank, had arrived at the Double R the day before and, accompanied by' Spur Treadwell, Bill McAllister, and a dozen cowboys, had started to check the number of Double R cows.

As the day's work progressed, Raine's face grew grave, and Bill McAllister cursed. Where there had been once a thousand cows, there were now a hundred. Late that evening, when they returned to the ranch, the punchers were already gossiping about the fact that the bank intended to foreclose its mortgage at once.

"Dot, things look mighty bad, but I ain't given up hope yet," Spur told Dot Reed that night.

Her face paled. With an effort she regained her composure. "It's not the money—but dad loved this place, an' I hate to see it pass into the hands of a stranger."

"Listen, Dot, yuh know I've always loved yuh, an' if yuh'll marry me, some day we'll buy the ranch back again—for I'll work an'—" A shake of her head stopped him. She looked up at him and asked herself why she could not care for him—he was kind, handsome, a real man. Yet deep down in her soul there was something that warned her against him.

"Yuh're still dreamin' of Slivers," he cried harshly. With an effort, he recovered himself. "I'm sorry. Do yuh—do yuh ever hear from him?"

"Yeh, I got a letter from him just the other day. He is goin' to prove he had nothin' to do with the murder of Iky Small an' that he wasn't near here when dad—He has a friend who brought—I mean is helpin'—" She came to a stumbling halt.

"Yuh mean he has a friend who is helpin' him look up proof. If he brought yuh the letter, he must be now workin' on the ranch," he said quickly.

She shook her head in denial, but the fear that had leaped to her eyes told him the truth.

"All right, Dot—I hope—an' yuh know I mean it— that this friend is successful," he said calmly, but it was only with a great effort that he was able to keep his voice steady and not betray the seething hate that was biting at his vitals.

He would smash her, find this Slivers, and hang him. To be spurned by a chit of a girl! He, Spur Treadwell, to

209

be spurned for a homeless cowboy! Instinctively he knew who Slivers' friend was—that boy, for he was the only new arrival on the ranch. His mind leaped back to that scene in the bunk house. They had been blind—both he and the twins. Well, it was not too late to mend that. The twins were in town; he would go there, start the wheels working that would pauperize Dot; and tomorrow the twins could attend to the boy.

With a savage haste, he saddled his horse and rode furiously toward town. Dot Reed watched him go, and a growing terror seized her. That night she tossed in her bed until long after midnight, trying to decide what was best to do. She remembered that one little slip Allen had made on that first day when she fed him, and she resolved to speak to him the first thing in the morning.

At dawn she was up and waiting impatiently for Allen to return from the cavvy. The sun had been up for an hour before she saw him riding toward the corral. She tried to walk slowly, but her feet would run. He was unsaddling when she reached him, and he turned and greeted her with a broad smile.

"Howdy, miss."

"Do yuh know Slivers Hart? Are yuh his friend?" she blurted out without any preliminary.

"Yep, I answers. Yes, twice. My name is Jim Allen," he answered simply, and then waited for her to go on.

She told him of what she had said to Spur the evening before and of her fears.

"Don't worry none, miss—mebbe I can fool 'em still," he said, grinning at her cheerfully.

"But yuh must go at once. He will bring those terrible twins back with him—they'll kill yuh!"

"Not any. I'm so darn small I'm plumb hard to hit," he said cheerfully. "If I has to run—yuh tell Bill

McAllister to keep watch on Hog Butte, an' if he sees smoke rings, first one, then three, to get what men he can trust an' meet me where the trail rounds Hard Pan toward Boston Jack's. Now, don't yuh worry none," he told her, and then walked toward the cookhouse.

"Where yuh goin'?"

"Me? I'm plumb starved an' I'm aimin' to get cookie to rustle me some grub," he replied.

She watched him walk nonchalantly toward the cookhouse. She noted he was wearing a gun in the holster by his side. This added to her fears, for it would give the twins an excuse to kill without any fear of punishment.

When Lefty Simms returned to the ranch, he had decided not to hurry things. He also noticed Allen was wearing a gun. He intended to wait until he caught Allen at a disadvantage and then, even while he called Allen's name, he would fire. Thus the whole reward would be his, and his name would sweep along the border like wildfire as the one who had killed the Wolf. He would be the most famous gunman of all time.

He lolled near the bunk house. Half an hour later, he saw Allen step from the cookhouse, glance about and then roll a cigarette. Allen sauntered toward the bunk house, where he started to joke with several riders, who were loitering there waiting for Spur to return from town, when they would take up that day's work of checking the cattle on the northeastern part of the range.

A minute later, Lefty Simms grinned evilly. Allen had squatted on his heels against the bunk house wall. It was practically impossible for him to draw with any speed while in that position. Lefty loosened his gun in his low-hung holster and walked slowly toward the outlaw. He stopped before him and looked down at the small, tattered figure, then grinned, for the thing was now sure. Allen was in the act of rolling a cigarette and had both hands raised before him.

"So yuh're the Wolf!" Lefty said thinly.

The grin left Allen's face. To the left of Simms, he saw three horsemen pounding toward the ranch from the direction of town. He knew the riders were Spur Treadwell and the twins, and something told him that their haste was due to him. He made no attempt to deny Lefty's accusation, for he was going to have to flee, anyway.

"I ain't denyin' it," he replied flatly.

The riders scrambled away and watched the two. From somewhere in the front of the house, Dot screamed. She also divined Lefty's purpose. From the direction of the corral, Bill McAllister pounded toward the two. His gun was in his hand. He realized that the little outlaw had been caught in a fatal position.

"Yuh lost any trouble?" Allen asked, looking up at Lefty.

Not a muscle in his body moved; he still held the cigarette paper and tobacco in his hands. Lefty crouched, his hand hovering like a claw above his gun.

"I always swore to kill the Wolf on sight," he snarled.

There came a spurt of orange flame, a whirl of smoke, a thunderous report, and Lefty sagged at the knees and sank to the ground. Even before the cigarette paper that Allen had held in his hand fluttered to the ground, he had sprung to his feet and was running toward his saddled horse.

The spectators were still staring in stupefied amazement at Lefty's huddled body, when there came a thunder of hoofs and Allen flashed along the corral fence and vanished behind some outbuildings.

"Gosh, he fooled Lefty clean—got a gun out with his left hand from a shoulder holster!" a rider cried in awe.

"Fooled him, hell! He outspeeded him. Lefty was standing all set, and look—he didn't even get his gun out of the holster!"

"Who is the little runt?" still another asked.

Spur Treadwell and the twins swung into the lane and brought their horses to a sliding stop at the group by the bunk house. A babble of explanations greeted them.

"That's the Wolf, Jim-twin Allen!" Spur roared. "Go get him! There's ten thousan' on his head, an' I'll clap another five on that to the man who brings me his scalp."

Men flung themselves on horses and streamed away in pursuit, but all save Spur's gunmen soon gave up the chase.

The grim-faced killers, however, heavily armed, followed that trail until far into the night.

Days passed, and Bill McAllister's eyes were glued on the Hog Butte, but there came no signal from Allen. The bank representative completed his tally and returned to town. Dot knew that his report would be unfavorable.

At last, the grim-faced killers gave up the chase, and came back to the ranch. They reported that they had followed the outlaw's trail as far as the Nations.

Then, just as both Dot and McAllister had decided that Allen had given up in despair, they saw smoke rings slowly travel upward in the heavy, overcast sky high above Hog Butte. It had rained all day, and the old horse wrangler was wet and tired, but when he saw those signs he raised his voice in a joyful whoop and then broke into song.

Just at dusk that night, Snoots Stevens and Flatfoot

led two grays toward the trail to Boston Jack's that skirted the Hard Pan.

When they reached the place where the trail skirted the Hard Pan country, Bill McAllister and three other Double R punchers joined them.

"Yuh boys use your ears an' button your tongues, 'cause yuh're apt to run into a bunch of gents what not only outnumber yuh but can fight a hell of a lot better," Bill McAllister warned them.

Just as night fell, it started to rain, a soft, steady drizzle. The men swore philsophically, turned up their coat collars, and rode steadily through the night. A little later, they were joined by three other men who were strangers to them all, except Bill McAllister. The old wrangler had a short whispered conversation with one of the three, a heavily bearded man, and the little troop plodded on again through the night.

They rode silently, with no sound save the creaking of the leather and the occasional clank of a shod hoof against the flint rock. They traveled in single file, and the blackness of the night was so deep that each one could see only the blurred figure of the rider who preceded him. Somewhere a cougar called, and a little later a heavy crashing in the brush and the nervousness of the horses told them of the passing of a bear.

"We're gettin' close. My ol' place is about a mile an' a half to the left," a whisper came from one of the men riding in the lead.

"Gosh, that's Slivers Hart!" Flat-foot cried.

"I'm sure gettin' curious about this party," Snoots whispered back.

A short distance farther on, Jim Allen loomed out of the darkness and called to his brother, Jack. The two whispered together, and then all rode on again. When

214

they were within three hundred yards of Boston Jack's place, they pulled up.

"Yuh gents stay put, an' if yuh hear shootin' come a-runnin'," Jim Allen ordered them briefly. Then he and Jack, Toothpick, and Slivers dismounted and vanished in the darkness toward the ranch houses.

Breathless, the men waited behind. Minutes slipped by, and they began to handle their guns nervously. Then a voice came through the darkness.

"All right. Come on!"

The horses were unsaddled and then turned into the corral. A guard was set, and the rest trooped into the ranch house. The main room in the house was large and square. At one side, there was a big, blazing fire, and the place was lighted by a stable lantern swung from the ceiling. It showed the untidy, dirty traces of several men.

Those who knew Slivers swarmed about him and greeted him.

"Darn my ol' bones, I'm sure glad to see yuh!" Flat-foot cried, as he wrung the boy's hand.

"Say, spill what this here is about," Snoots begged.

"I ain't kiddin' yuh—I don't know. The twins is runnin' this show," Slivers replied.

Slivers briefly told them how he had been framed and that, while they did not have sufficient evidence to prove it legally, they were positive that Spur Treadwell was the instigator of the plot.

"Sure he was—'cause of Dot. Where we goin' now?"

"I dunno. Yuh got to ast the twins; they're runnin' this show," Slivers said, grinning at them.

"Them McGills!"

"Not any! Jim an' Jack Allen."

The two swung about and stared at the famous sheriff

215

and the even more famous outlaw. Then, moved by a common impulse, they drifted toward the fire to have a closer look.

"I ain't sayin' Spur an' Boston didn't rustle Double R cows, but how did they get 'em out?" Bill McAllister asked. "Disposin' of several thousan' cows is a darned hard job."

Allen took a large piece of rawhide from a package and laid it out where the light from the fire would play on it. They all leaned forward and stared. It had been taken from a Crossbar Double A cow. They frowned and looked questioningly at Allen, who only grinned at them.

"Shucks, that's a blotted brand. Darned if it ain't an ol' Double R!" cried Snoots excitedly.

"Sure is—plain as the nose on your face!" Bill McAllister exclaimed.

"Sure it is—now yuh look at it!"

"If them Crossbar Double A cows was supposed to have come from a ranch near here, every one of yuh boys would have spotted them blotted brands pronto," Jim Allen explained. "But seein' they was supposed to have come from an outfit close to three hundred miles to the east of us, an' the cows bein' vented proper, yuh never thinks nothin' about it. An' if your eye did catch anythin' funny, yuh wouldn't have bothered to look close, 'cause yuh was sartin they couldn't be blotted Double R cows."

"The skunks!" cried Snoots. "They steal Double R cows, blot the brands, then sell 'em back to the Double R. Pretty slick, I calls it."

"That's why we couldn't get track of any big herds bein' sold that was suspicious," Bill McAllister said in disgust. He frowned for a moment and then asked a question: "But we buys only twelve hundred head, an' four times that many was stolen. How does that figger out?"

"I'm aimin' to show yuh the rest tomorrow," Jim Allen said.

"Ain't yuh afraid Boston will be comin' a-tearin' back here?" someone asked.

"Not any. He an' his whole gang left here just afore yuh gents arrived, an' where they was a-goin' is a good fifteen mile from here, so I don't figger they'll be back tonight," Allen explained. "I figgered it was worth the chance for yuh to sleep dry tonight, 'cause yuh sure are goin' to do a lot of scrappin' tomorrow."

For some time further, the punchers discussed the various phases of the rustling, and then they followed Allen's example and curled up by the fire.

Before dawn the following morning, Allen aroused them, and they saddled their horses and, after eating a hasty breakfast, took the trail. They traveled almost due east. On their left was the Hard Pan country, and on the right the barren stretches that led to the Nations. Just as the first light touched the distant hills, Allen stopped and pointed to the sheer bluffs that marked the boundaries of the Hard Pan country.

"Yuh know, I bet I traveled a thousan' mile tryin' to find a trail through the darn Hard Pan. But I didn't have no luck, 'cause there ain't none. So I circles aroun' here an' tries the back door, an' fin's how they get in. Yuh see them trees along the base of that bluff? That's where they goes through," he explained.

The men stared at the trees and shook their heads. It seemed as if the bluff continued on in an unbroken line behind the trees. But one among them exclaimed in wonder, for the bluff was cut by a smooth slide that reached clear to the top.

"Shucks, a million cows has come by here," Snoots cried out, and pointed to the chips that carpeted the ground.

Acting as an advance guard, the Allen twins pushed on up the slide; the others followed a hundred yards behind. At the crest, the trail again dipped sharply and wound its way between the familiar buttes, which slowly flattened out. Presently, the twins dismounted and waited for the others to arrive.

"Jack, suppose yuh take Toothpick an' sorta circle to the left, an' I'll wander to the right an' see if they has a guard set Snoots, yuh come with me."

Snoots hastily swung from his horse and, after thumbing his nose at those who were to be left behind, followed Allen through the brush along the slope to the right. Then, suddenly, Snoots drew his breath and swore softly to himself, for there before them lay a long, wide valley in the very center of the Hard Pan, and there were hundreds of cows in sight, contentedly munching on the heavy grass.

"If that ain't a rustler's paradise, I hope I never see one," he whispered.

Allen silenced him with a gesture and pointed to a man about fifty feet below them to their right.

"A guard," he breathed.

They watched the man who was squatting in a bit of shade and who was engaged in some occupation that he found highly amusing. He would burst into chuckles and then yank at a piece of cord. They could not see what was attached to the other end, but Snoots swore angrily.

"What's he doin' to that rabbit?"

Allen flashed a glance at him and then seemed to

218

busy himself studying the lay of the land immediately surrounding the guard. Momentarily silenced by what he saw in the outlaw's face, Snoots aroused himself when he saw Allen start to crawl off to the right.

"Let me go; I'm bigger. I can take him silently," Snoots murmured.

"He ain't goin' to be took prisoner!"

Before Snoots could voice a further objection, Allen had crawled silently and as rapidly as a lizard behind a projecting rock and vanished. Snoots stared stupidly at the rock a moment and then covered the man on guard with his rifle.

Twenty minutes later; they rejoined the other men. Making their way to the south of the gully, they rode silently to another break in the valley that led to an obvious cul-de-sac. Concealing their ponies there, they reached points of vantage above the valley and studied the terrain before them. About a half mile to their right, and almost in the center of the valley, were two rough huts, in front of which stood several saddled horses. About the same distance to their left, three other horsemen were driving several hundred cows toward the hut. Midway between these, there was a lone man on a buckskin pony heading for the gully Snoots and Allen had just left.

"He's goin' to relieve the guard," Snoots said.

"He's goin' to join the guard," Allen laughed. Then he added: "Yuh boys stay put an' let 'em all get in afore yuh starts shootin'." Before any one could raise any objection, he vanished, and presently they saw him advance coolly toward the lone rider.

"I dunno, but I'm sayin' I'm plumb tickled that I ain't ridin' a buckskin hoss, 'cause that little runt is sure mad an' awful homicidal.

"I ain't sayin' that guard wasn't treatin' that rabbit scandalous, but after Allen knifed him an' he's coughin' blood, Allen don't pay no attention, but looks broodin' like at that bunny. An' when he picks it up an' sees that its leg is broke, he goes white, an' I'll swear there is tears in his eyes when he regretfully uses his sticker to end its misery."

Snoots stopped, took a chew of tobacco, and then added reflectively: "Damn a knife, I say; it sure ain't no white man's weapon. Yet, I dunno. Someone had to stop that feller from yappin', an' a shot would sure have mussed up our plans. But he ought to have paid more attention to the feller he knifed than to the rabbit."

"Sure, he ought to have begged his pardon for stickin' him," Flat-foot scoffed.

"Aw, shut up!" Slivers growled.

They sank into silence and watched Allen ride directly toward the man on the buckskin, until he was within two hundred yards. The little outlaw made no effort at concealment, but suddenly swung his pony and headed toward the ranch house. The man on the buckskin fired two shots and then started in pursuit. At the sound of the reports, several men ran from the hut, threw themselves on their ponies, and started to cut off Allen, now circling to the left.

Still swinging to the left in a wide circle, the outlaw ended by pointing directly toward the riders with the cattle, who were riding pell-mell to intercept him. Again he swung sharply to the left and, driving forward with the utmost speed, headed toward the gully where the cow-punchers lay hidden. Soon after he passed between the two converging groups of horsemen, they met and scattered up the gully behind him.

"He bunched 'em like I would cows," Toothpick said

admiringly. "Pick your man an' let's go."

Thinking they had Allen in a trap, the rustlers pulled their ponies up and were dismounting, when the cowboys' devastating volley took them at point-blank range. The rustlers were all desperate men. In spite of the surprise, they stood their ground and attempted to fight back. But their enemies were concealed, and the rustlers were subjected to a deadly cross-fire, so, at last, what was left of them broke and fled.

Jack Allen, mounted on his big black stallion, and Jim Allen, on Honeyboy, dashed, side by side, after the rustlers. Their horses leaped the mound of fallen men and ponies in the entrance. The rest of the cowpunchers streamed out from the cul-de-sac after the twins.

"Goshamighty! See that black horse go!" Flat-foot cried.

"Black, hell! Look at that gray! He runs with his belly touchin' the groun'!" Snoots screamed.

Side by side, faster and faster, the twins overtook their quarry.Then they commenced to fire, first with their right and then with their left-hand gun. The rustlers started to drop and then scattered. Two jerked their horses to a standstill and held up their hands. The Allens swept by these and rode down the rest like greyhounds after rabbits. One man, and one man alone, reached the huts, and he slumped to his knees, as he dropped from his horse and tried to gain the house.

"Reckon we bagged the lot," Jack Allen said soberly, and methodically reloaded his gun.

"Yeh, an' that feller over by the hut that Jim plugged last is Boston Jack himself," Bill McAllister said.

They gathered up the wounded and dead and laid them in rows in the shade of the huts. There were six dead, three mortally wounded and five others injured.

Boston Jack had been shot through a lung, and his wound was fatal. He stared unblinkingly at his captors.

"Yuh aimin' to nuss these here bimbos back to health or are yuh goin' to string 'em up pronto?" Toothpick asked jokingly.

"Now—pronto!" Silent Moore said briefly.

"Naw, let's keep 'em to show Spur," Slivers jested.

The expression on Boston Jack's face changed. His fevered eyes caught Allen's.

"What's that about Spur?"

"Nothin'—but we're aimin' to keep yuh gents to show Spur afore we string yuh up—to sorta show Spur we—"

Caught by something in Boston Jack's eyes, Allen hastily laid a hand on Slivers' arm.

"Spur—he's comin'? He sent yuh gents here?" Boston Jack asked.

"Sure did," Allen replied easily.

Boston Jack was silent for a moment, then his lips opened and a string of curses poured forth.

"The dirty double crosser! He'd double cross his own mother! Damn him, tryin' to hog it all! I'd cook his goose, only yuh're his men an'—" He stopped suddenly.

"Naw, we ain't his men. This here is Jack-twin Allen, the Wyoming sheriff," Jim said, beckoning Jack forward.

Boston Jack stared with fevered eyes, then he nodded.

"Yeh, yuh sure is him. An' I knows yuh ain't working for no skunk like Spur. Come closer, an' I'll tell yuh somethin' that will cut that double crosser's horns," Boston muttered.

Jack Allen knelt beside the dying outlaw, who whispered to him. His voice grew fainter and fainter, and

Jack Allen stooped lower and lower, until his ear was close to the dying man's lips. Then Boston sighed and straightened out. Jack Allen arose to his feet and looked down on the dead man.

"Did he finish?" Jim asked.

"He told me enough to hang Spur a dozen times," Jack answered, "an' I reckon there'll be others who'll be willin' to save their necks by corroborating what he said. Usually, crooks will talk to save their own necks, so guard these wounded men carefully," Jack said.

Bill McAllister and three men were left as guards, and the rest started on the return trip to the Double R Ranch. It was not until they had reached Boston's ranch that Jack Allen told them of what the outlaw had confessed. When he had finished, they were all silent for a time, for it was a terrible tale of murder and treachery.

"But even if yuh hang Spur—that won't save Dot her ranch if she signs them papers this afternoon," Slivers cried suddenly.

"Sign this afternoon?" Jack Allen exclaimed sharply.

"Yep, Bill McAllister tol' me she was goin' to town today to see the bank man," Slivers said.

"But she's not to sign until tomorrow—that was the plan Boston and Spur agreed on," Jack countered.

"Hell," Jim Allen cried, "the kid's plumb correct. I'm bettin' that Spur is figgerin' on doin' just what we made Boston believe he done an' he fixed the signin' a day ahead."

"Then let's get goin'—an' the first man there tell Dot she's got thousands of cows in that valley all wearin' the Double R brand, an' there ain't no use of her sellin' the outfit!" Jack yelled as he ran toward his horse.

Flat-foot, Snoots, and Slivers were off first. They

were followed by Jack Allen on his big black, Tooth-pick on the dun and Jim Allen last on Honeyboy, followed by Princess. For the first two miles, the three leaders made a terrific pace and drew rapidly ahead. Then, step by step, they fell back. The big black passed them easily, one by one; then the dun sent her nose ahead. For several miles, Jack and Toothpick led Jim Allen, but at last the two grays rapidly drew abreast and then ahead. They were running like machines.

"Dang me, look at the little runt change horses! If he does that, no wonder they can run all day!" Slivers cried as Jim Allen, without stopping the machinelike gallop of his horses, lightly sprang from Honeyboy to Princess.

The black pulled abreast of the grays.

"Dang yuh, Jim, don't yuh go tearin' into town by your lonesome," Jack stormed.

"Get that elephant of yorn goin' then," Jim taunted.

Side by side, they raced on for another mile or two, then Jack felt his black commence to falter, and Princess shot ahead with Honeyboy pounding along behind her.

"No, yuh don't!" Jack cried with a laugh.

And when Honeyboy came abreast of him, he leaned forward, grasped the gray's mane, and swung to his back. Jim saw him and grinned joyfully.

"All right, we'll bust into town like we usta afore yuh was a famous man an' me a disreputable character," he cried.

Side by side, they thundered into town. As they raced down the street, Jim Allen spotted the twins coming slowly from the hotel. Miser Jimpson's house was almost directly opposite the livery stable, and so, when Jack flung himself from Honeyboy and hastily ran up the path to the house, Jim quietly turned into the livery yard and waited for the twins.

Jack Allen threw open the door and entered old Miser Jimpson's. He found several people there. Dot Reed was sitting at a table with a paper in her hand. W. A. Raine was standing beside her. On the opposite side of the table sat old Miser, while behind him Spur Treadwell towered above One-wing McCann.

They all turned and stared at the dusty, bewhiskered little man who entered so unceremoniously. Spur marked his two low-hung guns and longed for the presence of the twins.

"Who are yuh?" old Miser squealed.

"Me—I'm Jack-twin Allen."

"I've heard of you, Mr. Allen. You did some work for my bank once," Raine said.

"Is my word good?" Allen asked.

"I would take it," Raine replied promptly.

"Then, Miss Reed, yuh can believe me when I say yuh don't have to sign that paper," he said, smiling at the girl.

She flushed and looked in bewilderment from one face to the other.

"I don't understand! Every one—Mr. Raine, dad's old friend, the doctor—everyone says I must sign or lose everything!"

Spur Treadwell cocked his ears and listened for the coming of the McGill twins. He saw that old Miser Jimpson had grown pale, that One-wing was fidgeting. All knew that the end had come for them, unless they could stop this man's tongue or have the twins stop it for them.

Briefly Jack Allen sketched how Jim Allen had returned with Slivers Hart to help him clear his name, how little by little they had pieced various clues together. Then he went on to the events of that day and of what Boston Jack had told him.

Spur Treadwell knew that the little man would utterly damn him in another minute. He seized the moment when he thought Allen was not watching to snatch out his gun. There was a crashing roar, and the gun clattered to the floor, while he nursed a broken hand.

As if in echo to his shot, there came a volley from outside. When the last echo had died and silence again reigned, those in the room saw that Jack Allen's face had grown white and strained. He knew from those shots that his brother had met the twins.

The twins, Sandy and Mac McGill, saw Jack and Jim Allen flash down the street on the two grays and pull up before old Miser Jimpson's house. They watched Jack run up the path into the house and Jim lead the two horses into the livery-stable yard.

The same thought flashed into their minds. They were not sure of Jack, but they now knew the Wolf. Here was the chance to settle that question which had been argued so fiercely for years. Their eyes met, then, without speaking a word, they turned and walked slowly down the street toward the livery stable.

Gunmen, such as the McGill twins, were insanely proud of their reputation. This pride did more to rid the West of bad men than all the sheriffs and gallowses put together. Every man must admit that he was king or fight. There was no place on the throne for two kings. Gunmen went about with chips on their shoulders and said to all rivals: "Admit I am the best or go for your gun." A gun fight meant the elimination for all time of either the champion or challenger; no one had a chance to promote a return engagement.

For years it had been argued as to which was the faster, the McGill twins or Jim Allen. So Mac and

Sandy McGill marched down the street to prove definitely to themselves and to the world that they were quicker than the Wolf.

Their faces were always sinister and cruel, but now they were expressionless masks. People took one glance at them, hastily moved out of the way, and then followed them at a safe distance. Everyone recognized the look of the killer and knew the town was soon to have gun play.

When Jim Allen entered the stable yard, the hostler stepped from the barn to help him loosen the cinches. His mouth opened in an amused grin when he saw the two big guns strapped to the slender legs. His eyes took in the tattered little figure as well as the homely, freckled face.

"Don't yuh get tired packin' them two big guns?" he asked with a broad smile.

Jim Allen grinned good-naturedly at him, but made no reply.

"Say, kid, why for do you pack them guns? There's some real bad men in this here town, and they might take you seriously and you'd get hurt," he warned, for he had sudden liking for this boy.

"Maybe so," Allen said with another of his broad, loose grins. "No, don't go takin' the saddle off—'cause I figger I'll be leavin' in a hurry pronto."

"Hell and damnation!" the hostler exclaimed.

Sandy and Mac McGill had turned into the yard and were walking slowly toward them. The hostler rightly read the look on their faces and seized Allen by the arm.

"Quick, kid, get into the barn! Them devils has lost a peck of trouble and is huntin' for it," he said hurriedly.

Jim Allen turned and shook off the hostler's detaining hand.

"Yuh fool, they'll kill you!" the hostler cried in warning.

Then he thrilled, as he caught sight of the yellow flare in Allen's eyes and heard his low laugh, as he walked forward to meet the twins on stiff legs, like a fighting wolf. The hostler stared with open mouth; he had heard tales about those yellow, flaring eyes, and knew the owner of them.

"Gosh, the kid's the Wolf!" he exclaimed.

He crouched down against the barn and watched and waited. He saw Allen, hands swinging close to his guns, body loose and swaying, head straight for the twins, who, moving like two machines and side by side, advanced to meet him. When a scant ten feet separated them, they halted.

They stood there, silent, staring, for a time that seemed to the hostler to be hours.

"Gents, I'm countin' three," Allen said softly. At that all three went for their guns.

Six big Colts roared together. The barn walls caught and tossed back the echoes of the reports. As quickly as the uproar started, it hushed.

Mac McGill's hands had flashed faster than the eye could follow to the butts of his black-handled Colts. But, fast as he was, he was not fast enough. Before his guns came level, destruction smashed against his chest. Both of his guns exploded and the bullets sent up a shower of gravel at Allen's feet. Then he staggered and sank to the ground. Desperately he raised himself and fired again, then when another slug tore through his neck, he slumped back and lay still.

Sandy McGill's speed had been the equal of Allen's, but as the outlaw went for his guns, he had ducked and leaped to one side. One of McGill's bullets tore through

Allen's right sleeve, the other creased him on the side of the head. Allen's first shot took Sandy in the pit of the stomach; he staggered backward, and again his guns exploded. But his eyes were dimming and could not follow the figure that leaped first to one side and then to the other. Again and again his guns roared; a continuous stream of fire flashed from the barrels. But each time they roared and missed, a heavy slug tore into his body. At last, his body sagged and crushed to the ground. He was dead on his feet before he fell.

Silence settled over everything.

The Wolf stood there peering through the smoke, then he commenced to laugh—strange laughter that bit into the hostler's ears and left him shuddering—mocking yet mirthless.

Slowly the hostler recovered his senses. He saw Allen stuff fresh shells into his guns, then drop them into the holsters. After that he walked quickly to Honeyboy, tightened the cinch, swung into the saddle, and vanished out the back of the livery stable.

People ran to the livery yard, peered in and then, seeing nothing but those still bodies, they gained courage and crowded forward. A man, mounted on a dun, swung from his saddle, pushed through the crowd, glanced at the bodies, and gave a sigh of relief.

"The Wolf made his kill," he said grimly. Then catching sight of the hostler, he grinned at him and added: "What yuh think of Jim now?"

"He ain't human," the hostler said. "He was laughin' horrible—jumpin' about like a grasshopper, and his guns goin' so fast I couldn't see 'em. No, sir, he ain't no man, nor wolf, neither, 'cause he ain't like nothin' possible."

Jack Allen turned his prisoners over to the local sheriff and then told the story as told to him by Boston

Jack. This was later corroborated by two of the wounded rustlers.

It had been Boston Jack who had discovered that hidden valley. Spur Treadwell had refused to go with him unless things were so arranged that no one, except Boston Jack and One-wing McCann, knew of his connection with the rustling. They had blotted the Double R brands, driven the stolen cattle into the Nations, then swung them about and sold them back to old man Reed. Slivers Hart's ranch was too close to the secret entrance to the valley, so Boston and Spur Treadwell framed him for murder, drove him from the country, and later bought his ranch.

After that things were easy. Men each night kept the cattle drifting from the south of the range to the north, so it was easy for the rustlers to drive fifty or a hundred head each night into the hidden valley. Later, after Dot Reed had been forced to sell and the three had bought the ranch through an agent, they planned to return the cattle from the hidden valley to the open range. It was arranged that the day after Dot Reed signed away her ranch, Spur was to collect a number of honest punchers and raid the valley, wipe out the rustlers, and thus remove all men who even suspected his dishonesty. Boston Jack, of course, would not be there. But Boston Jack, when the valley was raided by Allen's men, believed that Spur had tried to double cross him and get rid of him at the same time he removed the rustlers. Hence, he had told what he knew.

"An' who killed old man Reed?" Slivers asked.

"The twins," said Jack. "Then they killed the two rustlers, who, thought, knew too much, and so they downed two thirds with one stone—got rid of Mr. Reed and silenced two tongues."

230

Dot Reed, her arm around Slivers, had listened in silence.

"And where is the—the Jim Allen now? I want to thank him," she said.

"I'm goin' to join him pronto—but he won't come back here, I reckon," Toothpick said, with a grin at the sheriff.

"You know where he is?" the sheriff asked sharply.

"Yuh figurin' on arrestin' him?" Toothpick asked sarcastically.

"Yuh is a fool if yuh does," the hostler warned." 'Cause your family will sure wear crape if yuh starts after him. I tells yuh the little devil ain't human."

"Of course, it's my duty—but I've only been married a couple of months, so I reckon I'll let the Wolf live a while," the sheriff said with a grin. He turned and looked at Spur Treadwell and One-wing McCann.

"Reckon I'll rest content puttin' the rope around these gents' necks," he added after a moment.

Six weeks later he did.

We hope that you enjoyed reading this
Sagebrush Large Print Western.
If you would like to read more Sagebrush titles,
ask your librarian or contact the Publishers:

United States and Canada

Thomas T. Beeler, *Publisher*
Post Office Box 659
Hampton Falls, New Hampshire 03844-0659
(800) 818-7574

United Kingdom, Eire, and
the Republic of South Africa

Isis Publishing Ltd
7 Centremead
Osney Mead
Oxford OX2 0ES England
(01865) 250333

Australia and New Zealand

Bolinda Publishing Pty. Ltd.
17 Mohr Street
Tullamarine, 3043, Victoria, Australia
(016103) 9338 0666